PULP
SCIENCE FICTION
FROM THE ROCK

A COLLECTION OF SHORT STORIES

Kim -
Thanks for the support!
Enjoy the read -
Andrew

PULP
SCIENCE FICTION
FROM
THE ROCK

EDITED BY ELLEN CURTIS & ERIN VANCE

Library and Archives Canada Cataloguing in Publication

Title: Pulp sci-fi from the rock / [edited by] Erin Vance and Ellen Curtis.
Other titles: Pulp science-fiction from the rock
Names: Vance, Erin, 1992- editor. | Curtis, Ellen, 1993- editor.
Identifiers: Canadiana (print) 20200166026 | Canadiana (ebook) 20200166077 | ISBN 9781989473382 (softcover) | ISBN 9781989473399 (PDF)
Subjects: LCSH: Science fiction, Canadian—Newfoundland and Labrador. | LCSH: Short stories, Canadian—Newfoundland and Labrador. | CSH: Science fiction, Canadian (English)—Newfoundland and Labrador. | CSH: Short stories, Canadian (English)—Newfoundland and Labrador. | CSH: Canadian fiction (English)—21st century.
Classification: LCC PS8329.5.N3 P85 2020 | DDC C813/.087620806—dc23

Copyright © 2020 Engen Books
Heroics 101 © 2020 Ali House
The Mouse © 2020 Lisa Daly
The Photograph © 2020 Melissa Bishop
The Daring Mid-Flight Heist on the Moonbeam Express © 2020 Jeff Slade
Green © 2020 CS Woodburn
Namaily © 2020 Matthew Daniels
The Pale Horse © 2020 Brad Dunne
Ceres © 2020 Alissa Hickox
First Visit © 2020 Andrew McDonald
The Cat's Meow © 2020 Shannon K Green
Close Encounters © 2020 Julie Aubut Gaudet
Freeson's Leap © 2020 Daniel Windeler
On Mission © 2020 Jon Dobbin
Breaking the Ice © 2020 JRH Lawless
The Final Invasion © 2020 Corinne Lewandowski
Slipdream © 2020 Andrew Pike
A Sticky Situation © 2020 Chantal Boudreau
Delay en Route © 2020 Peter J Foote
Parachutes and Grappling Hooks © 2020 Jennifer Shelby
The Swamp Cat and the Reckless Scout © 2020 Sherry D. Ramsey
For the Crown © 2020 Steve Power
Squid Wars © 2020 Nicole Little
Afterword © 2020 Ellen Curtis & Erin Vance
Introduction © 2020 Kenneth Tam

NO PART OF THIS BOOK MAY BE REPRODUCED OR TRANSMITTED IN ANY FORM OR BY ANY MEANS, ELECTRONIC OR MECHANICAL, INCLUDING PHOTOCOPYING AND RECORDING, OR BY ANY INFORMATION STORAGE OR RETRIEVAL SYSTEM WITHOUT WRITTEN PERMISSION FROM THE COPYRIGHT HOLDER, EXCEPT FOR BRIEF PASSAGES QUOTED IN A REVIEW.

This book is a work of fiction. Names, characters, places and incidents are products of each author's imagination or are used fictitiously. Any resemblance to actual events or locales or persons living or dead is entirely coincidental.

Distributed by:
Engen Books
www.engenbooks.com
submissions@engenbooks.com
First mass market paperback printing: April 2020
Cover Image: © 2020 Ariel Marsh

Engen Books thanks Ariel Marsh and Sci-Fi on the Rock for helping make this collection possible.
Printed in Canada.

CONTENTS

Kenneth Tam
Introduction..001

Peter J Foote
Delay en Route..005

Ali House
Heroics 101..008

Matthew Daniels
Namaily..019

Brad Dunne
The Pale Horse..029

Melissa Bishop
The Photograph..033

CS Woodburn
Green..044

Alissa Hickox
Ceres...057

Shannon K Green
The Cat's Meow..085

Andrew McDonald
First Visit...099

Andrew Pike
Slipdream...113

Lisa Daly
The Mouse...128

Steve Power
For the Crown..143

Jennifer Shelby
Paracutes and Grappling Hooks.......................................154

Sherry D. Ramsey
The Swamp Cat and Reckless Scout.................................159

Julie Aubut Gaudet
Close Encounters...185

Corinne Lewandowski
The Final Invasion..193

Daniel Windeler
Freeson's Leap...218

JRH Lawless
Breaking the Ice...243

Jon Dobbin
On Mission..268

Jeff Slade
The Daring Mid-Flight Heist on the Moonbeam Express..........292

Nicole Little
Squid Wars..301

Chantal Boudreau
A Sticky Situation...314

Ellen Curtis & Erin Vance
Afterword..322

Ariel Marsh
On The Cover..323

Introduction
Kenneth Tam

Clattering typewriters echoing through smoke-filled rooms. A glass of whiskey on the desk. A stack of dog-eared magazines made of thick, cheap, pulpy paper. An editor chomping on a cigar. A writer getting paid pennies for words that will captivate youngsters.

The start of a genre that we all owe a great deal.

I don't know how many people these days know what *pulp science fiction* is, or the significance it holds in the history of the genre. My own training is in history, so I'm naturally calibrated to look to the past for the roots of the present, and signals about the future. For me, the era of pulp science fiction — and indeed, pulp writing in general — represents a time when written stories became profitable commodities appealing not just to the upper classes, but for everyone.

Of course, it's not quite that simple — serial stories published in broadsheet newspapers had been around for decades before the pulp era, if not longer, and stories in different forms had always fueled imaginations. But the pulp industry was able to turn a profit with content directed at people who weren't going to read the stories in a drawing room, while being waited upon by servants. It was shaped by popular culture of the 1930s onward — for good and ill — and in the process, carved a place for the science fiction genre in the public psyche.

When Engen put out the original call for submissions for this book, the editorial team identified some of the tropes that are typical in pulp: macho stereotypes, a damsel in distress, low-art. The goal of this collection is to subvert those stereotypes, and the twenty-two authors represented within have done some fine work on that count. In the process, they've demonstrated that pulp science fiction's greatest contribution was giving so many different kinds of people access to speculative futures.

Before pulp made it popular, how many people might have looked to the future as a place for entertainment? Even seminal science fiction works like *War of the Worlds* (itself arguably a forebearer of the genre) was situated firmly in H. G. Wells' here-and-now. Sending future rocket ships to the stars for adventure was a concept that was very different than looking to the present or past for adventure, and though negative concepts like racism definitely permeated pulp science fiction stories, moving narratives away from Earth began changing ideas of who was the 'other', and illustrating the bond that all humans share.

It also broadened the number and demographic of people interested in science fiction. Thanks to pulp, vast numbers of people had access to a universal stage for entertainment and adventure — and those who didn't like the way the world worked had a place to safely offer alternatives. Pulp science fiction began as a way to sell a lot of paper to the masses; it became a way for the masses to explore different ways of being. People could read pulp, enjoy the adrenaline, but also wonder about the underlying ideas. They could nurture ideas of their own, and some even found typewriters and made their own contributions to the science fiction genre.

One notable figure who followed that route: Gene Roddenberry, who was known to love pulp series like *John Carter of Mars*. The genre obviously influenced the sort of writer he became, and shaped the opportunities that were available to him. Indeed, I've seen it suggested that *Star Trek* couldn't have existed if not for the success of the very-pulpy film *Forbidden Planet*.

Of course, the genre of science fiction has now extended far beyond its pulpy roots. We live in an era where comic books have supplanted pulp as a source for mass-market content, but you can of course argue whether comics would have happened without pulp. Either way, the progress has continued — in fits and starts, with some decided detours — from the pulp sci-fi era to today. If pulp's role in history was to open the floodgates of speculative future storytelling, its job is done.

But that doesn't mean we can't have an awful lot of fun returning to some of the tropes of the era, and using them to explore new concepts, ideas, and adventures. Indeed, pulp succeeded because it was, at its core, about taking readers on wild rides. So here are twenty-two new adventures, written by people who probably used newer gear than typewriters, and edited by people who almost certainly weren't chomping on cigars.

I hope you enjoy them.

Kenneth Tam
Author

Peter J Foote

Born and raised in the Annapolis Valley of Nova Scotia, and the son of an apple farmer, Peter studied archaeology in university. He is employed as a boiler and refrigeration operator, is an active Freemason, and runs a used bookstore (Fictionfirst Used Books) out of his basement in his spare time.

Through FictionFirst Used Books Peter strives to support the written word community, which he does by sponsoring the monthly Kit Sora Flash Photography Fiction prize.

Believing that an author should write what he knows, many of Peter's stories are a reflection of his personal life.

Peter's work has twice been awarded the Kit Sora Flash Fiction Prize: once in March 2018 and again in September 2018.

Peter holds the distinction of being one of only three authors to be featured in all the modern *From the Rock* collections to date.

Delay en Route

A strong wind blows down the main street, throwing up fine particles of sand into the air and causing a dented garbage can to fall over and roll against the curb. The flickering drugstore sign, marred by its rusting chains, swung as if a man in the gallows.

"Excuse me, do you have the time?" The voice issuing forth from the mouth grill of Dotty 83 is scratchy like an old record player but the words understandable.

Jeeves L-2 turns its head to face Dotty 83; the resulting dry rusty squeak is reminiscent of nails on a chalkboard. Dull eyes regard the domestic robot, its once proud shine now marred by bird droppings and the groceries in the basket on its lap spoiled and rotting. "I beg your pardon? It would appear that my audio input has developed a malfunction," Jeeves L-2 says and tilts its head, disturbing the hornets building a nest in its ear port.

Dotty 83 says again, louder, "Do you have the time?"

"Ah yes, the time," Jeeves L-2 replies, and with a series of creaks and groans, lifts its left arm up and peers at its wristwatch, the lens in its eye sockets zooming out. "That's odd;" and with a faint grinding noise, it pulls its right arm away from the weeds that have coiled themselves up its metal leg and arm. With a gentle tapping of an aluminum finger upon the watch face, it says, "I'm sorry, my watch seems to have stopped. The battery must have died."

"Oh, dear," Dotty 83 says. Its voice has regained some of its normal tone, the faint accent that hints at some place far away now clear. "I hope the hoverbus arrives soon. I have so many errands to do before Miss Sally gets home from school, and this is the programmed route. Madam Wong didn't give me another. Tsk tsk."

"This is also mine. I promised Timmy that I would play catch with him at the park, and Mr. Graham wants me to wash the hovercar for the family picnic. Perhaps they detoured the hoverbus? Is there construction on the multi-ways again?" Jeeves L-2 asks.

They hear the faint whirr and click of gears coming from the head of Dotty 83, the copper molded hair untouched by the windy day. "Perhaps. The last thing I heard on the Vox-box was a news story about an emergency alert, but Madam Wong was too busy to reply to my inquiries."

"That is unfortunate, but the humans are so busy... They are lucky to have us to assist them," Jeeves L-2 replies.

"Oh, I agree. Should we wait for the hoverbus for a while longer? What do you think?" asks Dotty 83.

Jeeves L-2 leans forward until a 'pop' issues from the robot's lower back, and the motion smooths. Gazing down the street, its eyes zooming in and out, Jeeves L-2 sees a road lined with motionless hovercars covered in dust, businesses with doors swinging in the wind, and no sign of human life. Leaning back, Jeeves L-2 turns to its fellow commuter and replies, "Yes, perhaps a while longer. I'm sure the hoverbus will be here soon, and this is our programmed route."

"I'm sure you're right," Dotty 83 responds as the wind continues to blow down the street.

Ali House

A native Newfoundlander, Alison is a graduate of the Fine Arts program at Sir Wilfred Grenfell College (MUN), and past recipient of the Golden Crescent Wrench Award. Her short story, 'The Price of Beauty' won the December 2018 Kit Sora Award.

Her first novel, *The Six Elemental*, was released in October 2016. Its sequel, *The Fifth Queen*, was published in March 2019.

She is the only person to have short fiction published in all of Engen's open-call short story compilations, including *Sci-Fi from the Rock, Fantasy from the Rock, Chillers from the Rock, Dystopia from the Rock, Flights from the Rock, Bluenose Paradox,* and *Kit Sora: The Artobiography*.

She currently resides in Halifax, Nova Scotia, where she works in arts administration and spends more time than a person should in and around theaters.

The first collection of her short fiction, *The Lightbulb Forest*, was released in February 2020.

Heroics 101

As Professor Rick Brawnly strode into the classroom, he looked at the eager young faces before him. It had been many years since he'd been a student at Space University, but he could still remember the excitement of his first day of hero class. Fresh from the Achilles Academy, he'd been ready to show his professors what he was capable of and to learn how to follow in his heroes' footsteps. After graduating from the university with top marks, he'd gone on to have a distinguished career as a space hero, fighting evil aliens, rescuing damsels in distress, and keeping the universe safe. But time passed and eventually he had to retire. His record secured him a job at the University, where he could mold new heroes and prepare them for a life of thrilling space adventures.

Although Brawnly still kept a strong physique, his thick black hair was greying, his stomach had a slight paunch, and his left leg bothered him when it rained. As much as he longed to still be in the thick of it, he knew that retiring had been a good idea. Being a space hero was, after all, a young man's job. And if he couldn't be out there protecting space, at least he could ensure that the next generation of heroes were more than capable.

The memories of his time at the university always

brought a smile to his face, no matter how many years passed, and he hoped that these students would look back on their time just as fondly. The fourteen young men sitting before him all looked like proper hero material – muscular, tall, with thick hair that was cut short enough to not get in the way, but long enough to be tousled by a stray breeze. They were broad-shouldered with biceps that could bench-press trucks, and dazzling smiles. Brawnly knew that some of these men would find hero training to be too difficult and would end up transferring to security or basic training, but at first glance he felt like they all had the potential to succeed.

"Good morning, future heroes!" he greeted them cheerfully.

"Good morning, sir," they replied in almost-perfect unison.

Brawnly stood in front of his desk, readying his first-day speech. "Now, I know that you're all here because you desire to be a space hero, but I want to warn you that there's more to being a hero than simply wanting to be one. You must prove yourself to be brave, strong, and loyal at all times. As a hero, you will be responsible for your crew's lives, and in times of crisis they will look to you for courage. I know that you've all gone through academy training, but this university will test you harder than you've ever been tested before. The next four years are all that stand between you and your dreams. Do not expect any of it to be easy, but if you remain determined, you can succeed." He could see that his speech was having the desired effect and that some of the expressions had changed from excited to serious. "Although there is a great burden that comes with it, the life of a space hero can be one of the most rewarding lives to live. Why," he smiled and leaned against the desk, crossing his arms, "I remember the time I was on Zantha-42, trying to locate the evil Morkane and the crate of assimodium that he'd absconded with. The sun was beginning to set as I approached from the west–"

A sharp knocking on the classroom door interrupted his memory. Startled, Brawnly turned to the sound, annoyance rising within. He'd never had a class interrupted on the very first day, and he couldn't think of any reason why someone would do such a thing.

The door opened and a young, brunette woman stepped inside.

"Professor Brawnly?" she asked.

"Yes?" he replied, confused as to why someone like her would be knocking on his classroom door.

"Oh, good," she smiled, relief washing over her. "I'm in the right place."

"No, I don't think you are," he said, straightening up. "Damsel training is on the first floor."

The smile fell from her face. "I'm not here for damsel training."

He was even more confused. "Science training?" he guessed. Sometimes the less important classes took on a woman or two to fill out the quota, but only if they showed exception skill.

"No, sir, I'm here for hero training. I'd have been here sooner, but everyone I talked to kept sending me to the first floor." She smiled again, although it was more of an effort this time.

Brawnly laughed, the kind of laugh that only came after a particularly wonderful and unexpected joke. "That's impossible. Women can't be heroes. Why, that's one of the first things we learn."

"But I received confirmation that my registration for

this class went through."

Brawnly picked up the class list that was lying on his desk. There were fifteen names on it, and doing a quick count, he saw that there were only fourteen men in front of him. "What's your name?" he asked.

"Riley Everheart."

Sure enough, five names down was *Riley Everheart*. It would have been a great name for a young heroic boy, but was all wrong for a girl.

"It says here that you went to Heracles Academy," Brawnly said, confused. Heracles Academy was one of the top schools for heroes-in-training and he had no idea why they'd let a woman into their classes, let alone allow her to pass. It had to be a lie, and he'd be damned if he let a woman try to sneak into his class using deceitful means.

"Does it?" She looked confused for a second, but then snapped her fingers. "It must be a typo. I went to Hera Academy. It's a great school, but relatively new. I passed all the necessary hero prerequisites while I was there."

Brawnly frowned. Admin must have thought it was a spelling error. After all, most heroes weren't especially known for their brains – that kind of thing was for the nerds in the science and engineering departments. He'd never heard of this Hera Academy and wasn't entirely certain that it existed, but he'd have to warn administration so that they could watch out for any more misunderstandings.

"Are you sure you wouldn't rather be in the damsel course?" he asked gently, placing the list back on his desk. "It's really a much better place for women."

She shook her head. "No, sir. I want to be a space hero. Have since I was a kid."

He paused and sized her up. She was tall enough, almost six feet tall, but there wasn't nearly enough muscle on her frame. Her brown hair was too long, and the braid it was in made it incapable of blowing delicately in a light breeze. Although she wore no make-up, there was a certain natural beauty about her. Her features were a bit too sharp, but if she took a damsel class, they would teach her how to soften those lines and make her complexion glow.

He couldn't understand why someone like her would want to be a hero when she was obviously all wrong for it. Perhaps it was that joke of an academy she'd gone to. They must have filled her head with all kinds of nonsense, misleading her about what it took be a hero. There was no way she could fight strange aliens or traverse difficult terrain or avoid traps while trying to rescue crew members.

"You say you've done the prerequisites, have you?" he said, an idea forming in his mind.

She nodded.

"Then you won't mind giving us a bit of a demonstration, would you?" He smiled, confident that she'd back down at the thought of physical exertion. Once she was put through the ringer and realized how difficult it was to be a space hero, she'd give up this futile thinking.

She looked at his smile, sizing him up, before matching it with one of her own. "I'd be delighted, sir."

The obstacle course had already been laid out in preparation for the first week of training, but it had taken Brawnly almost an hour to gather the other pieces of this test. He wanted Riley to run the course, but he also wanted her to fight enemies, defeat a Big Bad, rescue the damsel, and secure the McGuffinite. Some of these tasks wouldn't be taught to the students until their second or third year, but he had no desire to take it easy on her. The harder this test was, the sooner she'd quit, and the sooner he could go back to regaling his class about his many amazing exploits.

He rounded up some instructors who had free time and were eager to help reinforce the University's status quo. As word spread about this test, other teachers and students showed interest in attending, and soon the stands were full of onlookers.

Riley was standing at the starting line, alone. She seemed slightly nervous and well-aware that all eyes were on her. Some of the students had already started taunting her, yelling at her to go back to damsel class and leave this kind of thing to the men.

Brawnly held back a laugh and walked over to her. "Not as easy to be a hero as you thought, eh?" he said as he looked out at the course. "If you want to back out, nobody's going to blame you."

Instead of admitting defeat and giving in, she squared her shoulders and stood up tall. A determined look crossed her face as she crouched into a starting position. "Let's get this over with."

Brawnly hoped that this obviously false confidence wasn't going to be this kid's downfall. The course was safe enough, but it was possible for men to harm themselves by not realizing their limits. There was no way that she could complete the course ahead of her, but he got the impression that she was not going to back down. Brawnly almost admired her bravado, but he quickly pushed the feeling aside.

He looked out at the stands and raised his hands. The audience erupted into cheers, but none of them for Riley.

"Let's begin!" he shouted, blowing his whistle.

Riley took off. The first part of the track was easy enough, a length of sandy terrain, but it soon became inundated with large rocks to maneuver around, fallen trees to hop over, and holes to avoid. Brawnly had expected her to slow down, but instead she used her momentum to propel her slight frame over and around the obstacles. In record time she was at the next obstacle – the rock-wall. It was ten feet tall with unmarked handholds, but it proved no match for her determination. Brawnly knew where all the handholds were, but she was able to fit her smaller hands and feet into crevices that wouldn't have held the men. Using her legs and arms to lift herself up, she quickly made her way to the top. As Brawnly watched this incredible feat, he made a mental note to check into the Hera Academy and the type of classes they offered.

At the top of the wall were two of the second-year fight instructors, ready to attack. The audience cheered for the instructors, calling out for their success.

'This,' Brawnly thought to himself, *'is where we separate the men from the women.'*

The two men attacked, but Riley dodged their blows, proving too evasive for their punches and kicks. For a while it looked like all she could do was dodge, and Brawnly was about to interfere, but then one of the men came for her, aiming a punch at her head, and instead of dodging entirely, she grabbed his arm. Using his momentum, she threw him into the other man, knocking the two of them together. The men fell onto the ground, stunned, and Riley moved on.

The crowd was disappointed, but they started cheering even louder as she approached the Big Bad. Having watched her previous fight, the fourth-year instructor playing the Big Bad cracked his knuckles and readied himself. He started by throwing quick punches, all of which Riley dodged, but a few got close. Smirking, the man pulled a metal stick from his belt. In one fluid motion, he snapped both ends out into a long staff. Riley's eyes widened for a second before narrowing. She took a defensive stance and waited for him to come to her. The man approached cautiously. When he was close enough, he feinted before striking out with the staff. It caught her on the left arm and she winced in pain, but before he could bring the staff around again, she moved in towards him and delivered four quick punches to his stomach. He backed up, partly in surprised and partly in pain, and she deftly kicked him in the solar plexus, doubling him over. An elbow to his back and he was on the ground, groaning.

Riley stepped over him and waved to the crowd, who were now watching in stunned silence, their jeers and chants quickly forgotten with her defeat of a man who'd once brought down the evil Zerbzeb. She moved on nonetheless, approaching the cage where the damsel in distress was being held. The damsel, a third-year instructor, couldn't help staring at her with awe.

"You were amazing," she said in a breathy voice as Riley unlocked the cage door.

"And now you're free," Riley responded, smiling at her. She swept the damsel into her arms, dipping her. Only the smallest distance separated their mouths. "It's a pleasure to rescue one as fair as you."

The damsel kissed her passionately.

"Until next time," Riley winked as the kiss ended. She left the damsel breathless as she moved over to the platform where the McGuffinite was sitting. Taking hold of the metallic object, she held it triumphantly over her head.

Her victory was met with silence.

Brawnly's jaw was practically on the floor. His mind raced. Was he going to have to let this woman in his class now? The fact that she'd passed a course that most first-year students would have failed didn't change the fact that she was a girl. Or that she'd make all the other students in his class look bad.

He looked at the other teachers, but they were just as shocked as he was.

Riley walked over to him, tossing the McGuffinite in one hand.

"Thanks," she smiled. "That was actually a lot of fun."

"Uh..."

She waited for him to say something, but his mind was utterly unable to form words.

"So, did I pass?" she prompted him, holding out the McGuffinite.

"Uh..." He took the object and looked around again, hoping desperately to find help, but seeing none. "I mean, it's not... Um..." He felt like he was going to start hyperventilating. In mere minutes, his entire world had been turned upside down.

She frowned, looked around at the astonished room, and paused. Suddenly she smiled brightly. "You know what, Professor Brawnly? If this is the best that Space University can offer, then maybe I'm better off going somewhere else." She chucked to herself. "You know, I hear that Villain University is a lot of fun."

As Riley walked out of the room, Brawnly felt a wash of relief come over him. Good, now she was someone else's problem, and everything could go back to normal. But as soon as the doors closed behind her, the metallic clang reverberating throughout the room, he was suddenly filled with dread. Villain University? She was going to become a villain?

A different kind of fear gripped his heart. His heroes were going to need a lot more training.

Matthew Daniels

Matthew Daniels has been in every From the Rock book thus far. His story 'Healer's Hoards' appeared in 2016's *Sci-Fi from the Rock*, 'Living and Learning' in 2017's *Fantasy from the Rock*, 'Grow Gold Together' in 2018's *Chillers from the Rock*, 'Eggshell Revolution' in 2019's *Dystopia from the Rock*, and 'Rooftop Statistics' in *Flights from the Rock*.

In December 2019 he was named a member of the Engen Books Board of Directors.

His first novel, *Diary of Knives*, is set for a November 2020 release.

His flash fiction also appeared in *Kit Sora: The Artobiography* under the title 'Epilogue?'. Daniels has proven himself to be a renaissance man of genre fiction, capable of rising to the occasion of any challenge thrown his way. His short story 'Where With All' was featured in the *All Borders are Temporary* collection by Transnational Arts Production.

As competition over placement in the From the Rock series has improved, so has Daniels steadily grown in his authorial abilities. His newest story is titled 'Namaily.'

Namaily

The first step in Ipo's day was waking up. He did this unwillingly. Every time. Which made perfect sense to me. Sometimes I'd have to step on him to get him going, alarm or no. Neither of us needed our custom space suits because we were inside the Extraction Team Vessel, and this made it easier to step on him. The ETV looked like a habitable pinball from outside and a very complicated bachelor room inside.

Once he extracted himself from the bed, he broke his fast with Grey Goo™. It seemed to grow all of its own in its wall-mounted vat. Next to it was a second, smaller vat labelled Grey Goo™: Purrfection™. Ipo poured some of the latter into a bowl he set down for me. It was labelled Namaily in free-hand black marker.

Step two was what Ipo called SSS: shave, shower, and... uh... sit. On the toilet. This step included some minutiae and some important tasks -- such as recycling my litter. On this planet, which the Company called Buyome to be cute, it was hard to find good soil. The planet looked mostly like jungle, but everything was based on silicon. Which was why we came here. While that was great and all, it meant that we couldn't breathe the air or eat anything until it was broken down, filtered, and recombined.

Ipo pressed a button on the wall during Step Two, early in the mission. "Hailing Open Channel."

"Copy that, Extraction Team. Survey Team here."

"Our shift's not started yet, you buttheads," said a woman's voice.

"Good morning, Science Team," Ipo answered.

"That's Business Team to you," she answered.

"That's what he said," Survey Team chipped in.

"What do you want?" Business Team was so desperate for coffee that they could practically hear her rubbing her eyes.

"Any word from anybody about why our surface Wi-fi doesn't work, but all our other data and comms are good?"

"You bothered me before punch for curiosity?" Business Team grouched.

"There's punch?" Survey Team asked.

I didn't know you could feel an ellipsis until that conversation.

Business Team got to -- well -- business. "Base got nuthin'. None of my studies or readings are making any sense of it. There's no record from the scouting of the planet about signal interference of any kind. But I'm on it."

A few days later, we had to change how we did Step 3: Clock In. Punching for our shift was fine. All of the vessels were synced with atomic clocks to Earth, Indian Standard Time. We then went in an order: Business Team Vessel, ETV, Survey Team Vessel. Ipo had put on his space suit when the ETV ran afoul of a bizarre crystalline mushroom bog. We didn't always follow Business Team in a direct line because each vessel's driver made slightly different decisions about the terrain.

Ipo didn't bother suiting me up because he went

through the airlock and used the decontamination feature on the way back in. Apparently someone on the Design Team lost their job that day.

There was big money on this operation. Once silicon-based life was discovered, the Silicon Rally took off: without proof of intelligence, this life was a resource. None of the genetics laws applied outside of carbon-based life. It's why the space programs finally started getting real money and effort again. So now we go Survey, Extraction, Business. They even sent us better equipment for streamlining the process.

Over a month later, Ipo was taking his First Break -- which was Step 4 in the day. Sometimes he explored. Like admiring a waterfall instead of studying it. And though they'd done much for approaching lightspeed travel, they couldn't adjust for the lag of "just" lightspeed in their communications, so video contact home was pre-recorded and sent through relays.

"You're taking the giant leaps," his wife said in one of them. "So here are the small steps!" She'd done a monthly highlight reel to make the year's wait worth it. Their daughter had taken her first steps.

"Not as much as I love you," she said after a pause. That was what she used to say when he told her he loved her. N.A.M.A.I.L.Y.

The fifth step in the day, a segment that Ipo mutter-dubbed, "Solving Problems," was always the midday witching hour of technical difficulties that came for him when he tried to harvest the samples Survey Team flagged as useful. About a week after his daughter's moon landing, there were bugs in the system. Literally. They were like ants, but they covered their legs in discarded teeth like a crab wearing a shell.

It sounded like a helter-scatter of marbles.

"MAYDAY!" Ipo shouted into the radio. "BTV, there's an army of teeth in here!"

I was running around, jumping, hissing, and shrieking.

"They don't attack anything living," Business Team responded in a hurry, "unless you hurt them. They're after the machinery, but they can't actually get through anything airtight."

"I never let them in!"

"Yes, you obviously did. They're sneakier than you think."

"How do you know all this?"

"Remember that really grumpy morning I had?"

I was standing arched and watching the greenish pools of skittering bits, now that I'd noticed that they stayed outside of an invisible circle of each of us. "Yeah?" Ipo was nearing panic.

"They kept me up the night before. It's not until I put on a song with a harmonica that they fled."

Ipo was speechless.

"...you don't have anything like that, do you?"

"I like EDM," he answered.

There was a spark of distant sound from the radio. Was she sighing into the receiver, or changing something up in there? Then the sound of a harmonica came through. From the quality, either she had to jack up the volume or harmonicas were as bad as I remembered. He jacked up the volume on his end to be sure, and activated the airlock system. The little green ants, camouflaged in the vegetation outside, were soon out of his vessel. He performed full system scans sixteen more times and spent forty-five minutes searching for the last unaccounted foreign body before he realized it was the sample he'd taken.

Second Break, or the sixth part of the day, was when the teams got philosophical. I'd get my second helping of Purrfection™, maybe belly rubs and the like, sometimes a toy. As incidents like the Munchers (as Ipo called the ants) got more frequent and unusual, he'd read more or talk about the mission and what their work meant beyond the economy.

"I had a friend put together a hard drive with copies of all the project info right up until we launched," Survey Team told him one day.

"They didn't search you?" Ipo asked. His frown was so intense that surely it came through the other end of the radio.

"Of course they did. And they found it and knew what it was. I convinced them it was part of my project package," Survey Team explained.

"Sounds too easy," Business Team remarked.

"There's a lot of information. I've only poked at it because I was bored. I did find one thing you might like." A beat. "Here it is: the time credit budget for the planetary scouting."

Ipo's scritches stopped. I had to actually put a paw on his arm to remind him of his priorities.

...

Better.

Mostly the three of them seemed bitter or disappointed.

"How do you even short-cut something like that!?" Ipo demanded.

Standard procedure required a full month (based on Earth-synced atomic clocks) to investigate and secure a planet before sending human-contact missions. I'm finding my thoughts becoming clearer all the time. Random knowledge, memories of mentioned tidbits like this, keep flooding back to me now. Anyway, the Company's lobbyists had found ways to count certain exercises or information sources as credits towards X number of days explored.

All three teams had been sent on this planetary DNA harvesting mission with four days' intelligence.

Even calling them "teams" was...philosophical.

The seventh step of the day was what frustrated Ipo the most: Debrief, Report, and Document. Records were assiduous. I did most of my purring around this time as I crawled on or played with Ipo's devices, screens, and what-not. He had that half-grin from someone who's actually enjoying being tormented a little. What can I say? I am what I am.

Everything was documented. When we used the bathroom, how long it took, weeping spells, how often we communicated for non-mission purposes, how closely we followed daily scheduling protocols, the photos we took, weekly mental health assessments, complaints (sometimes I'd start loudly meowing to get Ipo to let up), digital and mechanical issues. They tried to have Ipo disciplined for the Munchers incident, but Business Team backed him up.

Discipline was easy: the orbital base had complete remote access to the vessels' systems. They could shut down whatever they wanted: bathroom mechanisms, heat, light, movement, radio contact, screens for reading. It wasn't until Ipo got a message from his wife that he realized -- based on some of her confusion about knowledge gaps -- that messages were vetted and censored.

The last of the reports were included in the day's genetic harvest, which was sent to orbit from an anti-gravity platform included with the vehicles. Orbital drones would retrieve these harvests and bring them to base. Only the ETV could harvest anything meaningful; Business Team was for deeper intel and Survey Team directed Extraction Team (that is, Ipo) to the best items.

Was I an item? I came from Earth with Ipo, they didn't need to study me. Plenty of cats out there. But still. For that matter, was Ipo an item?

Step 8 was Clock Out. Work was over for the day.

Step 1 was Wake Up. Again, Step 2: SSS. He shaved, he showered, he shortened my nails. And his own. Step 3, Clock In. Right away, flowers started blooming and it went downhill from there.

"Business Team!" Ipo shouted to the radio as he battened everything down and hot-footed the vessel away from the area.

"Something wrong?"

"ARE YOU TRYING TO KILL ME!?"

"Survey Team repor-"

"The flowers are attacking!"

"I'm sorry, what?"

"It looks like phosphorus or magnesium or something!"

"What does?"

"THE FLOWER THING!"

"Extraction Team, please."

Ipo looked at me. "When this is over…" it sounded like he was plotting with me. He'd been talking to me more often in the last few months. The orbital base was getting more insistent about the mission. The mental health assessments stopped. "Inefficient," they'd claimed.

It took hours to get out of the hot zone. The flowers

were literally setting their own forest on fire. Business Team was both excited and terrified. Ipo started laughing. I hid in a corner from him, because that just wasn't right.

Everything changed on Step 4 a week later, when Business Team interrupted Ipo's break.

"I've been making a special study of flowers since... uh..."

"That's a terrible idea," Ipo said.

Business Team sighed. "Probably, but I have news. I've found a connection with the ants."

"The Munchers talk to the flowers?" Ipo stopped eating his goo.

"No. Well, yes." Business Team faltered. "They're all connected! Which means...oh, gods..."

"What?"

"Hailing Open Channel," Survey Team started.

"Extraction Team here," Ipo said.

"Oh, hi, you're just in time. The whole planet has wi-fi!" Business Team declared.

Survey Team didn't absorb that straight away. "I have bad news, you guys. The landscape shifts I've- wait, what?"

Step 5 is Problem Solving. Ha.

"All the plants and animals. Fungi. Everything I can find. That's why everything's attacking us," Business Team said. "They all have a kind of antenna cell. There's no intelligent life on the planet because it's all one! An intelligence, a community!"

"That explains my findings," Survey Team said. "The forests, the underbrush, everything that's not actually water, wind, or stone. It's all moving!" A pause. "There's a tree outside, forty-foot diameter. It's...oh, no."

"It's what?" Business Team urged.

A massive crash. Ipo changed the radio channel because there was painful feedback. "Business Team?"

"Here!" She was breathing heavily, but not from exertion. "I've lost access to the data grid. No GPS. I could try to work out where Survey Team was…"

"That's a death trap," Ipo said. "I'm sorry, but that didn't sound like there was room for a rescue mission."

They started trying to contact the orbital base.

Step 6: Second Break.

Ipo had lost all contact. The anti-gravity platform was disabled. He didn't have a way of fleeing the surface.

Step 7: Report, Debrief, Document.

Extraction Team was in a full-on panic. I stayed where I was, snug atop a vent near the ceiling in a corner. He tried emergency overrides. Hailing the base, home, the whole solar system.

Only now am I starting to realize why I'm able to understand so much of this. I'm guessing it was the mushroom bog, though my body hasn't had any sign of mold. It's faint, and cuts in and out, but I'm starting to feel everyone around me. There are birds. Shrubs, vines, a windborne seed pod. The only living thing I don't feel is Ipo: struggling into his suit, trying to cobble together a weapon, and stopping up the gaps in the vessel that are being torn or worked into by all the life.

Clock Out.

Brad Dunne

Brad Dunne is a freelance writer and editor from St. John's, Newfoundland. He began his writing career as an intern at *The Walrus* magazine and has published journalism and essays in publications such as *Maisonneuve*, *The Canadian Encyclopedia*, and *Herizons*. His short fiction has been featured in *In/Words*, *Acta Victoriana*, and *The Cuffer Anthology*.

His debut novel, *After Dark Vapours*, was released in October 2018, to positive response.

His second novel, *The Gut*, is scheduled for a September 2020 release.

He maintains a blog at braddunne.ca

The Pale Horse

The Planet was death.

That's what Dr. Cheryl McLeod thought as she took a walk down to the lake. It was a conundrum none of the scientists could solve: How could a planet that boasted all the necessary life-sustaining elements not be able to sustain life? Planet Telex was chosen from other terraforming candidates for its Goldilocksesque temperature and atmosphere. It had an ideal proximity to a sun and there was a water cycle to transport any necessary chemicals to organisms. And yet, when they landed, there were no signs of life, like a ghost city that was waiting to be filled with people. The soil seemed to drain the life out of anything they planted. After the most recent crop failure, Cheryl felt like she'd better take a walk before she took a blowtorch to the entire lab.

At least the air was nice to breathe, unlike back on Earth where the air had become turgid and polluted. Cheryl considered herself fortunate to have grown up in Stornoway, Scotland; the Hebrides archipelago was one of the few remaining truly rural parts of the world. However, she didn't realize just how fortunate she was until she moved to London for university. After about a week, she was coughing up black phlegm in the shower and missing the ocean breeze of Stornoway. Despite the absence of foliage, Telex's air reminded her of fall in Scotland: that thick spicy fragrance of rotting leaves. Everyone on the mission agreed that for all its frustrations, a short walk on Telex's surface did wonders for the mind.

Cheryl crested the hill of bleached stone and looked out upon the small lake, which she'd taken to calling Loch McLeod. It was a little slice of home trillions of miles from Earth. She picked up a nice flat rock that fit squarely between her finger and thumb and skimmed it across the water with a graceful flick of her wrist. The stone skipped about four times before dropping into the lake, forming progressively smaller circles. Cheryl estimated it travelled about twenty metres. Not bad for a warm-up shot.

She began searching for another bit of ammunition when she was startled by an alien noise. Nearby there was the noise of heavy hooves clopping over the rocks and breaths drawn from loose nostrils. Before she turned her head to search for the noise's source, she heard a beastly snort and the sounds of drinking from the water. She realized the sound wasn't alien but in fact familiar, which gave her the nerve to turn her neck and see what it was.

A large pale horse was craning its neck to drink from the lake. The only animal the team had brought to Telex was a goat named Cans, so it wasn't theirs. Cheryl watched the horse drink and felt a terrible pang in her heart for home, where horses still roamed the Scottish highlands. Nostalgia overwhelmed her and she was compelled to approach the animal. Its ropey muscles flexed beneath its thick white hide. When Cheryl got close, the horse paused briefly from drinking to consider her, then returned to its business. She stretched out her hand to stroke its crest, a gentle convex curve from its ears to its shoulders.

"Where did you come from?" she asked aloud, overtaken by its beauty.

She continued stroking the animal and didn't realize anything was amiss until she looked down and saw that its hooves were backwards. Instinctively, she stepped backwards in surprise but was unable to pull her arm away. It was glued to the horse. She tried to pry it off with her other hand, but it was attached, like it had bonded to its skin. The pale horse was now emaciated, its muscles instantly grown gaunt.

Cheryl screamed. The backwards hooves began to march towards the lake.

"No, no, no," Cheryl pleaded, unable to get her hand loose.

Indifferent to her cries, the pale horse trotted into the lake, pulling Cheryl with it. Underwater, she could see the skeletal remains of a plethora of alien creatures, drawn to Telex like a fly to a pitcher planet. Cheryl screamed once again, and the water filled her lungs. Everything slowly went dark as she travelled deeper into Telex's digestive system. Before she went unconscious, a thought returned to her:

The planet was death.

Melissa Bishop

Born and raised in the St. John's /Mount Pearl area, Bishop is a newcomer to the genre fiction scene in Atlantic Canada whose fantastic prose has taken the provinces community by storm. Her work won two Kit Sora awards in 2019: July 2019 'Cycles' and September 2019 'Huntress of the Woods,' and has placed numerous other times.

Bishop describes herself as a loyal Tolkien fan and high school teacher, teaching at the same high school she attended in her youth. She started writing when she was very young and honed her skills in High School, when she started a pen pal friendship that has lasted for over 17 years, writing stories back and forth to each other.

She brings with her her short story 'The Photograph.'

The Photograph

Her husband was late coming home. Mary Anne was waiting in his study, looking at the vast valley that spread out before their second floor window. Rows and rows of trees swayed in the chilly autumn breeze. They had moved to the quiet town when they were first married, for Charles, a Canadian born and bred, loved the forest and wanted to be close to it. There was something about the way he looked at trees – this expression of wide-eyed amazement—that Mary Anne thought quite adorable. Charles found their woodland walks inspiring, and inspiration was essential in his profession.

Charles was a science fiction writer. His genre of writing was a rather niche one, but he had seen great success from his imaginative creations. Charles wrote a series focusing on the life of a lonely man trapped on a deserted planet earth, a Robinson Crusoe for the future, as he often described it. Mary Anne could never really read it. Her husband's words were so detailed that she could almost see the desperate man, trapped on that desolate planet. He felt real. It was such a foreboding story that she would rather not think about it. Now that Charles said he needed to speak with her, Mary Anne assumed he would announce the completion of his next edition. She hoped he would not ask her to review it.

Charles, however, had not yet returned from his errands. So she waited, listening to the tick of the grandfather clock and the soft echo of *All or Nothing at All* coming from the living room radio downstairs. Turning from the window, she began to look idly about the room, letting her gaze shift over the shelves brimming with books. She let a thin finger run along their spines, eyeing the titles one by one while the other hand ran over the small lump in her belly that would soon be their first child. Once she'd looked the titles over, she brought her attention to the photos Charles hung upon the wall behind his desk. If writing was his craft, Charles's passion was in photography. He was a man for capturing moments, and when he did, he hung them proudly on his wall. She eyed one photo of her and smiled. She remembered it very well. It was taken on July 15, 1939 at the county fair. Mary Anne had been riding the merry-go-round with her younger brother and someone snapped a photo of her, eyes shining and lips smiling. Her light brown hair, dark blue eyes, and yellow dotted dress were lost in the image of black and white, but Charles always said it was his favorite picture of her. She chuckled softly to herself in reminiscence, thinking of the moment Charles offered to help her down from the ride. That was the day they first met. How strange it is that one instant in time can change your life forever.

Her eyes flitted across the mosaic of photographs, each one commemorating a moment in their life. The picnic in Farmer Martin's field where Charles proposed; the view from the top of the woodland path they walked each day; the two of them on the doorstep of the chapel they were married in. She knew four months from now Charles would hang a picture of their firstborn proudly upon this very wall.

And then there was that peculiar one.

It was placed in the centre of them all, exactly behind Charles's desk, so that if he turned about in his chair it was the first one he saw. It was a picture from inside a great window, staring out at a gloomy desert. Two large trees stood, both stripped of greenery, bark, and life. One in the foreground and one in the back, the dead trees loomed over the window, as if reaching out towards the glass with their boney boughs. Charles had never said exactly where he had taken the photo, only that he had snapped it somewhere along his many travels. He had used the shot as inspiration for the cover of his first novel. She stared at it, examining it closely. The blackness of the trees peered back at her like two dark towers.

She straightened as she heard the front door open and shut. "Sorry I'm late, darling!" Charles' voice called from the porch. "I had to wait for Mr. Fisher to check out back for a few spare screws. I'll be up in a minute."

Mary Anne moved to sit in one of the two chairs facing a small fireplace to the left side of the room. They often had their tea here when Charles was mulling over an idea and needed an ear. A moment later, Charles' head appeared in the doorway, a broad smile stretching across his cheeks when he saw her. He was in all appearances an ordinary man— light brown hair, deep set brown eyes, an average stature and size—but when Mary Anne turned to him, she shined as she had in that picture.

"Hello, love," she said as he stepped into the room. She looked to his hand and grinned. "Stopped by Mrs. Humphrey's flower shop as well?"

"When I saw them, I couldn't resist," he replied, looking at the brightly colored bouquet he was holding. "Aren't they amazing? So vibrant and alive. No matter how many I see, I'm still surprised at the colors flowers can bloom in. They're beautiful, like my wife."

She chuckled at his foolish charm, rising from her seat. "I'll go fetch a vase for them."

"No, have a seat, darling. I'll lay them on the desk for now. There is something we need to discuss and I've put it off for far too long."

"Well, you'll wait one minute longer," Mary Anne insisted, taking the flowers from him before adding in a teasing manner, "I'll not let these die from your negligence."

When she returned, it was clear that Charles was nervous about this discussion. He had made himself a drink and was sipping it from a shaky hand. He was staring at his photo, at the two dark trees and empty desert.

"Charles?" Mary Anne called from the door, which brought his eyes to her. "What is the matter?"

He took a deep breath and, laying his drink aside, slowly took the photograph from its place on the wall. "We should sit. I don't know how else to begin."

As Mary Anne walked towards her chair by the fire, she could not fathom what was troubling Charles so. Had his last book been denied by the publisher? Was he ill? He had been rather pensive lately, unusually quiet in the evenings and on their woodland walks. She had often wondered but now she was certain something was wrong.

He sat across from her, eyes shifting to the photo he held between his hands. His deep brown gaze settled there. "Did I ever tell you when I took this picture?" he asked.

Mary Anne's brows furrowed in confusion. "In a desert somewhere on your travels," she replied. "What does this have to do with anything?"

"It was a desert," Charles said with a sorrow that Mary Anne did not understand. "A world of desert."

"Darling, what is going on?" she asked, hesitation creeping into her tone as Charles' expression grew grave.

He turned the photo towards her. "This was taken in a desert, yes. But what if I told you it was taken in the year 2070?"

Mary Anne starred blankly at him, then gave a shaky laugh. "I would say that you've been working on your stories for far too long."

Silence pervaded the room after her response so that her laughter died away and Mary Anne's eyes drifted back down to the picture resting in his hands. Charles seemed wary to carry on this conversation but had resolved to finish it.

"I told you I lived in northern Canada most of my life, and that is true. I've also travelled the world and have seen many things. But this is not about where I travelled to, it is about where I travelled from that matters, and where I must go again."

"Charles, stop playing this game," she protested. "You know your stories always scared me."

"They're true, Mary Anne," he persisted. "That was my life in 2070. Please, just give me a moment to explain it all. That's all I really need."

And so, Charles began a story, one that seemed to echo the words of his novels. He spoke of something called climate change that became a serious issue in the early 2000's and resulted in a worldwide famine in 2035. In 2041 there was what Charles called a 'nuclear war' amongst the countries that had survived famine and were desperate to keep what little food they had engineered. By 2050, the year that Charles was born, he was the first child born to his colony in 30 years. What remained of the world's population resided in what he could only describe as gigantic bunkers of heavy metals, sunken solidly into the earth. These immovable fortresses had only one window, made of a thick and impenetrable glass-like material. From it, his colony could stare out at the desert that was their dying planet. Two black trees stood outside, shadowing over them like harbingers of death.

No other children where born after Charles. His childhood was a hard one, filled with grim faces, disease, and death. His colony had one refuge as they lived through the desolation of earth—their photography gallery.

"By 2053, time travel became a popular form of entertainment. We had rudimentary Devices," he explained, lifting the cuff of his shirt to motion to the gold watch he'd always worn. He said it was his father's. "With them we could travel to any time for as long as we wished, but we needed a starting point. Photographs were the perfect medium. They gave us a time, place, and circumstances. We'd merely point our timepiece towards the photo and click the dial. My father and I used to sift through photos for hours. Our world was dying but the worlds we saw were beautiful." He eyes seemed distant as he spoke. "When he died, I was the last of my colony. My mother had died in childbirth and I had never really known her, for we never had a photograph of her. The others died in the epidemic of '66. For three years I was alone. I travelled; climbed mountains; swam in the Pacific Ocean; saw cultures long dwindled to dust. Then, in the boxes of boxes of photographs, I found you." He looked towards his photo wall, to the image of her on that merry-go-round. "I loved you instantly. In all the photos I had seen, nothing compared to your bright smile and beaming eyes. After some thought and deliberation, I decided to abandon my world -- to try and make a life in yours, if I could ever win you over. I took this photo just before I left my home," he stood slowly, bringing his eyes back to the desert image in his hand, "to remind myself of my resolve to go. So that I could be thankful for every moment with you." He moved once again towards the wall, gently hanging the frame in its place amongst the others. All that could be heard from the room was the slow tick tock from the grandfather clock.

"It all seems so fantastical, Charles," Mary Anne finally spoke through the quiet. "You are a beautiful writer, darling, but am I to believe you came to the county fair in 1939 to meet me? From the future, the very distant future, at that?"

He kept his back to her, the fading light of evening making him a silhouette against the photographs. "I don't need you to believe me," he said softly. "I just needed to tell you the truth. You and baby." He turned and brought his hand to rest on the small box camera that sat upon his desk. Mary Anne had bought it for him last Christmas, the first box camera with an indoor flash—a small metal plate tucked behind a bulb, perched atop the camera. "Now I must ask you one more favor. Can I take a picture of you? You as you are, right in this moment."

"Oh, darling." Mary Anne smiled nervously. "Of course, now that your story is over. You shouldn't play such jokes on me. You know I don't like them."

"Again, it is the truth, Mary Anne. I need the photograph so I can come back to you."

"Charles! Surely this has gone on long enough?" Mary Anne exclaimed, exasperated.

"I have to go back," Charles insisted. "Something's

gone wrong with my timepiece. I shouldn't be long, and for you, it will be no more than the flash of the camera. Your photo will bring me right back to this moment. But in case something happens, I needed you to know. I will be back. Shouldn't be more than a second," he repeated, trying to be reassuring in Mary Anne's hesitation.

"Oh fine, Charles. Take the picture," she relented, her patience wearing. "But please quit this game you're playing. You're frightening me."

He returned to the seat across from her, holding the camera delicately in his hands. "I don't mean to frighten you," he replied. "I love you, Mary Anne. I'll love you forever." His gaze lingered on her one minute more before he brought his attention to the camera lens. Something in his expression seemed sad. "Smile, darling."

She smiled. The flash was bright and left her blinking.

It took her eyes a moment to adapt once again to the dimly lit room. When they did, she found the chair beside her vacant. Her husband had vanished.

"Charles?" her voice called warily, unnerved by his sudden disappearance.

"Mary Anne?" a frail voice replied.

She rose from her seat and looked towards the photo wall, where the voice had originated. A pair of feet in shabby shoes peaked out from behind the desk. Someone was lying on the floor. "Mary Anne, is that you?" the weakened voice spoke again, a sort of desperate hope in each word.

The mystified wife moved cautiously towards the desk and coming behind it found a man lying there, a pool of blood seeping out onto the floor.

At first glance, he could have easily been mistaken for

Charles' father. He appeared to be a man in his fifties, his brown hair peppered silvery gray. Time had carved its ridges on his face, crinkled about his eyes, and furrowed his brows. On his right arm was the gold watch Charles had always worn. In his left hand was a black and white photo of Mary Anne, sat in the chair by the fire. Smiling.

When his eyes met hers, Mary Anne knew. No one had ever looked at her like he had. "Charles!" she exclaimed, panic rising as she dropped to her knees, her dress soaking up blood on the floor, wide eyes sweeping over a wound that looked as if he'd been through some sort of explosion. "What happened?!"

He smiled faintly, looking up at her.

"I got stuck," he said weakly. "Couldn't make it back. Everything was in such disrepair when I returned. It took me years to fix and modify my device and even then, it was risky to even attempt to come back. Thirty-two years and one great gamble." He coughed, a little blood trickling at the corner of his mouth. "For one last look at you." A trembling hand reached up to caress the side of her face. She brought her hand to rest on his as a tidal wave of emotions swept over her.

"I'll fetch Dr. Parsons," she said, her voice shaking with every word. "Perhaps he can help you."

Charles shifted his head from side to side, the gleam in his eyes slowly dimming. "My time is spent, darling," he whispered through cracked lips. "Just a moment more— to say that I'd do it all again. To say that I love you—you and baby."

Mary Anne held his hand to her cheek long after his last breath wheezed from his pale lips and the light faded from his brown eyes, forever fixed on her. When she could finally bear to look away from his face, she saw once more the photo still clenched between his fingers.

So, it had all been true. Taking the photo up with a trembling hand, she stared at her own image—the smile of a woman who had, mere minutes ago, been happy in her life. Now it lay shattered upon the floor like so many shards of broken glass. Tears began to flood her eyes, skewing her vision as the shock and sorrow of it all began to sink in. Her body shivered and convulsed. She sobbed for some time at the desolation of her life, her misery echoing through the empty hallways of the lonely house. With bleary eyes, she looked at the photos on the wall in lamentation. No more moments left to hang there. Her happy family dreams fading to nothing. How strange it is that one instant in time can change your life forever.

Her eyes suddenly settled on the photo at the centre of it all.

She knew what she had to do.

With shaky fingers, she folded Charles' hands across his chest, straightened his clothes with care and fussed over his hair. Carefully, as if afraid to wake him from sleep, she slipped the gold watch from his wrist and fastened it as best she could to her own. Standing slowly, she took one last look at his lifeless form, one more sweeping gaze of the room that had been part of their life. With a deep breath, she turned her back to it all, teary eyes fixed upon that photo on the wall. Those two black trees reached out as if hands extended towards her, welcoming her home.

C. S. Woodburn

Woodburn was born in Vancouver and currently lives on the West Coast. She has worked as an office cleaner, tea server, sales associate, and office assistant.

Her only previous writing credit is 'Sardines' from the short story collection *The Body Book*.

Green

The planet's sun was setting as the ship entered the atmosphere, the triangular craft barreling counter-orbital so that the oil-slick black hull played a mockery of the sundown in reverse: dark blue forced back through indigo-violet to salmon and fuchsia, tropical orange flaming into tangerine, molten gold, and honeyed butterscotch. It would have been worth noting amongst most people, but as it was, no one on board was awake, and if they had been, they were not the type to find anything of merit in the simple interaction between light and atmospheric particles.

Megametres sped past, and by the time the sun had been forced back up over the horizon, the craft had dropped within kissing distance of the planet's atmosphere: a perpetual mass of swirling thunderheads and inky tendrils that cloaked the gas giant in pewter and iron, shot with lightning and ignited with methane. Condensation burst over the nose of the spacecraft, warming panes left cold and dry by the sharp caress of open space, and steam burst and boiled from the black shell. Small streams and rivulets formed as the surface acclimated, artificial veins and arteries traced and then obliviated *ad infinitum* by the rushing wind.

Ahead in the distance a cluster of rods and antennas appeared projected out of the storm, burnished gold and copper by the dying sun, and the speed of the craft slackened perceptibly. Tiny stars blinked into existence the closer the craft flew, firefly specks deep in the roiling storm that faded from sodium brightness to afterimages, and with a last, gentle course correction, the ship slowed even further and dipped beneath the clouds. At the same time, lights came on inside the vessel—warm, friendly, yellow-white lights, designed to intrude on sleep in the gentlest possible of ways—and a mass of chemicals began to pump through the airducts: antivirals, antibiotics, antimalarials; taxanes; caffeine, nicotine, amphetamines. A bespoke inoculation crafted in response to atmospheric data and the biological statistics of the ship's passengers; a panacea to keep fraying biology intact, to hold disparate systems together: a chemical bandage, to smooth appearances and provide the illusion of control.

It had been only a few weeks since the two passengers had called on the gas giant, but in that time their needs had changed enough that the volatile mist stung Kai's lungs as she drew her first breaths, the very air itching and swelling her throat and nose. Automatically, she reached out with her left arm and passed her wrist through a metal hoop riveted to the side of her sleep pod. Red lights came on, scanning the pale flesh of her inner arm, while hypodermic needles darted in from four other angles; sharp bee stings followed by the welcome flow of cool liquid through her veins: antihistamines, anticoagulants, immunosuppressants, and a bolus of insulin. It was another remedy to get her almost functional, the equivalent of a cold cloth on the forehead: more specific treatments would be pushed as soon as analysis of her vital statistics was complete.

While she waited, careful to keep her arm in the diagnostic hoop, Kai reached across the pod and tapped a touchscreen in the wall, calling up a view of the planet from an external camera. Not surprisingly it was dark beneath the cloud layer, rain slithering repeatedly across the camera lens, warping and distorting what sights were visible. Even so, she could make out a vast pillar of light ahead: the Needle. An unbroken spindle of fluorescent-lined hatches and ill-fitting modules that pierced the planet *ex atmo* to icy core, it was tawdry and displeasing to her eye, and as the ship drew closer with nothing new to disturb the scene, she closed the vid-link with a sharp tap of her finger. Fringespace planets were such a bore, the Sabir so pathetically desperate for upgrades and repairs, so eager to get back to their little lives of digging things up and breaking them down…

So long as they didn't steal anything this time, thought Kai. The last thieves who'd tried it had been so riddled with inferiorities, it'd almost been hardly worth the effort they'd put into harvesting them.

Beeping from the wall let Kai know her scan was finished, and she slid her arm free of the band. Data tables ran freely down the touchscreen, and she flicked through the readouts impatiently. She'd need a new kidney sooner than later, which meant that either the printer she'd used was having problems again, or else—more likely—there'd been another damn mutation. Hers or the stock's she couldn't say; either way, the best thing would be to play it safe, to see if they could find a healthy donor or trader on-planet and secure a new kidney as soon as possible. And if no one came forth—well, then they'd adapt. Like they always did.

Kai scrolled through the rest of the information quickly, no other red exclamation marks jumping out at her, and jabbed the accept button at the bottom of the screen. Another, larger syringe slid from the wall, and pierced the meat of her upper thigh. Heat burned in her muscles this time, and Kai curled into a ball, fighting the urge to cry out.

Moments later, fully tensed and prepared for the day's work, the pod's lid skimmed open and Kai stepped out onto the deck of the common area. Rana, her eggmate, was already awake, checking the vast honeycomb of grow-pods that lined the ship's walls. Seeing Kai emerge, however, she put down her tools and walked over. "Your eye."

Kai's hand went to the right side of her face. A phage treatment meant to correct an infection two months previously had mutated after introduction to her eye, the bacteriophage designed to kill the infected cells instead slowly robbing her of her sight. She'd only injected the cells for replacement before the trip began, and as she'd slept during transit, they should have worked to replace the ruined tissues with a functioning eye. It had been a gamble though, the eye stock of uncertain provenance, but since there had been no discomfort or errors marked on waking, Kai had assumed it had been a success.

That was the problem with testing an unknown product on yourself: you never knew what defects might emerge, hidden in the junk DNA; or what sort of trick a seller may have played in order to gain a few extra credits.

"Is it imperfect?" Kai asked, her voice calm.

"It's green."

A mercenary smile crossed Kai's face and echoed on

Rana's. They had taken the sample because the seller had claimed it was dark blue, the same colour as Kai's left eye. Blue was valuable enough on its own, far more so than ordinary brown or hazel, but green— nothing held a candle to the amount they could get for green. They might even be able to further gem it themselves, developing a spectrum of greens. No wonder the seller had lied.

Overhead a glissade of lights marked the ship's final descent, and the two women, nearly identical in appearance but for one green eye, strode to the rear of the craft. Paper-thin suits of pearlescent chitin composite, tough and packed with hair-thin webs of biological sensors, were pulled on over their bodysuits, and a simple sustaining slurry consumed. A gentle jolt marked the ship's successful landing, and with the flipping of an array of switches, the hatch on the spacecraft's back irised open.

Damp air and billows of gas, the smells of exhaust and sweat and the mineral tang of stone and dirt blew into the compartment, along with the coughs and calls and shouts of the Sabir milling around the Needle. The Gemmers' visit was unscheduled, as always—the better to remind the Sabir of the magnanimity of the Gemmers—but the ship, unmissable beside the battered transports and ore shuttles docked next to it, had taken time to land, and already a crowd of Sabir was rushing toward them, abandoning the more commonplace food and repair stalls. Males with impossible musculature, or dark skin crusted into a leather-like hide; females with gills, or extra eyes, or long double-jointed arms; sexless Sabir with skin white as milk, breathing from tanks containing planetary atmosphere, without which they would die. Bald Sabir. Blind Sabir. Pale, dark; small, tiny, large. All plodding, limping, and striding toward them.

"Offer everything," said Rana—

"Promise nothing—"

"And don't get involved with what doesn't concern you."

The two women exited the ship as the first Sabir arrived, an impossibly tall man with muscles curdled beneath this skin. "Anti-rejection drugs," he lisped, through atrophied lips. "I need them."

Kai displayed her shopkeeper smile. "And we need credits."

The man clumsily offered a credit stick, and as Kai took it, her suit swept into action, reading details both biological and biographical. Early age gemming for muscular and visual enhancement, purchased at a hefty price from the corporation that owned the planet. Tumours and mutated cells clustered in his arms and legs. Blood-bound cyanide and sulfur dioxide. An increased white blood cell count. An average credit balance.

Kai deliberated. She could sell the man the anti-rejection drugs he wanted, preventing his body from attacking his supplemented musculature and allowing the tumours to grow and spread; or, she could correct his diagnosis and provide him with a course of antineoplastics to attack the cancers and destroy the root cause of the problem. Anti-rejection drugs would force him to come back time and again, earning them more credits; but, in the end he would die, and who knew how much they could fleece him for before that?

"Rejection is not the problem," Kai said. "Your modifications have mutated, become cancerous. I can fix it, but it will cost you."

"Anything."

Kai drained the credit stick, wiping out half the man's

life savings in seconds, and gestured inside the ship.

Within a half hour the man marched out again, muscles already unknotted, a week's worth of injections cached in a carry-pouch carved into his leg. Fringespace or central planets, theft was a problem everywhere. Kai had said nothing of the blood poisoning, the cause of his cancers, or that his body had begun to reject his eyes wholesale. He didn't have the credits for the additional repairs, and if she fixed him completely, he would have no cause to return. It wasn't good for Sabir to think they didn't need the Gemmers.

Hours slipped by, and Kai's and Rana's suits became pink- and then red-stained from their work. New lungs were purchased off the rack: new eyes, new hearts, new livers, new kidneys; the work was quick and dirty, cut and go, no time to craft the organs or them adapt to their new body. Immunizations were given, diseases eradicated; skins toughened, muscles strengthened, senses heightened. Kai restored fingers and toes lost to frostbite and accident, and draped raw-burnt frames in swathes of new skin; Rana implanted twinned-zygotes costing billions of credits each, one pair gemmed for bioluminescence and exoskeletons, the other for preternatural intelligence. There was no time to stop; petitioner after petitioner packed the floor, as those without the necessary credits were turned away with a mocking laugh, and those who could afford it were sped through with cool hands and avaricious smiles. Kai's and Rana's suits kept them smiling, hydrated, and alert through it all, trickling a stream of sustaining drugs and stimulants into their systems, with not a single drop of sweat sacrificed without reason.

The grow-pods were almost empty, and Kai had "allowed" herself to be persuaded to specially print an ear—

an increase in price demanded for the extra trouble, of course – when a leather-backed male shoved his way to the front of the crowd.

"There is a queue," Kai informed him, eyes on the cartilaginous form growing before her. "Unless you wish to pay an extra fee—"

The man barrelled forward and actually entered the ship. "Your eyes."

Kai stepped back reflexively—the man was large, muscular and craggy to go with his skin—and she saw triumph followed by rage cross his face.

"I knew it," he said.

"Hey, get out of there!" someone shouted. "Don't piss them off!"

"Wait your turn, Amon!"

"No cutting!"

Other voices joined in, and the man, Amon, turned to address the crowd. "These women—" He spat on the floor— "these things, murdered my brother." He half-rotated, his baleful glare alternating between Kai and the group of Sabir. "He was a trader on Turindat, a merchant, and when he wouldn't sell them the stock they wanted, they killed him."

Through the tide of drugs, Kai felt cold tickle her stomach and forced herself to laugh. "We are Gemmers, Sabir," she said, purposely not using his name. "We wove the stars and shaped mankind from its scraps; we do not kill for stock. What make what we need, and what we cannot, we buy."

"Like you bought that eye?" Amon asked, pointing at Kai's luminous right iris. "My brother told me about you—your people and their stocks. Recycled, reused, damaged—can't even make proper organs for yourself these days. But my brother, Brear, he learned how. He watched and he learned and he surpassed you—he, a Sabir! The only one in the system to gee-em green eyes in a decade. He was going to buy my contract out once they were ready—"

The leatherback had pressed closer as he spoke, teeth bared, and as he came within striking distance Kai reached out, a scalpel in her hand, and sliced across the centre of his cheek. Flesh split and sticky yellow ooze burst out, billowing and holding and binding, already trying to repair the skin.

"You see?" the man roared, clutching his face as the crowd behind him boiled. "We are nothing to them; nothing but test tubes and samples! Looking down on us, hating us—"

"You attacked me," Kai said. "My eggmate will swear it, and our word—"

"The word of liars?" hissed Amon.

"They killed my son," shouted a woman from the crowd. "He came in for new eyes and they took his kidneys!"

"Those kidneys were payment," said Rana.

"What about my brother's payment?" Amon asked, rounding on Rana, standing frozen-footed and empty-handed on the other side of the ship's door. "What did he get in return for you stealing his stock? For stripping his body of its blood and its organs and its marrow— *What did he get?*"

"My heart was fine before they replaced it, and now it's cancerous!" shouted a man.

"So are my lungs!"

"And my muscles!"

"They've used us for years! Charging us impossible

prices, selling modifications that break and mutate—"

"It's *their* turn to pay!"

"Fraudsters—"

"Monsters—"

"Make them pay!"

The crowd surged forward as Amon grabbed Rana's wrist. A subtle flex of Kai's muscles prompted her suit to release a reserve spike of epinephrine, and as Amon turned to grab her also, she glided forward, planted one foot, and snapped out a kick, transferring her momentum into the centre of his stomach. The Sabir man flew backwards with a grunt, out of the ship and onto the floor—dragging Rana with him. Kai had time to see her eggmate scuttle to her feet—so frail and delicate against the frothing mob of Sabir—and then she was slamming toggles, irising the hatch shut.

Dulled thumps and thuds sounded against the hull before silent engines raised the ship, carrying it forward and slamming it through the nearest section of the Needle's clumsy frame. Storm and wind instantly battered the ship, snatching and washing away the debris, erasing any trace the Sabir may have left. Kai settled behind the controls and ordered the ship out of the atmosphere, into the freedom of open space.

That done, she stripped off her used suit and fed it into a grow-pod. The microbes within would break the chitin down, recycling the proteins and nutrients, and then filter through the various fluids and solids left behind by the day's patients. Anything worth having—new antibodies, cells resistant to disease—would be plucked out, the DNA mapped, copied, packaged, and then sold back to the next planet-full of Sabir, blissfully unaware they were paying for something that had been right under their noses. The blind fools.

Though not as blind as Kai would've liked.

She returned to the controls.

The Gemmers would not be coming back here, not for many sols. Perhaps years. The Sabir had made their choice, and every hulking, infected, imperfect one of them would learn the consequences. Not because of Rana—losing her had been an unfortunate accident, but she should have acted faster; it was her own fault—but because the Sabir had believed themselves to be better than them; better than the Gemmers. Perhaps it was good after all that they had killed the Sabir on Turindat; from what his brother had said, he had discovered some of their techniques and replicated them, even improving upon them— but that couldn't be true, what did a Sabir know?

Still, it wouldn't hurt for someone to circle by and collect what they could of his research.

While Kai tapped away at the craft's controls, isolating and quarantining the planet on all Gemmer's maps, urgent data showing orange, red, and purple exclamation marks scrolled past her fingers: distant life signs from Rana's suit. The marks became more frequent, the colours more intense as Kai worked, until, at the same moment as she tapped the last key, the readouts spiked and ran patently blank.

To Kai's surprise, she felt a sudden flow of liquid from her eye. Touching her fingers to her cheek, she discovered a viscous fluid seeping from her right eye socket— her newly fabricated eye, dissolving into a mass of lysing cells.

As the spacecraft burst through the storm, reaching the upper limits of the atmosphere, a fine down of crystals rose on the vessel's exterior and then evaporated, unseen, into the cold clarity of space. Content with the ship's bearing, Kai wiped her face clean and began to prepare for the next day's work: the grow-pods reset, a list of the day's prices shared to the Gemmers' nexus, and Rana's biometrics erased from the system. Lastly, Kai set three grow-pods to producing three pairs of green eyes from the unstable green stock, each pair modified slightly in the hopes of preventing lysis. Then she dimmed the lights, climbed into her pod, and let the barrage of drugs lull her to sleep.

The sample had cost her dearly after all, and she wasn't about to take a loss. Not on something that mattered.

Alissa Hickox

Alissa Hickox was born in Dartmouth, Nova Scotia and currently resides in Hubbards. Her hobbies include camping with my family, walking with my husband, reading books to my awesome little boy, astronomy, and dreaming about space when I'm supposed to be working.

She brings with her her first published tale, 'Ceres.'

Ceres

Earth looked nice when it was far away.

The bright blue spark floated next to Venus and Mercury in the dusty blackness. The three planets formed a delicate line that pointed toward the nearby sun. It looked so quiet and peaceful.

Frank Moshan hovered next to the fuel pump and smirked. In real life, Earth wasn't peaceful, and it certainly wasn't quiet. Still, it did look nice from far away.

Frank was happiest floating like this in the silent black – and he wasn't happy often. Being in the asteroid belt, in a spacesuit, with a view like this was his idea of a perfect vacation. Too bad he had to work.

`"Ceres 1, this is` *`Unity 5`*`, permission to approach for docking,"` a woman's clipped, formal voice squawked in his ear.

The captain of *Unity 5* had a pleasant enough – if overly businesslike – tone, but Frank's headset was cheap and shitty. Everyone squawked.

"Permission granted," Frank answered gruffly. He turned and watched the huge passenger vessel glide toward him.

It was a complicated puzzle of turning rings, gleaming in the unfiltered sunlight. A ship like that wouldn't like stopping the rotation to fuel up; he would have to move fast to keep everyone happy. On the plus side, big ships meant big money – and hopefully a big tip.

"Dock 15," Frank instructed, "you will have to stop your rotation."

"Acknowledged," the captain replied, "please be quick about it. We have a lot of passengers on board and most of these twits go into space thinking they'll never have to feel zero G. I'll have hundreds of complaints from people who didn't listen to the announcement, didn't secure their valuables and didn't strap into their safety seats. Then, when the gravity comes back on, I'll have to send housekeeping everywhere at once to clean up broken tourist junk and puke on the ceiling."

Frank laughed despite himself. He was starting to like this woman. "I'll do my best, ma'am," he said. "I'm no dirtside rookie."

"No, you're not," she answered approvingly. "I didn't have to tell you to get away from the engine spray until we stopped moving."

Frank was attached to the station's largest robotic arm and fuel pump. He'd retracted it as far as it would go as soon as the passenger ship had matched the station's orbit. He continued waiting.

"Confirmed engine shutdown," the captain said. "You want the large module between the first two rings. Intake B."

Frank was already guiding the arm between columns of metal the size of skyscrapers. The gleaming titanium was speckled with tiny windows. He could see objects and people floating around in them.

The arm reached as far as it would go. The valve hovered one hundred meters away.

"Looks like they built this thing to the limit of code," Frank grumbled. He detached the fuel pump, fired his jet pack, and glided toward the intake valve. A smile crept onto his face. He liked the jet pack and didn't get to use it often. Frank tapped a button and a tiny spurt of nitrogen rotated him just as he reached the ship's metal skin. His boots magnetized and stuck to the fuel tank with a clang that rang through his suit.

"Very impressive," the captain said. "I've never seen anyone land that perfectly. What's your name?"

"Frank Moshan. What's yours?"

"Diane Mirror."

"Nice to meet you, Diane." Frank attached the pump and started the machine. "That will be a few minutes. Sounds like you've been to Mars 5."

"I have indeed. Four fuel attendants instead of just one, and it took fifteen minutes just to attach the fuel pump."

Frank shook his head. "They tried to make me work there and I refused. The Mars 5 manager is an idiot. He sends people into space after three months of training."

"Only three?"

"Yep. There's a reason Mars 5 has the most fatalities of any fuel station." Frank checked the pump readout. "So, I take it there are cameras everywhere?"

"Oh, yeah. It's to check the status of the ship, but unfortunately, they pick up a few passenger windows. You wouldn't believe how many people forget to close the panels."

"I believe you," Frank muttered. He stopped the pump, detached it and glided back to the robotic arm. "You're done," he said. "Just wait until I get clear."

"Of course. Some people don't?"

"At least once a month."

"Are they *trying* to kill you?"

"Sometimes I wonder." Frank sailed between the rounded skyscrapers. He passed a window that showed a woman floating upside down. She flipped him the bird. Frank smiled and saluted her.

He returned to his original position and waved at the huge ship. "All clear," he said.

"Five and a half minutes," the captain replied with approval. "That's the fastest I've ever seen."

"Thank you," Frank responded, genuinely pleased.

The giant ship undocked and slowly began to spin. It picked up speed as it slid away.

"Thanks, Frank," Diane said. "I'm dropping this crowd off in the Jovian system and then I'll be back with fresh twits. See you in three days. Over and out."

"Looking forward to it. Out," Frank responded. He looked at the display on his spacesuit's right arm. Tiny green letters appeared: **Payment received: 22,000 credits. Tip: 4,500 credits.**

Frank grinned. He decided he definitely liked Diane.

"Hey, Frank, what's open for me?" a familiar voice squawked.

"Hi, Charlene," Frank responded cheerfully. "Take number 1."

Charlene was a cargo runner. Some of what she hauled

was legal, some of it wasn't. She came to Frank for fuel because Frank didn't give a damn. Charlene tipped when she could and shared valuable gossip when she couldn't. She was also real smart ass. Frank liked her.

Charlene's ship was an ancient cargo runner called the *Freedom Star*. The large, rectangular structure was a patchwork of different metals – different parts that had been replaced in the ship's long life. The clumsy-looking freighter slid into the dock with surprising grace.

Frank climbed up the station to fuel pump 1. "So, how's the rust-bucket been treating you?" he asked playfully. Charlene adored her ship – insulting it was the quickest way to get some backsass.

"The ship's fine, but I need to dock the passenger tunnel," she replied.

Frank blinked. He had never known Charlene to ignore the bait.

Something was wrong.

"Okay," Frank said slowly. "I take it I have a visitor."

"Yeah, you do. Her name is Mary Richmond. She's a scientist coming to study the salt pools. She says she'll only be here for a few days."

It was hard to tell through the squawk, but Frank thought he heard a slight edge to Charlene's voice.

"I wasn't aware I would have company today," he said carefully. "Can I see her clearance certificate?"

"She's sending it now."

Frank looked at the display on his arm. The documents were either authentic or made by the best forger in the universe. Mary Richmond would be staying with him in surface quarters for five days studying those darn salt pools... And he was to be her EVA guide.

He groaned inwardly at the thought of babysitting a rookie for five days. Frank sighed and tapped through multiple screens on his arm until he reached the airlock controls – would it kill Earth to tell him these things in advance? "The certificate looks good," he said resignedly. "Tell her to cross when ready."

The short tunnel from *Freedom Star* extended slowly – and jerkily – to Ceres 1 main airlock. Frank wasn't sure he'd trust a passenger tunnel that old, but the docking went off without a hitch.

"She's crossing," Charlene reported. "She can't hear us now."

"Good. What aren't you telling me?" Frank replied immediately.

"Nothing, exactly."

"Out with it. Why is she coming on your old freighter when a passenger ship just came here. She could have traveled in relative comfort and gotten here faster – but she would've had to be on their passenger list – and you don't have one."

He heard a sigh laced with static.

"That's exactly what I thought," Charlene admitted, "but the *Freedom Star* needed bad engine work last month and this simple transport job offered more than enough to pay for it."

"An offer you couldn't refuse right when you needed it the most," Frank said sarcastically. "Sounds a bit convenient, doesn't it?"

"That it does."

Frank was liking this less by the second. "So, you drag me into this... whatever... even when your gut says something's up? I thought you were a friend, Charlene," he finished bitterly.

"I am!" she sputtered guiltily. "I had her checked out. I have a friend who... knows how to do that. I called in a favour. Birth records, credit history, the works. Everything checks out. Her clearance certificate is from Cerebus – your company. Everything looks good... All I have is a feeling."

"Did she do anything weird on the ride over?"

"No, she was perfectly polite. Uh, Frank?"

"Yeah?"

"I still need fuel."

"Oh, right."

Frank was deep in thought as a fuel pump ran. Like him, Charlene worked alone on the frontier of space. They both lived with the uncomfortable knowledge that if they suddenly disappeared, no one would notice for days. "Did she make any arrangements with you for the return trip?" he asked.

The fuel pump finished, and Frank removed it. He climbed out of range.

"No," Charlene replied. "She said that she had already made arrangements with someone else."

The *Freedom Star* retracted its tunnel and undocked. Frank's arm display flickered. **Payment received: 9,050 credits. Tip: 2,050 credits.**

His heart jumped. Charlene had never tipped him that much.

"There's a little extra for the times I couldn't tip," Charlene said anxiously. "Just in case. Be careful, Frank."

Frank tied down his spacesuit and floated warily into the cramped station. The small, hexagonal ring was crammed full of tools, knickknacks and food packets all tied to the wall and floating on their strings.

His visitor hovered near the second airlock. She was dressed in an expensive surface EVA suit, carrying her sleek grey helmet in one arm and a floating blue bag in the other. Glistening black hair fluttered around her face. She had high cheekbones, a prominent nose and cold, grey eyes.

Crap, she's beautiful.

This was an added nuisance. Frank had not had a visitor for three years, let alone someone female. He liked it that way – in his opinion romance was more trouble than it was worth. However, he wasn't dead.

"So… You're Mary Richmond," he said awkwardly.

"And you're Frank Moshan," she replied, equally deadpan.

"No ships are scheduled to come for days," he continued, "so I guess I can escort you to the surface now."

"Yes," she replied coolly.

He pushed off from the wall and flew into a doughnut-shaped opening in the floor. The space elevator was only slightly smaller than the station itself. Titanium support girders and rivets threaded the thick glass that dominated the outer walls and floor. The inner wall was solid plates of metal dotted with bright yellow handles.

Frank grabbed the handle near the control panel and checked that his unwelcome guest was inside. Mary Richmond was hanging on a short distance away. He closed the ceiling hatch and waited for the elevator to do its pressure checks.

Mary looked down and started. "That's trippy," she said.

Through the clear floor they could see the jet black cable that ran through the centre of the elevator. It looked like a perfectly straight pole that narrowed into nothingness before it reached the cratered grey surface.

The elevator began to move. The craters grew slowly larger, but the illusion of narrowing graphene remained the same. Frank always enjoyed the sight.

He looked up. Mary was staring fixedly at the inner walls. Her obvious discomfort amused him. Perhaps he could catch her off guard.

"So what do you hope to learn from the salt pools?" Frank asked casually.

"What?" she muttered distractedly. "Uh... How the salinity affects refraction." She went back to staring at the wall.

Frank didn't buy it. The salt pools had been studied decades ago when they were somewhat famous. Salinity would've been the first thing they checked. The mirror bright pools looked arresting from space – and growing ever larger through the floor – but they were basically just frozen, briny lakes. Earth had lost interest long ago.

Frank felt his feet touch the floor. The weak gravity of Ceres was starting to take hold. Mary looked like she was struggling with nausea.

"What research company do you work for?" he prodded.

"Cerebus," she muttered.

"They have a not-for-profit division?" *Yeah, right.*

"Huh?" She looked at him blankly.

"You can't make money studying the refraction of salty ice – not if you're a fuel company, anyway. I was surprised Cerebus was spending money on pure science."

"Oh, right. Well, it's a very new division," she said quickly. "Only five of us work there."

"Who are the other four scientists?"

"What?" the woman blurted.

The habitation complex resolved into individual rectangles.

"You just said there are four scientists working with you," Frank reminded her. "Who are they?"

"What is this, twenty questions?" she snapped.

She's definitely lying. "It's called human curiosity," Frank said guardedly. "I don't get many visitors out here."

The elevator came to a gentle stop on the roof of the complex. A loud beep signaled the end of pressure checks. Frank absentmindedly slapped the button and opened a small hatch in the floor.

He crawled down the ladder as quickly as he could. Mary followed slowly in her EVA suit.

They entered a small, white hallway packed on either side with vacuum sealed bags of food, clothing, and other storage.

"Watch your step," Frank muttered as he walked through the hallway and crossed the lip of the hatch.

Frank's home was made of several connected boxes the size of shipping containers. He stopped in the middle box – the kitchen. It was also white, but small, square windows, old couches and pictures taped to the wall made the room less severe.

"Obviously, this is the kitchen," Frank said awkwardly. "Your room is there." He
pointed to the first door on the right. "The toilet and shower are next to it – let it run for five minutes or it burns you – and my room is on the other side next to the gym," he finished. "Make yourself at home."

Mary Richmond looked around coolly. Now that they were off the elevator, the unreadable mask was back. "Shouldn't we get going?" she said firmly.

"You mean outside? Now?" Frank looked at his watch. "It's almost sunset. We'd have an hour at most before we had to turn back. Don't you know Ceres has nine-hour days?"

"I have a lot of work to do," she said, turning away. "My orders come from the company. If you have a problem with that, complain to them."

Frank stared incredulously as she passed him for the airlock.

The bubbly field of frozen salt was bright even with Frank's sun visor down. The pinkish white expanse contrasted sharply with the dark grey dirt of the huge crater that surrounded them. Frank looked west and frowned. The unnervingly small sun was getting far too close to the rim of the crater wall. They shouldn't be out here now.

No sane person would want to do an EVA this close to sunset – and the nightly radio blackout with Earth and Mars… Unless, of course, they were doing something they wanted to hide.

Mary was bent over her equipment at the edge of the closest salt pool. Her back was to him.

"We need to get inside now," Frank said nervously.

"Hurry up and get your samples."

"I just need a few minutes," her voice squawked through his headset.

Something in her tone came through the static and made Frank's neck prickle. He took a step backward.

Maybe that was what saved him.

She whirled around and flew at him with a large, glinting needle pointed at his knee joint. She was smart enough to try to puncture his suit in a limb rather than the hard chest wall.

Frank hopped sideways and avoided her.

Now that the surprise was gone, he had the advantage. Mary – if that was even her name – was still used to Earth's gravity. She overshot her jump and landed stomach first in the graphite powder.

Frank judged his lunge perfectly. He stumbled forward and landed with one knee on the arm that held the needle, and the other on Mary's life-support backpack. It wasn't the most graceful maneuver, but it worked. He gripped the oxygen hose above her backpack.

Spacesuits were designed to avoid coming apart accidentally, but they all needed to be disassembled and cleaned. There was no mechanism to stop him from simply yanking the hose out.

"Drop it or I disconnect your life support," he growled. He was just angry enough to mean it.

For a minute he wondered if her radio had been knocked loose. Then a long sigh hissed through his mic. She tossed the needle a short distance away.

Now Frank was in a predicament. The immediate danger was gone, but they would both be slow and clumsy getting up. She could always attack him again. On the other hand, Frank couldn't hold this position forever. Kneeling was difficult in a spacesuit – his legs were already hurting. The simplest solution would be to disconnect the air of his would-be murderer before getting up, but Frank wasn't quite cold-blooded enough to kill someone after they'd surrendered.

"Are you going to let me up?" she coolly echoed his thoughts. "You're not a killer."

"And clearly you are," Frank said grimly.

"No."

"Then why were you trying to kill me?"

She sighed again. "I wasn't trying to kill you. There was a spray that would've knocked you out. I was going to drag you back and leave you in the hab complex when I'd finished."

"Finished what, exactly?"

The ground shook beneath them. The sound vibrated through his boots as a muffled roar. Frank stumbled backwards into the soft, grey-black powder – and found himself sinking like quicksand.

Mary screamed through the radio.

"What the f – " Frank's helmet bounced off a rock. He rolled down a slope and landed in a heap of dirt.

Frank cursed. He sat up, lifted his visor, and wiped the graphite dust off his helmet.

The world was pitch black.

Frank turned his headlight on and saw swirling grey dust against a wall of black. He was underground.

He stood and looked at the dirt slide. The cave-in had blocked the ceiling. Mary was nowhere to be seen.

He moved a few handfuls of rubble, but fresh gravel immediately poured in its place. If he kept doing that, he risked causing another cave in. He would have to find another way out.

"Mary, are you there?" he asked hesitantly.

His radio came alive.

"Frank? Where are you? I need your help with something."

He turned and looked for an exit. "Are you alright?" he said warily.

"Yeah, but my briefcase is stuck. Help me get it out and we'll be rich."

Frank squeezed through a narrow passageway and found a dead end. He backtracked. "You just attacked me. Why should I trust you?" he asked.

"I'm sorry about that. I should have told you the truth from the start. The company stiffs seemed to think you wouldn't do the job, so they hired me. They told me to knock you out so you wouldn't be in the way. They underestimated you."

The cave opened up into an enormous cavern. His headlight caught a huge mass of silvery blue.

Eggs. Thousands and thousands of shiny, translucent eggs filled the cavern. Each one was the size of a basketball. The ceiling was covered with pinkish white ice. He was under the salt pools.

Frank stared and realized his mouth was open. He couldn't believe it. He was looking at alien life.

"Frank! Over here, your left."

He turned and saw Mary digging her stainless-steel suitcase out of the rock pile. She yanked it hard and fell over as it came free.

Frank walked closer to the eggs. "This is incredible!" he said with awe.

"I know," Mary said. "They're worth a fortune."

He looked at her quizzically.

"Did you really think Cerebus built a fuel station here just for the location?" She opened the briefcase and took out a scalpel and several large syringes. "The first survey team found the eggs by accident. The ground around the eggs becomes unstable near hatching time. That's why they are always under the salt pools. The team watched the hatching and took eggshells back after everything had left. They didn't get very much because these things eat the eggs as their first meal."

"Cerebus knew about this for how long?" Frank asked incredulously. "Keeping it a secret violates the New Mexico convention."

"Yes, and they had good reason." She took out several large sample bags. "The eggshells are made of the best superconductor ever discovered. Whoever can figure out how to make it will become the richest company on Earth – a tech supergiant. Unfortunately, the survey team only got a tiny amount and the aliens only lay eggs every four years – so they built your little gas station as cover." She prepped the syringes.

Sinking dread settled in the pit of Frank's stomach. "That explains why they were willing to risk jail time hiding alien life. They sent to you here to collect the eggshells after the babies hatch?"

"No, weren't you listening? If the eggs hatch, the young eat the eggshells." She held up a syringe. "This is poison. It will kill the eggs and keep them stable for transport." She put down the syringe picked up the scalpel. "We have to cut the hard shell to get the poison in, and then we take as many as we can carry."

"We?"

She stood. "Yes. Today is your lucky day. I meant what I said about sharing the money. I need some to pay off my debt, but we can split the profit after that. Are you in?"

Frank turned around and looked at the eggs. They shone back at him. Silvery blue shadows moved beneath the shells, as if they were attracted to his light.

"No," Frank said with disgust. "I'm not in the business of killing things for money."

"Suit yourself. You might as well look for a way out then. I have to get started. This is my ticket to freedom," she said excitedly.

"Money won't make you free, especially blood money."

"What are you? A shrink?"

"No," Frank sighed. "I'm the guy who's stopping you." He faced her and stood reluctantly in front of the eggs.

"Wh-What?" she stammered. "You can't stop me!"

"Yes, I can."

"You don't understand!" Her voice was almost pleading. "This is my escape. Without this, I'm going back to the slums. I can't go back."

Frank's voice softened. "I understand, more than you

know, but I can't let you do this. It's wrong."

"I'll kill you if I have to!" Her voice gained a flinty edge.

"You can try," Frank replied quietly.

She looked at him wide-eyed. He could see her shaking through her helmet; she was trying to psych herself up to kill him.

This was stupid and Frank knew it. Three years on Ceres had weakened his muscles. She was fresh from Earth with at least ten times his strength. She was half his age. She was armed. No patch kit in the solar system could fix a slice from that scalpel. One touch in the right place and he'd be dead in minutes. The smart thing to do would be to move aside, but something deep inside Frank refused to let him budge.

She took a deep breath. "Please, get out of the way."

It was the most heartfelt plea Frank had ever heard.

"No," he whispered.

Her eyes hardened and turned his stomach to ice. "I'm sorry," she said.

The lunge was as sudden as it was brutal. The scalpel came flying toward his shoulder. This time, he couldn't dodge it.

He fought his initial instinct to raise his hands and leaned toward the blade – watching the scalpel head straight for his eyes.

There was a nerve-racking screech as the hard edge left a diagonal scratch along his faceplate. He headbutted the woman and sent her tumbling onto her backside.

If he was lucky, he could take a few blows to his hard helmet and chest plate. A touch on a joint, a limb, or a glove – and he was a dead man.

She scrambled up and came at him again, this time aiming for his knees.

He threw himself forward and caught the blow on his chest. A warning alarm beeped in his suit. The glow from his arm display flickered and went out.

Frank was pulled roughly forward as his attacker tried to retrieve the scalpel. It was stuck in his electronics.

This was his chance.

Frank thrust both arms out and slammed her helmet. She toppled backward in flailing slow motion.

He grabbed a scalpel and tried to pull it out.

She tripped him.

Frank floated toward the ground on his stomach. His arms saved him from falling directly on the scalpel. He rolled and tried to sit up.

She scrambled on top of him and yanked the blade out. She was fighting like someone who really knew how... On Earth.

Frank kicked with everything he had. He saw the surprised look on her face as she flew backwards and bounced off the ceiling – hard. The scalpel fluttered out of her hand. She careened to the ground and bounced again. Frank scrambled to his hands and knees as she rolled to a stop.

Mary groaned through the radio.

He looked frantically for the weapon, feeling mild irritation at the diagonal slash floating in front of his vision.

A glint caught his eye. The scalpel was half buried in the charcoal coloured sand.

He plucked it out of the dirt and threw it as far as he could into the pitch black cavern. She would never find it again.

Frank stood and quickly moved to the briefcase. He

threw everything inside and locked it. He had to destroy this thing or keep it from her somehow.

"No!" she screamed.

The woman came out of nowhere. She flung out her arm and caught him square in the chest.

Before he knew what had happened, he was flying across the cavern.

Frank crashed into the rough rock wall. His head slammed the back of his helmet so hard his ears rang. He fell slowly forward and dropped the briefcase. The room was spinning.

She had finally realized her strength was her advantage.

Frank landed on his hands and knees and winced at the pain in his head. His back and life support were exposed. *Get up, get up, get up, get up, get up!*

He got to his knees as she collided with him. His head bounced off his helmet again. Her gloves reached for his neck – she was trying to take off his helmet.

He caught her arms and resisted, but he knew it was useless. He had no chance in a contest of brute strength. He glared into her eyes and radiated his anger and his fear. If she was going to do this, she was going to have to look him in the face and watch it.

She blinked. Hesitated.

Red warning lights began flashing in her suit. She screamed – he saw it a second before he heard it through the radio. *What the hell?*

She went limp and slowly slid off him. A glowering set of black eyes hovered behind her.

The eyes belonged to a large, spiky ball that reflected crystalline blue in his headlights. It had at least ten long, spindly legs that bent at odd angles. Shining green machinery covered its body.

Frank tried to backpedal and scraped the wall behind him.

Three more creatures appeared around the first one. Frank could see even more moving shapes behind them. The cavern was quickly filling up.

The one nearest to Frank was holding a long, thin instrument that had punctured Mary's suit at the back of the knee. Apparently, this nightmare creature was his saviour.

The strange beings ignored him. The closest one withdrew the metal rod from Mary's suit and flipped her over. Frank watched in horror as it drove the rod into her chest plate and began fiddling with it.

Frank closed his eyes and looked away. His stomach churned. He couldn't watch them pick apart her corpse. The thought that he might be next had him covered in cold sweat.

"Frank Moshan," a strange, metallic, and perfectly clear voice rattled through his headset.

Frank nearly jumped out of his skin. "Wha-what?" he stammered.

"Frank Moshan. You have saved our eggs. You protected them from damage until we could arrive. We thank you."

"Uh... You're welcome," he mumbled. Frank looked back and realized the rod had not gone far into Mary's spacesuit. The creature was merely using her radio. "How do you know my name?" he asked.

"You have been here for three years. We have studied you and learned your primitive language. We left you alone because you did no harm. We believed your species was not a threat." It looked down at Mary. `"We were wrong. We will no longer let humans trespass on our world. We will attack and destroy all humans. Except you. You will be spared with our gratitude."`

Frank's throat went dry. The thought of being the last man alive was heart stopping. "Whoa, hang on," he stammered. "I appreciate the gratitude, but can't the solution be a little less drastic?"

`"You wish to die with the other humans?"`

"No! I don't think anybody has to die!"

`"Explain."`

"What if I can guarantee no human ever comes to your world again? We won't even go near it."

The leader stared at him for a moment. "Please wait," it said. It withdrew the tool from Mary's spacesuit and turned around.

`"- Go! Frank, get out of here! Why aren't you trying to escape?"`

Frank started as Mary's voice sounded in his ear. He hadn't known she was still alive. The puncture must have been small enough for her spacesuit to temporarily compensate. In any case, she wouldn't survive long with an air leak.

Frank glanced at Mary but remained silent.

`"Come on, move!"` she yammered. `"You don't deserve any of this."` She sniffed. `"He can't hear me; those bastards broke my radio. I should've known the money was too good to be true. Stupid, stupid... Oh no -"`

The alien reattached its tool to her radio. "Your solution is acceptable," the voice rasped. "We will destroy everything humans built on our world."

Frank blinked. "Okay," he said quickly, "but please give me time to get off your world. I need to return to my home and use an escape pod."

"You have thirty of your minutes."

Frank nodded. He looked around. "How do I get out of these tunnels?" he asked.

"We will help you get out as soon as you are ready."

He nodded again. Frank looked down at the other astronaut. Her eyes were closed, and she had turned away from the being holding her – away from oncoming death. Tears ran slowly across her cheek. Her expression was a strange mixture of fear and... relief.

"What will you do with her?" Frank asked casually.

The alien looked down. "We haven't decided yet. It would make a good specimen for a museum, or perhaps, we will give it to the young. They will need to practice hunting."

Frank winced. "Why don't you let me deal with her? She is a human criminal, and I did promise to keep all humans off your world."

It paused. "Very well. It is awake again. Would you like us to put it back to sleep? This will make transportation easier."

Frank grinned. "Sure, thank you."

She screamed silently and went limp.

"Are you ready, Frank Moshan?"

He looked into the black eyes. "Yes," he said.

"Good. Goodbye, and thank you."

A brilliant green flash blinded Frank. When his vision cleared, he was standing in front of the habitation complex – right beside the airlock. Mary lay prone next to him. Impossibly vivid stars hovered above in an endless clear void.

Frank had no time to gawk.

He dragged Mary into the airlock and started repressurization. The second he heard the all-clear beep, he ripped off his EVA suit, padding, and cooling suit. He left Mary in the airlock and ran to the escape pods.

Earth was behind Ceres – he would have to program both escape pods to broadcast emergency warnings once they were clear of the planetoid. He worked as quickly as he could.

Bringing Mary may not have been the best idea, but Frank thought even she didn't deserve to be alien baby food. The pods were automatically piloted. She could float unconscious in space until she was picked up.

Frank hurried back and awkwardly removed Mary's spacesuit and padding. It wasn't easy when she was so limp. He left her cooling garment on and carried her to the escape pod.

She moaned and opened her eyes.

The woman kicked and jumped out of his arms. She landed clumsily next to the escape pods and looked around wildly. Frank backed away and groaned inwardly at his foolishness.

"… How are we back here?" she said finally.

"I negotiated our way out. We have twenty minutes to get out of here before they blow it up."

Her eyes grew wet. "You got me out?" She looked down. "Thank you. That's more than I deserve. Just leave me here."

"Leave you to die?"

"Yes. I told you, I can't go back to Earth. I won't."

He stepped toward her. "Mary –"

"– My name isn't Mary. It's Jade."

He raised his eyebrows. "What's your last name?"

"I don't have one." She shifted her feet. "At least I don't remember it. My parents abandoned me when I was four or five… I grew up in the Cairo slums."

He nodded. "That's rough. I grew up in the Detroit slums, but I had a family – at least until I was twenty-five."

She looked like she honestly wanted to know more.

He sighed. "TB mutagen 5A got my whole family. A bottle of antibiotics could've saved everyone, but we couldn't afford it. The pharmacy didn't care that we would die without them: no money, no pills. I was the only one that survived." He swallowed. "I decided Earth was a greedy, rotten place and I wanted to get as far away as possible. Eventually, I did."

He checked the clock. "We're running out of time. We have to go now."

Jade shook her head firmly. "You go."

"I have a better idea. I set your escape pod to go toward Vesta – not Earth."

She looked up in shock.

"I'm guessing that other than Cerebus, Charlene, and I, no one knows you're here. Cerebus will think you're dead – if you stay here they'll be right – but if you take the escape pod it will head to Charlene's ship. I left a message with strict instructions to pick you up and leave you locked in the cargo bay until you reach Vesta. Once there you can sneak into the black markets. It's a good place to disappear."

She looked like she was about to cry. "You of all people… Why?" she choked.

He shrugged. "The universe has enough death. I try not to cause more."

She reached forward and grabbed both sides of his head.

Frank gasped and tensed his body – expecting another attack. Instead, soft lips pressed his.

She drew back and looked down.

"Wha...?" Frank exhaled.

"Sorry," she muttered, "I had no other way to thank you. Goodbye."

She turned away and climbed to the escape pod, pausing only for a last glance over her shoulder. The door closed and hissed as the tiny spacecraft moved away.

Frank shook himself and scrambled into the adjacent escape pod. He grimaced as it closed.

He was lying in a space the size of a coffin.

A hiss and jerky motion signaled his approach to launchpad. The narrow passage opened up and Frank could see stars.

The escape pod tilted up and the engines rumbled to life. Frank looked at the simple, blocky complex that had been his home for three years.

His tiny craft flew rapidly into space. Frank grunted as the G force pressed down on him.

The rocky horizon quickly curved into a round asteroid. As he stared, the habitation complex shattered like a puff of confetti. The glinting shards arranged themselves around the planetoid as of each one had a mind of its own.

As Ceres retreated, Frank realized the debris was uniformly covering the asteroid in a stable orbit. The shrapnel would let light through but make it impossible for a human craft to enter the world's gravity well, let alone land.

Ceres slid from view as the spacecraft turned. Frank stared into an endless black sky. He suddenly realized that as much he loved space, he didn't want to die alone in it.

He felt a prick in his hand as the escape pod injected him with a mild sedative – designed to make him sleep and use less oxygen. His eyelids grew heavy.

Frank fought it and stared fixedly at the stars.

Bright lights assaulted his bleary eyes.

"He's coming around," a familiar voice said.

Frank blinked and his vision cleared. He sat up. It was much harder than normal.

He was in a hospital room: standard cot, standard chairs, standard white walls. Even the doctors wore standard white coats. What was not standard was the fact that every piece of furniture was bolted to the floor. Loose objects were kept in a cage mounted to a desk. The sun moved rapidly in a tight arc across a small, triangular window. Frank was on a rotating ship with Earth-strength-simgrav.

The woman who sat across from him was wearing a uniform-- but not a white coat. She had blonde hair shot with grey, authority in the straightness of her back, and kindness in the wrinkles around her eyes. She waved the doctors out of the room.

Frank tried to stand. The woman held out a hand to stop him.

She smiled warmly. "Easy, tiger," she said. "You're not used to 1 G anymore. You'll need to walk with a cane for a few weeks."

Relief flooded his body. It had been a long time since he'd seen a friendly face. "Diane?" he asked.

She beamed. "You got it in one. We heard your SOS and your message. I turned the ship around. Actually had a few asshats bitch about the delay – and I told them if their vacation was more important than a man's life they were welcome to get an escape pod themselves. That shut them up." She rolled her eyes. "Anyway, we passed on your message and confirmed that Ceres 1 is gone. I think you're out of a job."

"Damn, I never got to tell those bastards I quit." Frank smiled. "Thank you for saving me."

Diane beamed and leaned forward eagerly. Her eyes were shining. "You can thank me by buying me a drink and telling me everything. I've been doing this for ten years and this is the most exciting day I've had!"

Frank grinned. "Throw in some dinner and you've got a deal."

Shannon K Green

A gifted author with a talent for the strange, Green has been recognized in both the genre community and the contemporary literary community for his pursuits. In the past, he has been shortlisted for the 1996 Arts and Letters Award, and later won the 2015 Audience Choice Steampunk Newfoundland Showcase.

Green's short fiction has appeared in *Fantasy from the Rock, The Hamthology, Jibbernocky* and the bestselling collections *Chillers from the Rock, Dystopia from the Rock,* and *Flights from the Rock.*

The Cat's Meow

How'd you end up in Alpha Centauri Settlement One you ask; well, that's a bit of a yarn to untangle.

My sister and I, we got ourselves onboard the *Bondar* by hiding between two unmarked crates on a metal pallet. I say unmarked, but the truth is they were marked in a language we couldn't read, one of the spacer languages that Earth had adopted in the years since we had made contact with Mars; it smelled like rice though. We hunkered between the crates while the crew ushered the pallet to the galley pantry area -- thankfully not just a normal cargo hold -- and attached the strapping and mag-locks to the whole shot. These things need to be properly secured to keep them motionless, at least during take-off and landings.

How did we even get into a space dock, you might be asking? Well, it wasn't hard, truth be told; we walked through a "side gate," a simple hole in the fence which can be found at nearly every shipping yard if you look hard enough. After that, it was a simple matter of watching the guards and longshoremen patrol to find a path through to a ship that would be leaving the planet. We'd done it with our mother a few times before she decided to settle down on Pluto, leaving Jenna and I alone at the ripe age of six.

(Not much of a mothering type I guess.)

Me and sis had itchy feet anyway, and we decided to hitch a lift on any likely ship. First, we went to Earth, but we found that a bit crowded and decided to try our luck again. We never meant to hitch a lift on the *Bondar*, and certainly didn't know she was headed to Alpha Centauri; we were just looking to put the stench of Earth's overly industrialized atmosphere behind us.

We kept ourselves out of sight between the crates on our little pallet until after lift off.

If you've never experienced lift in a deep spacer, you've been missing out. At first the whole ship shudders, like an old diesel truck when the engine starts. That seems to be common enough among all internal combustion engines. Next, the anti-gravity drives kick in with a rumble that feels like sitting on the side of one of the larger volcanoes of Venus, not just a shuddering of the ship but a tooth chattering, bone shaking experience that leaves your hair standing on end. The stoker that explained all this to me told me that once the anti-gravity engines start, the diesels are shut off -- something about the vibrational frequencies tearing the ship apart if both engines are run together for any amount of time -- but the diesel is required to start the anti-gravity, but it can run on its own once started... I don't claim to really understand it.

Anyway, after the tooth rattles, and hair standing, and your bones coming out of your body, the ship lifts. It feels like those bones you just left behind are pulverized, your hair forced back into your skull, and your teeth all sent to the tooth fairy. This goes on for what feels like forever, but in actuality is something more along the lines of ten minutes. Then everything goes back to normal, except you feel like you've spent a day in the sun getting a relaxing massage as the ship's gravity kicks in and you're back on standard gravity for whatever planet you've just left. Most ships will slowly transition you from the originating planet to the destination planet in the course of the voyage; this works out better for everyone aboard according to science, and according to my own experience as a seasoned stowaway.

We'd been on board for about three weeks before anybody noticed us. My sister and I had been surviving on what fell from the crates the cook had been using and scavenging whatever else we could find. It had been easy to keep ourselves hidden once we'd figured out the schedule the galley kept, so it was purely laziness and over confidence on my part. One of the galley hands saw me asleep on a crate. His response surprised me though; he just walked out of the pantry while I scrambled myself back into hiding. I heard him return, with a second person, a few moments later.

Carefully, I looked through a peephole in my hiding space at the pair. The galley hand had brought the head cook with him. "Well? Where is the wee stowaway?" she asked the lad before turning her voice on the whole room. "You should know we aren't one of those ships that spaces hands we can turn to work. We may put planetside on our next refuel, but you'll be safe until then." With that speech, she laid a dish of something that smelled suspiciously like a seafood chowder down on one of the sealed barrels near the door before ushering herself and the lad out of the room.

As soon as we heard the door close, my sister and I raced to the bowl. It was chowder, chunks of fish and lobster in a creamy broth, still warm if not exactly hot. We demolished the first hot food we'd seen since before we'd come aboard the *Bondar*. We even went so far as to take turns licking the bowl clean. Then we hurried back to the little hiding place we'd made for ourselves in the back corner. With full bellies and a basic sense of safety, we slept like babies…

But I awoke alone.

I woke up on a strange bed in a room that looked more like a laboratory than any kind of bedroom I'd ever seen. It took me a moment to realize that I must be in their med bay, and then another instant to see Jenna on the bed next to mine.

Then I heard a man say, "Well, they seem healthy if a little malnourished and I've updated all their vaccines to make sure they stay that way. You did right to slip that sleeping pill into the chowder you gave them, by the by, much better to get them a proper physical than let them hide in the pantry uninspected. The captain will have no trouble letting them stay aboard as far as Station Gamma, maybe even as far as Alpha itself. If they're willing to work that far." He approached me as I started to stagger to my feet. "Ah, you're waking up. Did you hear that? I'll have to check with the captain, but I think he'll let you stay aboard as long as you pull your own weight with ship's chores. We're too far out to turn around and she does hate to unnecessarily waste lives that could add to the colonies."

Jenna and I quickly voiced our agreement as she, being somewhat steadier on her feet than I, made her way to my bed. We hadn't spent a night apart since we'd been born and didn't like to be separated. It was a twin thing for all that we were fraternal; me most closely resembling Molly, our mom, and her favouring Tom, our pa.

"I think they've had to rely on each other up to now," the cook said in a melodious voice. "But we'll take good care of you too, as long as you help us keep the pantries clear of..."

"And do our little stowaways meet the health requirements as laid down by the intergalactic settlement committee, Doctor?" a new voice interrupted her from the door. The voice was followed into the room by the largest woman I had ever seen. Shoulders broader than a Plutonian axe handle, she stood head and shoulders taller than the doctor, who wasn't exactly short himself. Her stern face softened as she was informed that we would indeed get the all-clear on whatever planet we next made landfall on, though we hadn't been given proper identity chips yet.

"Give them the chips and release them to galley duties," the captain said simply and left the med bay.

And that was how we went from stowaways to ship's exterminators. It turned out that some of the supplies brought aboard had stowaways other than Jenna and I. Rats, mice, and a variety of insects had made their way into space with us. A common enough occurrence, to be sure, and one every space crew battled from liftoff to touchdown. The insertion of us two now welcome stowaways meant that there could be two crewmembers dedicated to the task of cleaning the vermin from the ship without taking others away from their normal duties. And it was work that my sister and I, having grown up sometimes relying on the vermin as our primary food source in back alleys and cargo holds system wide, excelled at.

I know some of you will be shocked at that, but remember that food costs money and money isn't something most poor folks ever have. So, we had learned from a very young age to eat whatever you could get into your mouth; sometimes that meant chilled chowder, sometimes it meant something less than savoury to the average person. Though it did take sis and I a while to get used to the idea of perfectly good food, even if it wasn't the most appetizing at times, simply being jettisoned into the outer reaches, as it were; but the food we were given as crewmembers was much better than the things we caught.

And, oh, the food they gave us: seafood from the ship's aquariums; the algal proteins bred to taste like beef; chicken, real chicken and real eggs like you could find on any settled planet; and the beef, well the beef was a little dry as we got closer to refill, but it was still beef that we didn't have to drag in from a dumpster. That was perhaps the biggest change for us; we were fed. Everyday we were fed. If we had a good hunt, we ate. A bad hunt, we still ate. We were part of a crew, with food everyday and our own place to sleep. That simple fact, more than anything else, is what kept Jenna and I aboard as we stopped at first Pluto, then Station Gamma, and past New Hadfield; all the way to Alpha Centauri.

As I'm sure most of you know, the *Bondar* wasn't the first colony ship to Alpha Centauri; it was in fact the third. The rudiments of Earthly civilization had been prepared on the planet, but the *Bondar* was destined to be converted into its first major living and production space. The first two ships had each carried pioneering crews to prepare a landing site for us. The major offerings of settlers were to follow us once we had landed and begun to establish a firm foothold on this new alien landscape. But the *Bondar* was fully set up as a farming and seeding vessel, meaning it could produce not just sufficient food for itself, given the fuel and water, but that it was meant to produce enough for a full colony for at least a decade. Besides that, it was also meant to be the management center main dwelling for most late coming settlers, with some hot shot thinking it was smarter to drag the whole enchilada with you than it was to count on being able to harvest from whatever planet you were being sent to. That was back in the days when the Interstellar Resettlement Plan was still getting funds from Earth-side. This meant a lot of ship to explore for vermin to hide in.

Usually by the time we'd reached our next port of call, Jenna and me had managed to clear out whatever had made its way aboard on our last landing, but some parts of the ship we just never made it to. Other parts, like the cargo hold and the empty spaces around the fuel tanks where vermin were more likely to creep in, we made part of our regular circuits. But about three Earth weeks from Alpha, we decided that the common areas were well cleared and it was time to sweep those places we hadn't been seeing to as regularly. We knew it might take us a few days, but we made it known to the cook and the galley boy what our plan was and set out.

The main part of the ship -- the living quarters, bridge, galley, and cargo holds -- were all to the fore of the ship spread over five or six decks. But each of the areas we all used were at most a quarter of each of those decks. The rest of those decks were sealed by Earth standards; that is, they were locked up tight, but they still had breathable atmosphere available. There might have been some way to vent those decks to space and dump all the vermin that might have been in there, but to the best of everybody's knowledge there was no such plan for us beyond the standard vacuum exposure vessels were required to make before planet fall on the most planets.

Our first couple of excursions went about like you'd expect: rooms inhabited by trackless dust that puffed into the air like dandelion fluff on a breeze as we made our slow circuits. Then back to whatever entryway we had used to be let back into the portions of the ship still in use to spend the night in our little bunks. There was some minor excitement on the fourth day of our little jaunts.

We were on the seventh deck, one that had been set aside for use as office space for settlement administrators. We had entered to the normal layer of dust that accumulates from the in-ship air exchange with the scrubbers turned off; why put the extra use on the filters if nobody will benefit from it? And we were making our usual rounds in the ambient light which the captain made a point of supplying us for these excursions: bright enough to see, dim enough not to startle most of the vermin we were hunting. Jenna was walking slightly ahead of me; for whatever reason she was anxious to be moving, so I let her take the lead.

We had just finished with maybe the third room -- might have been the fourth, I'm not sure now -- but we weren't very far into our normal pattern of checking all the doors on the port side of the ship for a given corridor, then doing all those on the other side as we made our way back. Anyway, we were just exiting one room and turning toward the next when both our ears perked at a new sound: a low whistle coming from a room up ahead of us on the starboard side.

Now I know you've all heard the horror stories about space travel: instant decomp, stale air, air loss, heat loss, lost rations. Let me tell you that there is so much that can go wrong on an interstellar rocket ship that many people won't set foot on one in any circumstances. On a gravdrive, like the *Bondar*, just as many things can go wrong, plus about a million others. And the biggest fear for both is still a breach in the hull, watching your breathable air leak away into the emptiness of space as the temperature drops below absolute zero, knowing that at any second the slow leak can, and usually does, simply tear away a chunk of the fragile surface that separates you and life from the freezing airless expanse of space. So, we were understandably concerned to hear the sound of air moving in an unoccupied portion of the ship.

I ran to the room the sound was coming from. Jenna held back a little, almost like she was suddenly timid. I have seen her face rats, spiders, all manner of nastiness without hesitation; but this was something new for her. Truth to tell, it was new for me too, but I'd heard stories and knew how important it would be to fix such a thing. In the room, the dust was swirling, funneling upwards to one of the interior walls. One of the air circulators had shifted into a reverse-cycle, drawing the contents of the room into itself. I could feel it pull at my hair as it sped up, drawing dust from the corridor as well as the room now. The breathable atmosphere on this deck was noticeably thinning.

I turned back to Jenna, reaching a full run in two strides. "Get below!" I shrieked. "We need this deck sealed."

She spun with me, soon drawing ahead as she caught my panic. "What is it?" she called back at me.

"Busted air circulation!" I howled as we reached the access to the live portion of the ship. I continued howling it as I threw myself at the bulkhead. What felt like hours later, the cook opened the door. Jenna and I flew through it, trying to put as much distance between us and the malfunctioning air unit. The cook obliged, stepping into the access where she must have either heard the moans coming from within or felt the difference in the air, before she slammed the door, secured the seal, and called for a repair crew.

Moments later, the repair crew appeared decked out in their finest hazardous environmental gear. They asked Jenna and I if we would take them to the malfunctioning air circulator; I stepped boldly forward and was fitted with a portable breather. Feeling naked alongside their reinforced bodysuits with little more than a helmet to ensure my air supply, I stepped through the hatch ahead of them.

The trail, still plain in the dust of disuse, was easily followed at first. As we neared the malfunctioning air cycler, the path became much easier to spot -- just follow the dust as it was sucked towards the unit. The crew set to work: one of them removed a panel to one side of the unit, another went to the unit's control console near on the opposite wall, while the third crewmember and I paced the office. I had just completed my fifth or sixth circle when I saw it.

There was a flash as bright as a rocket's engines at takeoff from the air unit and the helmeted figure there was thrown backwards into the opposite wall. The bright side of this was that the malfunctioning air cycler stopped working, and all movement of air in that portion of the ship ceased. The not so bright side of this was that the crewmember, who I could now recognize as one of the pilots, lost the helmet which had obscured her face. As the other two members of the repair crew rushed to her aid, one replacing her helmet while the other attempted to lift her, I ran towards the hatch linking this portion of the vessel to the living quarters.

As I made my way through the corridors, I noticed that it was not just the air circulator in that specific cabin which had failed; all the circulation units in this portion of the ship were quiet. The ambient lighting was gone now as well, with the only illumination in these hallways now coming from glow strips embedded in the walls. Panic drove my steps ever faster. Making the trip faster than I had with Jenna, I found the hatch by hurling myself into it bodily and repeated the action until the crew appeared behind me. Adding their force to mine, we all battered the safety sealed hatch until the cook let us back in.

"Fetch the medic," the navigator said as he removed his helmet. A needless request as the galley boy had run off, hopefully for just that purpose. The navigator and the cook fell to, getting the pilot out of her hazviro suit, then starting to perform CPR.

Jenna and I hovered, watching, waiting to see if the pilot would snap back. The rest of the crew hovered too truth be told. Right up until the doctor appeared and shouted, "If you aren't actively helping, then you're just in the way!" and took the navigator's place.

We all began to edge away, hovering just a little farther from the injured woman when the ship's alarms sounded. Then the captain announced through the ship wide public announcement system, "Lock all access to outer portions of the ship. Engineers to bridge."

Cook bustled Jenna, the galley boy, and I back to the pantries, checking every hatch we passed. Once there, she set to work preparing the next meal, exiling Jenna and I to our pantry bunks. I remember she threw in some food for us at one point, and let us roam the kitchen and dining areas for a little while, but she wouldn't let us into the corridors, not even the ones in active use by the transporters.

That was our territory for the remainder of the voyage: the pantries, the galley, and the public galleys; no matter how hard we tried to go further, everybody kept us inside. It made for a rather dull finish to the voyage. That was nice in its way, but still boring. There was some minor excitement day to day: the cook burned her hand cooking breakfast and the galley boy had to take over for the rest of that day and into the next, one of the deck hands spilled a full bucket of mop water on the freshly cleaned floor and ruined more than one pair of socks in the process.

But there was only one piece of major excitement before we touched down planetside.

The pilot, who went by the name Sonia it turned out, appeared in one of the galleys two days after her accident with the air circulator. She had a few electrical burns, and a lump the size of a kitten on the back of her head, but "nothin' lasting" as she put it. She was relieved of active duty for a few days to recover and spent much of the time in the galley, drinking tea and reading. So, Jenna and I spent a lot of that time with her. Sometimes she read to us, other times she just let us be near, keeping us out of Cook's way really but in a way that we didn't much mind. Even after she was returned to active duty, Sonia made a point of visiting Jenna and I every day. The day before we made planet, Sonia came to the galley to bid us farewell. We all cried a little until Cook asked, "Why is it goodbye? The two wee ones will need somebody to care for them, at least for a while."

"I thought they were yours," Sonia said. "They've always been down here with you and I just assumed."

Cook laughed heartily in response, then told the story of how she'd found two stowaways napping in the pantry. How she hadn't the heart to see us put out and insisted that if we could pass the medical examinations, we had to be kept alive and onboard. "If anybody has a say of what happens to Jenna and Cato, then it'd be the captain, at least if we make a decision before we land."

Sonia rushed out of the galley, Jenna and I at her heels. Not just excited at being freed of our small prison, but also by the hopeful look on Sonia's face. She burst onto the bridge like rapid decompression after a hull rupture.

"What is the cause of this commotion on my bridge?" the captain asked.

Sonia took a moment to catch her breath before she spoke calmly. "Captain, I would like to officially adopt Cato and Jenna before we land. They have passed all quarantine and medical procedures required by the settlement commissions but are aboard the *Bondar* alone. I will give them a…"

"I can think of no better home for them," the captain said flatly. "Now go enjoy the end of your off shift before I call you back for the landing."

She thanked her as we went to the galley to celebrate, milky tea for everyone.

And that's how two scrawny cats came to live in Centauri Settlement One. Maybe not as exciting as you'd thought, maybe more, but that's the story nose to tail.

Andrew McDonald

Andrew McDonald is from St. John's, Newfoundland, where he lives with his wife and daughter. He is a long-standing fan of horror, science fiction, and Heavy Metal.

He brings with him 'First Visit,' an astonishing tale to expand the senses. It is McDonald's first published work.

First Visit

The neighborhood was so typical of a modern American suburb, Howard thought, that the only thing one could consider suspect was the car he and his partner were currently sitting in at the end of the cul-de-sac.

The developer had only broken ground a few years ago but they put up two hundred houses in record time. The same three house styles repeated continuously, making the drive through the area seem like they were going in circles.

They had parked in front of 12 Cedarview Crescent for ten minutes as Elliot poured over his notes, rereading the same two pages. Howard was getting impatient, but he was trying to give his new partner a chance. This was new to Elliot and god knows it took Howard a while to get used to this kind of visits.

Howard had spent the latter half of WWII hunting Nazi spies all throughout Europe, and then followed that up by rounding up the war criminals that had tried to run. Now he had another list of people exhibiting suspicious behavior and with instructions to go ask some questions. Elliot, who was younger than Howard by nearly twenty years, had no similar experiences to draw from and no idea where to begin investigating people for suspicious behavior based on anonymous tips.

Howard did not hold his partner's lack of service against him. He understood the need to replenish the ranks with new blood; most of the men he served with were dead or retired and Howard suspected if he stayed in the army much longer he would end up an attraction at a military museum right between a captured Panzer and the scale models of Fat Man and Little Boy.

"Are we sure?" Elliot kept asking. "Do we know for a fact that this Intel is good?" He flipped back and forth between the pages. "This is someone's life we are dealing with."

Their intel had come from police reports. Three days previously, residents of the nearby town reported flashing lights in the sky accompanied by small bangs and rumbling in their homes. Pieces of strange rocks were found stuck out of the ground next to craters no bigger than a melon. Most struck dirt, some hit homes, and one punched a fair hole in the bed of some poor guy's Chevy pickup. *Small meteors* is what army intelligence had told them.

Most of the fragments had already been collected, but it could be assumed some citizens had rummaged through these impact sites. Footprints were present around some of the craters.

Reports started to trickle into the local police stations of strange and sometimes hostile behavior. Husbands and wives reporting that their spouse was a completely different person now. Violent incidents increased. Then the factory at the edge of town exploded. Windows rattled for miles. Nobody was sure what caused it so far, but the local police had their hands full.

The army stepped in to offer help, but with a caveat:

they only wanted cases that involved people that lived near the meteor strikes. The police, swamped with work, took any help they could get.

This was the First Visit. Cheryl Ellis had come into the police station the day before to file a report about her husband, Franklin. She had awoken early that morning to her husband looming over her. He was standing over her on his side of the bed, looking angry. Furious is the word she used. She vaulted out of bed and sprinted to the bathroom. Her loving husband gave chase and was inches behind her when she slammed the door, locking herself in. He slammed into the door full force, almost buckling the door, but it held. She called out to him and received no response but a pound on the door. This wasn't like her Franklin. He was an even-tempered man, not one to get angry. When she peaked under the door, she could see his feet. He stood there for five hours. Sometimes he jiggled the handle, but he mainly just waited outside the door

She sobbed in the tub, eventually falling asleep. When she awoke in the morning, Franklin was no longer there, but she wouldn't open the door in case he lay in wait. Cheryl opened the bathroom window and squeezed herself through. She ran to a neighbor in nothing but her nightdress. She was frantic. They called the police. The police passed it to the army and here the two men where, outside the Ellis' cookie cutter home.

Howard was tired of waiting. "The only thing we can do is talk to the guy. If he is clean, we walk, no harm done."

"Just talk?"

"Yup. All we do is talk."

Elliot still looked nervous. "I think I can do that," he replied, as relief washed over him.

They exited the car onto the dark street. It was nearly nine and the sun was down. The only light came from the streetlamps and porch lights. Howard moved towards the back of the car and opened the trunk. The trunk contained an assortment of government issued firearms. Howard selected a Thompson submachine gun and fifty round drum mag for it. As he loaded the weapon, Elliot watched wide-eyed.

"Thought we were just going to talk?" he asked, looking more worried than ever.

Howard smiled. "Just in case he doesn't feel chatty." He motioned for Elliot to arm himself, but Elliot shook his head no. Howard could feel the unease building in Elliot and turned to him as he closed the trunk.

"Look, we have to take precautions," Howard said. "One time, after the war, they sent me the house of this old man. He must've been in his seventies, he was so old and feeble, no way this guy was a Nazi, right? But headquarters was sure, so myself and this private pay him a visit and he turns out to be this sweet old man in a hand knit sweater who couldn't hurt a fly. He invites us in, puts on the kettle, and tells us stories of his childhood and where he hid during the war. I'm not pressing him too hard, softball questions, and he was so cooperative. Kettle boiled and he goes to make tea. Then the old son of a bitch pulls a potato masher on us"

"Potato masher?"

"German stick grenade." He reaches down and pulls up his shirt to reveal a jagged scar. "Geezer blew himself and the private all to hell, I barely made it." He tucked his shirt back in. "The old guy helped run one of the camps, knew we would hang him, wasn't going to let us take him alive. I'll never let my guard down like that again." Howard paused, thoughtful. "I can't even remember the name of that private anymore," he added, mostly to himself.

Elliot nodded slowly, and then took out his sidearm, double-checked that it was loaded and holstered it again.

Howard held his weapon down and covered it in his trench coat. The weapon disappeared from sight as he walked towards the house, Elliot trailing after, clipboard in hand.

As they approached the door, Howard motioned for Elliot to proceed. His partner waved him off, held up his index finger and took a deep breath. He raised his fist, hesitated, then rapped on the door. Elliot almost face planted as the door swung inward.

"Unlatched," Elliot said to himself. Howard motioned for Elliot to stand aside and Howard stepped through the doorway, Elliot following after like a younger brother afraid to get in trouble.

The house was dark and didn't smell right. Something had spoiled and needed to be tossed out. They moved further into the house. Every room was dark, except for a faint light flickering from down the hall.

"Hello? Is anyone here? The door was open," Howard bellowed, then paused, waiting for any kind of a reply. All he heard back was faint static. Following the light, they turned at the end of the hall into a kitchen, the sour smell getting stronger. There was no one in the room. Elliot looked around the dingy kitchen and made to announce their presence once more, but Howard hushed him and pointed towards the other side of the kitchen, to an open door that led to another room, where the flickering light seemed to emanate from.

They entered through the door. It was a living room, again dark and foul smelling. The light was coming from the TV with no signal, so the only sound was static at a low volume. Sitting on the couch was a man in his early forties, staring at the flickering lights on the TV. He did not appear to be aware of the two men that had entered his home. After a few uncomfortable moments of silence, Elliot raised his clipboard and checked the information on it one more time.

"Mr. Ellis?" Elliot asked.

The man on the couch didn't react.

"I'm sorry, sir, the door was open."

No response.

"My partner and I are looking to ask you a few questions."

The man blinked. The first sign of life.

"We wanted to talk to you about your activities this past week, mostly pertaining to the explosion at the factory. I understand you do the night watch there, is that correct?" The man's empty eyes kept staring at the static, Elliot looked to Howard again for assistance, but Howard motioned for Elliot to keep going.

"Did you see the incident?"

Nothing.

"Were you harmed?"

Nothing still.

"Sir? Are you okay?" Elliot was getting uncomfortable with the silence, while Howard stood in the doorway, his body partly concealed by the door frame. He kept the Thompson out of sight.

"Sir?" Elliot asked again. The static on the TV seemed to get louder to fill in the silence.

"Sir?" Elliot raised his voice, not quite a shout but loud enough for the sound to fill the room.

The man on the couch snapped out of his daze and

suddenly became aware of the presence of the two strangers in his den.

"I'm sorry to bother you, sir, it's just we have some questions. Once we ask them, we will be out of your hair."

The man was now darting his eyes back and forth between the two men that had invaded his home. He started clenching and unclenching his fists, eyes still jumping between the two men. He was beginning to look like a caged animal. Howard knew the look, having seen it dozens of times.

"Can you answer some questions about-"

The man exploded from the couch, rising to his feet and lunging at Elliot, the closer of the two, hands stretched out, looking to strangle the young man. Elliot stumbled back, shielding himself with his clipboard. Howard raised the Thompson and fired a short burst one-handed. All four rounds struck the wild man in his stomach and chest. He staggered and fell back on the couch, striking his head against the wall hard, leaving a dent in the wall as he slumped further down.

Elliot stood in shocked silence. "Jesus, Howard," was all he could muster.

Howard stepped forward with a two-handed grip on his weapon. "Run out to the car and radio the base, they are going to want more troops here before the police arrive."

Elliot didn't budge, his gaze was fixed on the body. He reached up, rubbed both eyes with his free hand and looked at the body again in disbelief. "Was he sick?"

"I have no idea what was wrong with him"

"His blood, Howard. His blood is green."

Elliot was right. The man's wounds were leaking a foul

looking liquid. Elliot slowly walked to the body, stepping in front of Howard. Howard lowered the gun and started to scold his partner when the dead body on the couch shot to his feet. Unable get a clear shot, Howard tried to sidestep Elliot, but the body was too fast. It grabbed Elliot by the collar and threw him at Howard sending both men to the floor. Ellis tore off down the hall.

Howard was on his feet first and gave chase. "The car!" he yelled back over his shoulder.

For a dead man, Ellis was fast. Howard was having trouble keeping up. He zigged and zagged through the halls of the house, following drops of green liquid. He got to the front door and saw Ellis already running down the street. He raised his weapon and let off a short burst, unsure if anything connected. He was not worried about bystanders. The road curved away from the homes, and any missed shots would go harmlessly into the nearby woods. Howard followed Ellis down the road, choosing to walk fast and keep shooting instead of running. A few shots hit the runner, but he did not slow down. In fact, he hardly seemed to notice. Howard heard the rumble of the car engine behind him and Elliot pulled up. Instead of getting inside, he stepped onto the running board and grabbed onto the inside of the door, holding the Thompson in his right hand.

"Drive," was all Howard said. Elliot floored it and started to gain on Ellis who was still running like neither man had ever seen. Howard continued to fire small bursts that hit the target repeatedly, but none of the shots brought Ellis down. The .45 ACP that the Thompson fires is primarily a handgun bullet and while great in close quarters, lacks stopping power at distance. While Howard had seen men in the war take a burst and try to run, none ever got nearly as far as Mr. Ellis who showed no signs of stopping

They had now exited the cul-de-sac and were heading towards the city. The subdivision was new and the area around it undeveloped, mostly consisting of recently bought out farmland. To the right was a high wall of sedimentary rock and a small hill, to the left of the road was a steep incline covered in shrubs that lead to a field. Ellis broke off to the left and disappeared into the shrubs. Howard yelled for Elliot to pull over. The car came to a rest on the wrong shoulder and Howard was running before it fully stopped. He ran around the car and fired down into the shrubs at the movement. He saw spots of green and knew he hit something. The Thompson was empty.

"Keys!" Howard yelled out to Elliot. He quickly tossed them to Howard who caught them without breaking stride. He popped the trunk and tossed the Thompson in, opting for something with more stopping power. He selected a Springfield M1903 rifle. It lacked the speed and capacity of the Thompson, but more than made up for it with sheer power. Quickly walking back to the edge of the road, Howard surveyed the hillside. Ellis was nearly at the bottom of the hill, some two hundred feet down. Howard shouldered the rifle, took aim and fired. The .30-06 caught Ellis on the back and he tumbled down the rest of the hill, landing in a heap at the bottom. Elliot was out of the car, with binoculars, watching Ellis.

"He's getting up," Elliot said, shocked. Howard worked the bolt and chambered a fresh round. Ellis was getting to his feet when the second round struck him in the upper back again, sending him sprawling. Howard put another round in him before he could stir again.

"Jesus, Howard, he has to be dead now," Elliot exclaimed as Howard loaded the fourth round.

"The guy had enough .45 in him to stop an elephant, I'm not risking it," Howard replied as he shot Ellis in the lower back.

"Enough!" cried Elliot as Howard worked the bolt again. "He's dead, Howard. Stop!"

Howard didn't take his eyes off the prone man at the bottom of the hill. "Sure moves a lot for a dead man," Howard said as he gestured down the hill.

In disbelief Elliot peered through the binoculars and saw Ellis was still trying to get up.

"How can he-" was all Elliot was able to get out before Howard fired once more. This round blew a hole in the back of Ellis' head. Elliot retched. Howard returned to the trunk of the car to stow the rifle and extracted a Winchester shotgun and a box of shells before closing the trunk. He tossed the keys to Elliot, who missed them entirely and scrambled to pick them up.

"Take the car down and far as that gate and cut across the field and meet me by our friend down there," Howard said to Elliot as he started down the hill. "I'm keeping line of sight on him. This sucker might have some fight left in him."

The trek down the hill was a hard one as Howard almost went ass over teakettle more than once. He could see and smell the green blood on all over the hillside. It smelled both rotten and clean, like someone poured bleach onto roadkill. He fought to keep from gagging, as the scent grew stronger. He made it to the bottom without falling and slowly walked up to the body, eyeing it for the slightest twitch. He sure looked dead, face down in the dirt, riddled with bullet holes, the .30-06 looking especially nasty. The coup de grâce to the back of the head looked to have finished him. Howard looked at the wound, holding a handkerchief to his nose. The smell was eye watering. The head wound puzzled him. He had seen people shot in the head during the war, but this was different. The head had split open in the back, but it looked like a tree that he had seen in France that had taken an artillery shell. Instead of brain, blood, and bone, it looked like pulped wood. He stepped back. What was this?

The body twitched. Howard brought up the shotgun and fired, buckshot sprayed all over the body. He held the trigger down and worked the action. Howard quickly slam fired the other four shells into the twitching mass. Ellis no longer resembled man, or much of anything for that matter. Howard stepped back and started to reload the shotgun, when Ellis sprang to his feet once more. Howard staggered and nearly lost his footing while he plucked shells out of his coat pocket and jammed them into the gun. Ellis took a step towards him. Howard dropped a shell and cursed his fumbling. Ellis turned his shattered face to Howard and lurched on unsteady legs. Howard finished loading and was about to fire when he heard a noise from behind him. He turned to see the car roaring across the field.

Howard threw himself out of the way as Elliot rammed the vaguely man-shaped mass with the vehicle, sending it flying back ten or fifteen feet. Elliot was out of the car in an instant and popped the trunk, disappearing from sight. When he reappeared, he had the Thompson with a new drum. Elliot ran to the body and let what was once Ellis have it. Bullets tore up the body and everything within a foot or so. It was evident to Howard that Elliot had spent little time with the Thompson before as he struggled to keep the muzzle down. He held the trigger down until the drum ran dry, then he dropped the drum, pulled a thirty-round stick mag from his jacket and proceeded to dump that into the green mass on the ground. Howard was speechless. When that magazine ran out, he pitched the gun into the dirt, drew his side arm and put seven more rounds into it. Elliot was attempting to reload his pistol when Howard finally got his attention, shouting his name repeatedly.

"That's plenty," he said to his nearly hyperventilating partner. Neither of them were ready to let their guard down yet. Howard had an idea. Keeping the shotgun trained on the mass, he told Elliot to get the Jerry can from the trunk

Elliot disappeared shortly, returning with the can. He poured gas all over the remains, being careful to keep himself dry. Elliot left a trail of gas back towards the car. Elliot struck a match and set the gas ablaze. The heat was sudden and immense, the flames were bright green and shot fifteen feet into the air. The smell was oppressive, worse than anything Howard smelled in the war. The body twitched. Howard put five more shells into the pillar of flame. Elliot joined in with his pistol. Finally, it was still.

Turning towards the car, Howard saw the extent of the damage for the first time. The car was toast, the front crumpled in as though they had struck a brick wall.

Howard reached in and grabbed the radio from the car.

"The suspect was hostile and was put down. Whatever this is, it is not normal. The suspect shrugged off most small arms. .45s are useless, .30-06 slowed it down. Buckshot pissed it off. Headshots ineffective. Advising the issuing of B.A.R. machine guns to troops, vehicle mounted heavy machine guns and flamethrowers; fire seems to work."

Elliot nudged Howard hard in the ribs. When Howard turned, he expected to see Ellis again, but the body still smoldered in the dirt. Instead, Elliot silently pointed up to the road. There, lined up shoulder-to-shoulder, stood hundreds of people. Men, women, and children. They were not simply people being curious. This wasn't normal. They stood motionless, not making a sound, watching the men. They looked like mannequins, or target dummies.

"It's okay, folks! You are now safe! we are with the army!" Elliot shouted.

No one made a move. Those were not people anymore.

Howard picked up the radio again. "The whole area has is affected. We are overrun. No further commutations."

Dropping the radio back in the front seat he walked back to the trunk and started loading the Springfield.

"What do we do?" Elliot asked, panicked.

"We make them work for it," Howard replied as he tossed the reloaded Thompson to his partner.

They stood by the corpse of their car and waited. As one, the hordeon the ridge started down the hill.

Andrew Pike

Andrew is a St. John's native who holds a degree in English from Memorial University of Newfoundland, as well as diplomas in Journalism and Music from College of the North Atlantic.

He nurtures an unhealthy addiction to coffee, has written for *The Telegram*, and plays classical piano.

His first published story was 'Escape from Selenous Valley Retreat' in *Dystopia from the Rock*.

Slipdream

1893

The young hero stumbled forward, arms bruised from the fight, eyes blurry from sleep, calculator tucked into his breast pocket. A series of explosions erupted from the battleground, stirring fallout into the gray Martian atmosphere.

"You'll never do it!" he yelled.

"Useless, my boy. It's already done! Look behind you!"

The boy turned to see the alien landscape had been obliterated. There would be no chance of the human base surviving.

"Now you'll meet my new experiment, see?" The villain pushed a button on his control pad. The cliff beside him revolved revealing a swivelling robot with a minigun.

"Little Terror will follow my every command from my wireless control pad! And I'm commanding it to *kill* her!" The robot pivoted, beginning its stiff trek toward a yellow-hued alien woman chained cliffside.

"Monster!" the boy cried, as the villain laughed maniacally. The scene slipped into slow-motion with the alien speaking directly to the boy.

"Hack the control pad!"

The boy tapped his calculator as fast he could, but to no avail.

"Come on, Hugo! You can do this!"

Sweat dripping down his face, he dove deep into his subconscious, then keyed it instinctively. The robot turned and pelted the villain with its minigun. The villain cried out as he fell to the ground.

"Amazing! You did it! Great job!"

Hugo dashed over and grabbed the robot control pad, revelling in its potential. He guided the robot to shoot missiles into the air. The alien rolled her eyes.

"You know, Hugo, there is science beyond robots."

"But they're so awesome!"

The alien sighed. A beep in her ear distracted her from the dreamer.

"Well, Hugo, thank you for saving me. I have to go. Remember: humans first. Sweet dreams!"

The alien's light rose up, up to the stars, into the revolutions of space...

Ashlyn disconnected from the dream. She removed her REM-Link visor and waited for her pupils to dilate to her cabin's soft nocturnal light. The transition always took about five seconds and she was careful not to stand up too quickly to avoid vertigo.

"Bridge in five minutes," her com beeped.

She sighed, gently sitting up and leaving her bed, unphased by the motion-blur of slipdream stars outside.

The bridge door swished open to a bustling crew preparing for the mission briefing. Grudgingly, she took her place next to the captain's chair.

"Late again, Ash. This is an important briefing." Her father's militaristic punctuality negated any clever reply, so she just rolled her eyes. Their guest appeared on screen addressing her father.

"Captain Findlay. Great to speak to you. It's been a long time."

"It has indeed. It is good to see you, captain. What is the situation?"

"I'm saddened to report that the nanos have multiplied tenfold in this last future result. They are expanding beyond earth. Not that they are close to unlocking the collective unconscious, but—" the captain trailed off, his expression reading of deep concern before snapping back to his professional poise, "—Captain, we need all remaining ships working on a new strategy. Our precognizer is in the midst of establishing a plan with shorter exposure times and more frequent jumps."

"Understood. We have work to do. Nice to meet with you, Captain. Helm, get our precognizer on the next channel, let's hit the next jump date ASAP."

1934

A bluish glow looms over the silver city, lulling in the silent hum of machinery, thousands of machines going about their business with not a human in sight; they must have been left like this for centuries. Barely a star in the sky; exhausted. Perhaps through the eyes of a hitchhiker, this could be the end of a world obsessed with technology…

"Is this the future you want to create, John?"

Campbell turned to face a woman emerging from the mechanized city.

"What a surprise, I didn't expect to meet anyone here."

The woman gestured towards the city.

"*This* is what happens when humans lose the passion to imagine, to create. These machines have been running automatically for millennia, for what? Some short-sighted command in an unrecallable history?"

Ashlyn was interrupted by a beep from her com. "*Rap it up, we're making the next jump.*"

She stepped aside and quietly responded, "I've only just started!"

"*Extract immediately. We're making a jump in two minutes. That's an order.*" She shut off the com and faced her dreamer.

"Well, John, apologies, I have to cut this short. Keep inspiring others with your work. Keep imaginations soaring through the rough times and remember: as glamorous as they may be, machines are not the way forward; they will lead to nothing but ruin! Sweet dreams."

Campbell wiped the sleep in his eyes as Ashlyn's consciousness rose up through the fantasy of faint twilight.

1990

After selecting her new dreamer, Ashlyn touched down gently on an imaginary field of wheat swaying in a warm breeze. She was ready for her next mission. Soft horizon light suggested dawn. Quiet. Her sympathetic nervous system kicked into action. Is there a risk of unruly robots? Nuclear annihilation? Is the perimeter teeming with predators?

No.

Strange.

No dreamer in sight.

Was this correct?

A forest in the distance compelled exploration, but she

took a moment to breathe in the air. It was a full, hearty air, unlike that of the smothering industrialization in the dreams of 19th century architects. No, this was something new. She looked at her suit: a green tunic and long cap.

The morning light grew as she walked to the forest. What was the nature of this dreamer? Usually projects were clear-cut; feign capture by a rogue android, embolden the *great hero* to save the day, preach aversion to the machines, etc., etc. On this mission there was no direction. She considered reaching out to command but ruled against that for now.

Songbirds sung from the forest branches, playing Call and Answer with a musician's melody. She followed the sound. A clearing revealed a young man in a tunic with a shield on his back playing a wooden flute. The performance exalted every note, each inflection heightening her perception drawing out the ambiance of the nearby stream.

Then he stopped. The moment stretched on and the silence became palpable.

"It's amazing" she said.

"Thank you," he replied, looking up at her. "What is your name?" The question took her off guard; normally the dreamer projected a desired identity onto her.

"I'm Ashlyn."

"I'm Blaire. Will you join me on a trip to Starsow Mountain? It's the best view in all of Linwood Dale."

"Well… Okay."

She followed him up along the stream, discretely contacting command to verify the situation. "Do you have any record of any prominent figures named 'Blaire' in 1990?"

"*No.*"

"Do I have the right dreamer?"

"The number was assigned by the precognizer. Just play it out. Follow the brainwashing playbook, assume it's a person-of-interest."

She spent the whole day with Blaire following the stream. It was unusual but calming. He was interested in where she'd come from. She said she was from a spaceship far away. As a cognitizer, honesty within dreams did not forsake the *subtle interference* principle because anything that happened in a dream was written off as fantasy.

By the end of the day they'd made it to the top of Starsow Mountain. The view was astounding. No stuffy cities in sight, just forest for miles and the ocean in the distance. Each cliff, each shoreline beckoned to be explored. She actually wanted to stay, but then the beep sounded in her ear. She shuddered.

"Blaire, uh, it was very nice to meet you. You have a fantastic imagination. It's just, I have to return to my ship now."

"Okay. It was great to meet you too. Thank you for joining me."

"You're welcome. Keep it up!"

"I will, Ashlyn. Sweet dreams!"

She paused, taken aback. She began to say goodbye, only to be interrupted by the familiar daze of her consciousness lifting up into the stars.

"Cognitizers: your work is invaluable. Thank you all for joining me on short notice." The precognizer raised both hands together in a fist in front of her shiny head and shooting star insignia, a salute honoring the shared commitment to protecting humankind. The audience followed suit.

"I have called you here to discuss our change in strategy. The future currently holds over five-hundred thousand potential outcomes of the nanomachines discovering slipdream travel. They have now expanded beyond Earth and consumed all human colonies. Gravely, there are no nano-free humans left beyond the 60th century." The precognizer remained calm and astute in her presentation, despite the heavy subject-matter. The bright stars of the slipdream outside luminated the conference room's attentive audience.

"Our first plan of action will be to increase the frequency of jumps. Your job will remain the same: apply the principles of cognition to the most influential figures of history.

"For our second action item, we will need you all to increase the intensity of brainwashing. Fiction-based cognitizers: you will continue to colour dreams with gray goo, liquid metal killer robots, and out-of-control swarms—the more doomsday the scenario, the better. Science-based cognitizers: continue to emphasize the hazardous real-world scenarios we've seen, like mesothelioma, genetic modification and of course the eventual dominating of humans as hosts by the nanomachines."

"Above all please remember to teach that dreams are sacred. They show us where we need to go and, more importantly, where we need to avoid. They help us craft better futures. Let's help our ancestors understand their value so as to strengthen the power of the slipdream. The nanomachines must *never* discover it. Now, I will present your new slips for the jump to 2020…"

Ashlyn was distracted by the hypnosis of the slipdream stars. It was mesmerizing to ponder that humanity's whole defense against subservience to the machines was owed to the collective human imagination. She recalled the creativity of Blaire's Linwood Dale. He had no idea the dark future that lay ahead, but maybe in his optimism there was hope of victory over the nanos. Maybe it was possible."

"Ashlyn."

She snapped out of her daydream to see the precognizer standing in front of her with small piece of paper. The rest of the crew had left.

"Your Freudian slip," she joked, handing Ashlyn the numbered paper used in the REM-Link system to sync her up to her next dreamer.

"I have to apologize," she said. "It seems you were assigned an erroneous slip for this jump date. Your dreamer was meant to be Kevin J. Anderson. Unfortunately, it's a moot point now as we will be jumping to 2020 shortly."

Ashlyn paused in contemplation, then spoke.

"How do you do it?"

"Do what?"

"How do you choose the dreamers?"

"It's complicated. It involves forecasting timelines, ranking historical figures, etc. Generally we choose jump dates that coincide with significant events in the nanotechnology movement, but there can be variance. Ironically, it's a task better suited to machines, but we do what we can."

Ashlyn looked out the window, then spoke again.

"You lived on Earth before the nanos took over. What was it like back then?"

"People were a lot more ignorant of their potential. They didn't know the cognitive possibilities of the slipdream, they were over-dependent on machines to do their bidding. They were closed-minded."

The precognizer stopped, seeing Ashlyn stare longingly out the window. Then she spoke sternly and out of character.

"It's important for us to remain determined, Ashlyn. Remember the first principle of cognitizers: subtle interference. We can never *return to Earth*, to the way it was before, it's too dangerous. We can only move forward. Someday our work *will pay off*, and we will return to a future devoid of the nanomachines."

Ashlyn thanked the precognizer and headed back to her room, briefly encountering her friend Tara in the hall.

"Who did you have this jump?" she asked.

"Oh...no one you'd know."

"I had an engineer, 'Bill Joy.' I gave him enough info on self-replicating nanomachines to last him for a good article or two. But geez, I wish I was a fiction-based cognitizer. Mark got Arnold Schwarzenegger! Can you imagine? And I heard someone else got Steven Spielberg. I'd *die*."

Back in her cabin, Ashlyn sat on her bed observing her small library. Campbell, Stephenson, Crichton, she had quite the collection but longed for something more. She opened Frey causing her makeshift bookmark—her last REM-Link slip—to fall out. She held it up next to her new slip, deliberating. Her com beeped.

"Heads up, Ashlyn, we're making the jump to 2020. Get ready for your next project."

2020

Ashlyn touched down in the warm grass in a cool evening breeze. No twilight; it was dark, but she was not apprehensive. She felt strong and confident. She crept through the wheat field carefully, her face ripe with a guilty wonder.

The dark forest bore no one. She found the trickling stream and followed it upwards. A heavy rain began. How did people live with weather? Such an inconvenience, but it did not stop her.

Exiting the forest, she made her way up the mountain. As she got higher, she saw castles with lights on below where once there was forest. Then she remembered—of course, the jump! She was thirty years forward in time from the dreamer's original dream. It was coincidental he was even having the same dream.

She approached him wearing the same tunic and shield sitting on the edge of the cliff, blond hair swaying in the wind.

"I knew you'd come back," he said.

"Blaire?"

He stood up and turned around, a flash of light revealing his rain-drenched profile. He was definitely older, stronger, experienced. Thunder erupted in the distance.

"My dreams aren't the same," he said. "There are others, but they're not friendly. They build castles and speak through electricity. The storms grow worse and they just hide inside, ignorant of all peril."

Ashlyn stood silent, not knowing how to respond.

"Something dangerous is coming." He pointed up. The sky flashed again as if an electric skeleton hand reached down. Ashlyn began to run to Blaire, but as the thunder rumbled through the air, she felt herself falling up into the sky.

"What the hell are you doing?"

Ashlyn woke to a furious Captain Findlay accompanied by two security officers.

"You know damn well this is a direct violation of cognitizer protocol! We never use the same dreamer slip on a separate jump date!"

"I… was curious."

"I can't believe this. My own daughter!"

The captain's com interrupted them.

"Captain, we have a problem. Scientists on earth have uncovered a breakthrough nanotechnology treatment for cancer."

"No! Get our precognizer on the next channel. This is a disaster! Mark, deactivate her REM-Link visor!" He scowled at Ashlyn. "You won't be cognitizing anytime soon. We'll talk about this later. I'm very disappointed."

"Code red. All personnel report to the conference room for an important meeting."

Ashlyn turned the volume down on her com. The entire ship went to the conference room to discuss a strategy for the new risk. When it was clear, she snuck out of her cabin and headed towards the ship's hanger.

She unlocked the door to the hanger and ran to the emergency pod, just as the emergency response procedure instructed in 4065. Back then, as a kid, working in the hanger was fun; new ships, new people every day. No nanos, no endless slipdream.

She opened the escape pod. It was absurdly dangerous, but she was sick of having to influence the ignorant prodigies and the self-absorbed scientists. No more.

"Damnit Ashlyn, what are you doing?"

She ignored it. Her heart weighed a million pounds.

"ASHLYN!"

It was too late. She had to do it. The screams continued through her com, but she opened the bay door.

"All personnel take to your cabins; jumping slipdream in

two minutes."

She panicked. She had to get out NOW.

"ASHLYN!!!!"

Security personnel appeared at the door to the hanger. Her ship lifted off the ground and turned towards space. The hanger door began to close. She revved the engine moving towards a vortex of stars. The reality of what she was doing washed over her in a wave of fear as she broke through the forcefield.

Seagulls meandered through the overcast sky above the small harbour city on earth as a building filled with curious folk—princesses, furry beasts, mermaids, superheroes, evil villains—all types. Kindred spirits gathered in a lofty sunroom with tall trees and brick pathways for the convention's opening ceremonies.

"Hey, what's that?"

A boy pointed up to the sky. There was a light falling slowly, but gaining speed. A crowd gathered by the bay window to get a better look, but it quickly withdrew into a frenzied exodus.

The glass exploded, screams filled the air; a giant metal craft had destroyed the window and was now in flames. Most fled the building but several remained.

The door to the craft opened and a dark-haired woman stepped out, dressed all in black with a shooting star insignia on her collar. She was covered in blood. A man dressed in a green tunic and shield stepped towards her.

"Ashlyn?"

2057

The enchantment of Blaire's forest dream had changed

a lot since Ashlyn's arrival on earth. The castle gates had opened; she had taught others how to link their dreams together rather than relying on technology for communication. Together with two children, their dreams resonated with the dreams of others, strengthening the slipdream.

Ashlyn stood on their shared fantasy of Starsow Mountain, contemplating how peaceful her life had become. She was older now, without the promise of extended life that nanotechnology had advertised in her childhood. But in the slipdream, she would always remain young through the dreams of others.

A light fell behind her.

A star?

She turned around. Her father stood behind her in king's attire.

"Why did you leave, Ash?"

She ran to him and they embraced.

"How are you here?"

"It's against protocol, but… your presence on Earth has changed everything. I've just been advised by our ship from the future that the dreams you've incited have opened up more opportunities for influence. With many minds now open, our message has been better received throughout history, and humanity has veered away from a dependence on machines. There are no nanomachines in the future."

She began to cry. He held her, visibly moved, but stoic.

"I'm sorry for getting mad at you, Ash."

She stared at him with wet eyes, realizing that he'd only just seen her leave; the jump had been instant for him whereas she had lived out her whole life on earth.

"I have to go… I shouldn't be here. The work for our

future victory still needs to be done, and it will be done. You are a hero, Ashlyn; you will live on in the history books as the one that saved humankind. We are all very grateful for what you've done."

"Must you go?"

"I have to. But... I will be back. We will speak again. Thank you for keeping the slipdream alive in the minds of humankind. Until next time... sweet dreams."

Lisa Daly

A native Newfoundlander, Lisa is an archaeologist, historian, professional ballroom dance instructor, crafter, and avid baker.

Previous non-fiction writing credits include essays *Sacrifice in Second World War Gander* and *An Empty Graveyard: The Victims of the 1946 AOA DC-4 Crash, Their Final Resting Place, and Dark Tourism*.

She made her fiction writing debut with 'The Island Outside the War' in *Dystopia from the Rock*.

Lisa acted as the guest editor for the Summer 2019 *Flights from the Rock* collection.

She returns to fiction writing with her short story 'The Mouse.'

The Mouse

The door banged open and two men joyfully stumbled in, allowing sunlight to highlight the dust motes. They made their way down the steps to the bar as the door closed, letting the shadows overtake the tavern once again.

"We need beer! Beer for everyone!" shouted one of the men.

An unassuming man emerged from the back room and started drawing pints of ale. The two men were settled at the bar when they noticed the stranger in the corner. He was a big man, tall even while seated, his broad shoulders enhanced by a thick leather jacket adorned with pins, spikes, and a pocket watch decorated with skulls. His dark hair looked a little greasy, and a little messy. His scarred features gave him a permanent intimidating scowl.

The newcomers were in too much of a good mood to be intimidated.

"Hi, stranger!" one called out. "What are you drinking? We're celebrating! Bartender, please get this man an ale."

The Mouse looked at them through his lank hair, finished off his current drink, and accepted the new one with a curt, "Thanks."

Taking that as encouragement, the first speaker continued, hand extended. "I'm J'rd and this is Sam," he said as Sam nodded while counting coin to pay for the drinks. The bartender pocketed the coin and left for the back room again.

"Social fellow," noted Sam.

As they each drank deeply, the Mouse looked them over. They were both tall, lanky fellows, dressed in the matching uniforms of the Union of Galactic Hierarchies labour class, cut to accommodate their extra arms. The Mouse thought of what work was in this sector, and figured they must either be linesmen or hyperway workers. Both wore the hard lines of labourers, lighted by their wide, happy smiles. Except for the hair they shared many of the same features, aquiline noses, high foreheads, and dimples. J'rd had a shock of red messy curls sticking out every which way, while Sam had tightly clipped blond hair. The Mouse guessed they might be brothers or cousins, and liked the look of them. He shifted in his seat, opening himself up to further conversation.

J'rd and Sam each put their glasses on the bar, and turned toward the larger man. "What brings you here? You're not a worker, and you don't look like a Hi'er, not in beat up clothes like that. I ain't never seen a Hi'er in anything but fancy suits and dresses that would get dirty and ripped if they ever had to do real work," commented Sam.

"That's not a fair comment," added J'rd. "You just insulted the fellow's clothes."

"It's fine. It's fine," assured the Mouse. "I've had much worse said about me than that. I just finished a job, and that always makes me contemplate the world, and there's no better place to do that than in a dingy bar with a pint of ale."

"That don't sound like our type of work," interjected Sam. "At the end of the day we're happy for the ale, but too tired to contemplate nothin'. Must not be hard work then."

With a glare toward Sam, J'rd said "Forgive my cousin. We've been going through a tough time at work and have been risking our necks for UGH, but the Hi'ers in charge keep cutting staff, pay, and equipment. But let's hear your story, you don't want to hear about us working on the lines."

Urdian Linesmen, the Mouse thought, and not happy ones. But yet so happy...

"Well, I just found a new owner for a turbo-jump that I borrowed and neglected to return to its previous owner. It sort of became necessary when I was being chased through the Federation Spire a few months ago by UGH guards. Something about how they wanted their emblematic ruby back..."

"Wait now!" J'rd almost yelled. "I heard about that. You're not the Mouse? The famous thief no one's ever seen?"

"Don't be ridiculous, J'rd," shot Sam. "This big fellow can't be the Mouse. The Mouse is never seen, and whole crowds would notice someone with his size and looks. That's the whole point in them being 'the Mouse'; they get in and out of impossible spaces. Like a mouse."

"But it's been all over the line, how the Mouse stole the S'dighit ruby. They claim the Mouse just barely escaped, but I didn't believe it until now. No one's ever come close to catching the Mouse." J'rd looked at the big man in awe.

"Well, I wouldn't say they came close, but there was

a chase. See, I had managed to find a way in by rerouting the signal in the air exchange system. The S'dighit need sulfur in their air, and no S'dighit would ever touch the ruby for fear of the curse, so their main security was the air tight chamber that only they could enter. But a few tweaks to the air exchange in the middle of the night, and suddenly the air was fine for us carbon based life forms. So I went through the supply tubes, snuck into the room, and retrieved the stone. I miscalculated or was using old intel."

The Mouse paused to take a drink.

"How did you get out?" asked J'rd.

"Turns out," the Mouse continued, "they had a secondary security patch in the room that recorded any movement too close to the ruby. That set off the alarms. Going back the way I came would have taken too long, so I blasted through an internal wall and ran. The guards were on me in a second. Funny, I would never have expected that with all that fancy regalia that they could run as fast as they do. I guess their skirts are made for it, even if they look fancy when they're standing still. They chased me, blasting spears firing and scorching the walls around me."

The Mouse pulled back his leather sleeve and showed an angry scar as he said, "See, they even got me here."

The other two men leaned in to look at the wound, raw and wrinkled where the flesh was healing. The Mouse pushed his sleeve back down, reached for his beer, and drank deeply.

Sam looked concerned. "This is a great story and all, but if you're really the Mouse, why would you tell us. We could go and tell anyone what you look like. The guard are offering big money for just a description. Last poster I saw said we'd get more than both our salaries combined for the next five years. And that's just to tell them what you look like. Imagine the money if we told them where you was!"

"True," said the Mouse, waiving his beer at them, "but you wouldn't have told me that if you planned to do it, now would you? See, I'm good at reading people, and you two seem like men I can converse with."

"Sam, shut it," grumbled J'rd, leaning forward on his stool with interest. "I want to hear the story."

The Mouse grinned at his eager audience. "Alright, so they gave chase, and I did catch a blast to the arm. Those blasting spears hurt! I mean, they don't look like much, but I guess like their dresses, they're meant to look unthreatening. I don't recommend getting hit by one." The Mouse raised his arm again for emphasis as he added, "This was just a graze.

"So, the Federation Spire is pretty big but I had the floor plan memorized because I had to avoid the S'dighit living quarters. Running into one of those rooms, either I'd collapse from lack of oxygen, or I'd kill a whole room of them by letting the air in. That's got to be tough, being confined to certain rooms in that great big tower, but that's off topic."

The Mouse paused and took another drink. He eyed the other two and watched as they thought about the lives of S'dighit. The S'dighit were ugly by most planetary standards, somehow both hard and jagged, but oozing with their bodies always moving around and shifting. It was hard for non S'dighit to identify individuals, and not being able to recognize one you had met before was highly offensive. Plus, most life forms couldn't share the same air as them, so they were typically avoided. The Mouse watched as the two men seemed to share some sympathy for the S'dighit, and understood the Mouse's reluctance to do them harm. After all, the Mouse had a reputation as the universe's greatest thief, not as a killer.

"I had to weave around the corridors, trying to make my way to the port. I needed out. At one point, I turned down one hall only to be greeted with another squad of guards. Boxed in by guards and S'dighit chambers, I could only go up or down. Now I don't have legs like you two," he said, indicating the strong muscles and joint angle of the Urdian labourers. "Nor do I have spare hands if I need to climb."

J'rd and Sam glanced at their secondary pairs of arms as the Mouse's nod invited them to share his little joke.

"So up wasn't really an option. So I blasted a hole in the floor, and jumped! I must have hit one of the support tubes, you know, for air and current and access to the comm systems, because there was a blast of air and a nice round hole to jump down. I knew it couldn't go more than four floors, so it was my best option. I jumped."

Ever the storyteller, the Mouse paused and finished his beer. As if summoned, the bartender reappeared to pull them each a fresh pint. The Mouse dropped some coin on the bar to cover the drinks.

As the bartender shuffled away, the Mouse continued. "It was tight, which was good, and slightly angled, which was even better, because they couldn't fire straight down at me. I did have a pulse shield," he added, waving the elaborate ring on his hand for emphasis. "So I used that to both protect me from the blasts, and to keep me from falling too fast. It wasn't easy to hold against those blasters, let me tell you. I was about to make myself another hole for an exit when I saw a door. Probably best I hadn't blasted the thing again, really. It was a support, and I could have brought part of the building down on myself! I made it to the door, dropped my shield so I could open it, and shimmied through the tunnel until I found a maintenance room. From there it was a straight run through the labour tunnels to the port. Thankfully, all the floors through from 150 to 400 have ports. I found myself a nice turbo-jumper, and got out. Guess no one thought to lock down the whole building. I brought the ruby to the buyer, and played with the turbo-jumper. But now I just got rid of that as well, so I guess the job is over."

"Wow," breathed J'rd, leaning back as if to take in the story as a whole.

"I'm still not sure I believe you could be the Mouse," Sam piped up. "It's a great story, but there are still too many holes in it. There's no way you could fit in those tunnels. They're made for folks like us, or the Sophscars, or the D'sinvians. You're just plain too big."

"I have my secrets. Wouldn't be a good thief if I didn't, now would I?" the Mouse stated, leaving it clear that no questions would be answered. "Now you two, you said you were celebrating something. What brings you two such good spirits after a hard day's work?"

"Well, you see…" started J'rd.

Sam punched his cousin's shoulder hard. "J'rd, shut it. We can't tell anyone."

"He told his story, and it's far worse than ours," J'rd countered.

"But if he's who he says he is, then he'll never be caught. We will be."

"Don't be foolish, Sam. If he is who he says he is, then he wouldn't tell because why ever would he report us? He'd have to go to the Hi'ers or the guard for that, and they'd take his info and he'd be caught."

"I guess, but I don't like it," Sam said, expression still wary.

"Nonsense. We're here to celebrate, remember. He's probably the only one we could ever share our story with."

"Alright, I suppose..."

The Mouse said nothing during the exchange, just sipped his beer while the cousins argued. He knew they'd tell their story. His story helped build trust, and he knew his appearance would help convince them that he wasn't the type to go to the authorities.

J'rd turned from his cousin and started.

"So, me and Sam work on the comm lines in the inner and outer orbit. We make sure all the platforms are working, and all the relays are talking to each other and to the other ones outside the atmosphere."

"It's long days and hard work," interrupted Sam.

"We used to have a bigger team, but the Hi'ers don't seem to want to pay anymore. Something about less money available, so it's austerity all around. Well, for us labourers it's less, but for them it always seems like they have more. We used to have a team of a dozen for this sector, but now it's just the two of us."

"And we have to cover the whole sector!"

"Yes, Sam, I just said that," J'rd sighed. "And the safety gear is designed for Sophscars, not for us, so there's extra material in some places, and not enough space for our knees. Their secondary arms are longer, so we can use the sleeves, but not well or comfortably."

J'rd and Sam shared glance, an unspoken sadness passed between them.

"About a year ago, Sam had a scare," J'rd continued as

Sam looked down at his beer. "That extra fabric needed for a Sophscar's tail got caught in a fast-moving relay and dragged Sam for miles across the inner orbit. He got beat up awful bad, hitting against all the debris out there, and if it had been one that went from inner to outer orbit, he would have suffocated. It was scary, I almost lost all the family I have left." Jr'd paused and took a slow drink.

Sam reached up and put a hand on his shoulder, but said nothing.

"We complained about the equipment, but the Hi'ers ignored us. Said we had everything we needed and we should just be more careful. But we have so much work to do that sometimes we have to rush, or the planet won't have comms. And we couldn't bring in anyone else because of their new rule that won't allow training, so anyone new already has to be trained to do the work, but anyone already trained is already working or too old to work. We knew nothing would change until someone was seriously hurt, or killed. And we didn't want it to be us." J'rd slammed his palm on the bar, punctuating his words angrily. "We came up with a plan. We'd create someone, and kill them."

Now it was the Mouse's turn to lean in to the story.

J'rd looked proud in spite of his anger as he went on. "We created another Urdian, another cousin. They had training, but wanted to move to be closer to us, to family. So we had them work the lines with us. We didn't think it through, because we did have to do something with their pay. We couldn't open a credit for them, or put it with ours, someone would notice, so we gave it away. There's a charity, my uncle, Sam's dad, spent his last days there when he couldn't work the lines anymore. They help the old ones, help them live with dignity when there's no more money. So we took the notes and mailed them in every month, each time from a different comm point, so they couldn't track us down."

The Mouse nodded, thinking how it was exactly that dispersal that narrowed down the potential suspects.

"We didn't intend for it to go on long," Sam put in, looking a bit embarrassed.

J'rd nodded agreement, adding, "No, just long enough for someone to notice if they were hurt. But then we heard there was an audit coming, so we had to kill them off before that. We fixed it so one of the outer orbit platforms misfired and pushed the suit off. Since you need all four arms to work up there, it's the kind of accident that can happen all too easily. If you've ever seen it, the travel boosters and the oxygen will both explode in the vacuum and there will be nothing left, just ash."

An uneasy silence settled over them, both J'rd and Sam clearly thinking how easily their staged accident could have been real. The Mouse let it linger while he finished his beer.

Before things could grow too morose, the door opened and sunlight shined in on the three barflies. A well-dressed man looked around the gloom. When he saw the Mouse his face brightened and, distracted, he missed the steps from the door down into the room. Faster than expected for such a big man, the Mouse was on his feet and across the room in time to catch the man before he fell.

"Thanks, honey," the newcomer greeted sheepishly as the Mouse set him upright. "I don't know why you love these places. I find them so dark I can't even see my feet."

"I know, dear, but I appreciate that you always come to meet me. You're a little early."

"No, I think you've lost track of time. You're a little late."

The Mouse looked at the pocket watch on his coat. "So I am," he said, and leaned in for a kiss.

The two embraced, just that little bit too long for propriety. Sam started to feel like they were intruding and nudged J'rd to suggest he should also look away.

As they separated, the man looked the Mouse over with a raised brow. "Darling, why haven't you changed? I thought we were going out tonight, and you know I would much rather spend time with your real face."

"Of course, just a moment." For a second it was as if the Mouse blurred, dropping slightly out of focus. In place of the broad, leather-clad man stood a tall woman in a figure accentuating purple dress. The pocket watch was now on a fine chain around her neck, and the skulls were now jewels that sparkled even in the dim light of the bar.

The man eyed her and said, "You still seem short..."

"Oops, almost forgot." She lifted the hem of her dress to show she was still wearing large, leather boots. With another blur they changed to three-inch silver stiletto heels and she went from the same height as him to just a little taller. "That's better."

"Fellows," she said to the two at the bar, "this is my husband, Dema."

J'rd and Sam were agog. The rough looking, burly man was gone, and now this beautiful woman was here with this well-dressed man. They both looked like Hi'ers.

The Mouse read their expressions. "I am sorry, fellows, you did catch me just as I finished a job, and I hadn't yet changed. To be honest, I wear so many faces, I don't always think of it until Dema reminds me."

Dema smiled at her, a man obviously in love.

"Do you mind if we both join you and you finish your story. You can trust him."

Before they could answer, the bartended returned as if summoned. The Mouse ordered ale for herself and the cousins, and a fruited Camorillian brandy for Dema. The bartender served their drinks and once again left for the back room. Sam gave him a worried look before eyeing Dema and the Mouse again.

"So is that how you do it? You shift. I didn't think shifters really existed. And this guy, you're sure he's not a Hi'er. J'rd, I don't know if we should stay. I don't know if I like this."

"Don't be silly," responded J'rd. "We now know more about the Mouse than anyone. If he, sorry, she, wants to hear the story, I say we tell it."

"Fine," replied Sam, obviously displeased, but knowing he would lose this argument.

Dema carefully sipped at the brandy while the other three drank deeply.

"Please J'rd, please Sam, I would really like to hear the rest," the Mouse pleaded.

J'rd obliged. "So, after our not real cousin was killed, we filled out all the paperwork, and set up a small memorial in the workshop. It took a month, but it worked! The Hi'ers are now giving us suits that fit! Turns out, they always had Urdian suits, they just never bothered to have them brought out of storage. They're even letting us train is someone as a replacement, so we'll have more hands to share the work. Sadly, someone had to die. Now only us here know that no one actually died, of course. One thing we didn't think of was insurance. Turns out, when we die at work, our family get a nice big payout, and that's what we're drinking now!"

"That's wonderful!" exclaimed the Mouse. "Oh, don't worry," she consoled when she saw Dema's shocked expression. "No one actually died."

She took another large drink. "Listen, I might need some help from linesmen in the near future, and I think you two are just the ones I need." She lifted the hem of her skirt, fished two cards from a garter on her calf. With another long swallow, she put her beer on the counter and slid the cards towards the other two. "Use this to get in contact with me, and perhaps we can work something out. The pay would be significant, and I could show you how you can actually spend it yourselves without the Union finding out."

The Mouse and Dema slipped from their barstools, leaving their unfinished drinks on the bar. The Urdians picked up the cards. Walking toward the door, the Mouse paused and looked back to make sure they were each holding a card before tapped one of the gems on her pocket watch. The two men stopped moving and stared forward, unseeing, while a black dot appeared under each of their thumbs.

"Getting their information?" asked Dema. "Will you be reporting them? It seemed like they committed fraud. These were the guys you were looking for, weren't they?"

"They are, and I don't think so," replied the Mouse, opening her watch and scanning the genetic and biographical information being collected by the cards. "They weren't trying to hurt anyone, and the Union really does have a problem with taking care of the labour class. They're just trying to make things a little safer for themselves and others. I won't begrudge them that. Plus, I wasn't lying when I said I might call on them. I have a job coming up that involves spying on a potential terrorist cell and having access to the lines would make it much easier. I might not even have to cover up the job with a theft."

"Now where would be the fun in that? I know you love being a spy, but you do seem to love being a thief more."

"Well, it is much more enjoyable. And how else would we keep you in such fancy clothes."

"Speak for yourself. I know you love Anderian silks," Dema said with an appreciative smile.

The Mouse gave a little turn, the slight fishtail on her dress flaring out. "You know me too well."

The bartender re-emerged and gave the Mouse a subtle salute just as her pocket watch beeped. She shut it with a click and the cards J'rd and Sam were holding changed, the black dot disappearing. Dema and the Mouse turned for the door, and the dust motes once again danced on the sunlight. Walking out, the door closed, letting the shadows take over once again. The two left at the bar slowly came back, as if emerging from a fog. They each looked at the cards in their hands.

"Where did these come from?" J'rd asked the bartender.

"Bar special," he replied.

Sam looked suspicious. "A bar special of three free drinks? That don't seem right."

"I don't set the specials. You don't have to use 'em if you don't want."

"We'll use them, we'll use them," interjected J'rd. "After all, we're celebrating, right."

Steve Power

Power is a writer currently living in St. John's, Newfoundland. His inspirations include the Stephen King, Ridley Scott, William Gibson, and Robert E. Howard. 'For the Crown' is his first published work.

For the Crown

Whelan remembered blue skies. He remembered green fields, and more than anything, he remembered spring air. It seemed a lifetime ago. In the spring of 1865, on Whelan's seventeenth birthday, he had been handed a redcoat and a magnesium musket and stepped into the HMS ALIS AQUILAE. He and hundreds like him had signed on with the First Queen's Royal Fusiliers; they would breathe stale air in a state of ageless half-sleep as the vessel made its twenty-seven-year voyage to the morning star. The steel grey flying mausoleum would carry 217 souls to the second planet from the sun, bound for the heart of the Ishtar Terra colony.

The nausea of the Tempus Serum was washed away as soon as he saw the grey-green Venus sky streaked with yellow cloud. He recalled the first gulp of sulphurous fumes. Breathing was like swallowing a loose-rolled smoke of stale tobacco, and it smelled like a pig farm. Everyone had been issued filter masks that mitigated the harshness you were inhaling, but they smelled of tar, rubbed your throat raw, and made you look like a warthog. The alternative to inhaling tar for half the day was a condition called "bloody lung", which was exactly what it sounded like. At night, everyone slept at the dorm, where the air reminded Whelan of the isolation wards and sanitariums he'd spent his early teens in as his parents slowly succumbed to tuberculosis. Whelan had concluded that he missed fresh spring Dover air more than anything. He would cut a man from chin to shin for the swallow of an Atlantic breeze mixed with fresh damp grass. He'd never take air for granted again.

21,535 days. He was in for twenty-seven years out, five years on the ground, and twenty-seven years back. When he'd signed, he was an orphaned sixteen-year-old barely man with a chin of brown fuzz and a thick blanket under a bridge, lots of book knowledge but no street smarts. Thanks to the Tempus Serum, he would return a twenty-two-year-old knight of the British Empire, with a fortune in his hands and no further commitments to King, country, or anyone else. He just had to last. The long ride home was waiting on the other side of 527 more days.

He absently pulled the magazine from his rifle, checked the primer, gave it a rattle. It was the routine; a misaligned shell could detonate in the magazine, the magnesium would catch, and the rifle would erupt in a cloud of white-hot flame. A horrible way to go. Whalen peered down the line of the trench where over a hundred men nervously fumbled with sabres, rifles, and masks. They adjusted their caps, fiddled with their armor, tightened buckles. The once vibrant redcoats were streaked with blood, mud, and dust, and the cobalt grey plates they wore made them look more like a Roman Legion than a modern fighting force. Everyone was anxious; it had been a long and bloody campaign, and somewhere out there, barely half a mile from the line, the last remnants of the 13th Prussian Hussars, the "Death Knights" lay in wait. His Royal Highness wanted Venus; he'd already lost

Mars, and he would not be content until the Union Jack was planted knee-deep from Mercury to Pluto. The end was nigh. Orders were to fight to a man; they die or we die. This was to be the final charge.

A whistle blew from somewhere, and men began to form up in ranks; seventy-five in the front, seventy-five in the rear, a piper, a drummer, and a flag bearer at either end. Somewhere behind them were the officers, though the captain was front and center. Whelan often laughed at what he deemed to be an impractical wall of flesh.

The front line propped themselves on the low ridge, and Whelan peered off into the yellow haze; the vicious steel points of the Prussian helmets stood like a valley of spears. Beyond that was the murky wall of green and yellow foliage that was the impenetrable Ishtarian jungle. Regiment had no idea how many of the Prussians were left; they'd estimated less than fifty men. Fifty hardened veterans of the Mars campaign. Without their gear, they were killers; with their full plate armor, "Zweihander" swords as tall as a man, and fearsome bolt throwers that fired five-inch hunks of iron death, they were nightmares.

The captain spoke loudly to the men. "Twenty strides, men!" he reminded them. "Twenty strides, then fire! Ten more! Fire again!"

Somewhere a whistle blew; once, twice, three times. Drums began to pound, and the pipes cried. Over the top. Whelan's feet sank in the shallow dried mustard dirt as he hurled himself out of the trench. The pace was fast, this was no orderly march -- the first line charged. Somewhere behind, the second line made a more measured pace. The shouts of men drowned out the din of drum and fife.

Hussars responded in kind; they stormed forward,

some carrying nothing but their swords while the rest shouldered their fearsome rifles. The clattering of their black plate mail was audible across the field, and their faces were covered by the skull shaped death shroud, a symbol of Prussia's elite. These were soldiers who feared not death. One man carried the "black eagle" banner while the rest wore one as a sash at their waist.

Whelan almost lost count of his strides. Ten... Eleven... He knew their magnesium bullets would have greater range than the giant hunks of metal hurled from the Prussian guns, and the magnesium would burn through their steel plate.

Twelve... Thirteen... He could see them clearly now, like a moving wall of burned black spikes, polished and glinting in the hazy midday sun.

Fourteen... Fifteen... He cocked the hammer back on his rifle; he could see the miniature blue flame of the priming hammer. He hoped all this running hadn't knocked his cartridges out of alignment.

Sixteen... Seventeen... Eighteen... men began to slow around him. Winstead,

heavier set and in his late twenties, was coughing, his warthog mask dangling loose. Woolridge, another fellow marching beside him, lost his footing, but quickly bounded back. He was halting early and taking aim. The captain was just ahead, his cap had flown off somewhere during the first charge.

Nineteen... Whelan brought up, dropped to a knee, and shouldered his rifle. The hammer fell, somewhere in the cast iron frame, the primer flame hit wax coated paper, powder exploded, magnesium bullets sparked to life, and expanding gasses propelled balls of white-hot fire across the open space. Death Knights fell, smoke hissing from glowing red-rimmed holes in obsidian steel. Whelan pulled the bolt back, spewing smoke and ash from the rifle's breech; then the charge resumed.

Ten more strides, then fire again!

Five strides less and they would be in range of the Prussian guns. Five strides and all hell broke loose.

The Hussar response was loud, savage, and angry. The Prussian guns roared, spewing death with each trigger pull. Hunks of black iron skimmed across the turf like stones skipping on a pond, spinning end over end. An errant bolt bounced, struck Winstead near the shoulder, a fist sized pound of flesh torn from his body as he crumpled to the dirt. The Hussar Death Knights roared as they charged, their shoulders low. Whelan heard another sickening thunk. A rifleman spun, eyes wide, viscera dangling through the hole in his abdomen. Whelan halted and dropped to his chest, firing. Woolridge howled nearby as white-hot flame engulfed his arms, his torso, his face. In seconds he was a smear of ash and charred meat. Misfire.

Both lines fired again. A swarm of white-hot death struck the nightmarish dark horde. Their advance slowed. Whelan fired again; several others had similar ideas. Shots were no longer organized waves, but a steady stream now; wild, inaccurate, but effective. He rose to his feet, and another volley flew over his head. He could hear the fife and drums closing behind now. Men began to run past him, howling. He let out a roar of his own, and his legs started pumping. The Prussians were close enough now that he could see their eyes, cold and soulless. As they closed ranks, a cry echoed across the field:

"FOR THE CROWN!"

Chaos followed. Bodies slammed together, men fell, crimson clouds of blood, flesh, and bone mixed with the yellow haze. Whelan's bayonet lunged into the abdomen of a charging attacker who swung wildly. Whelan could see thick liquid pouring from the wound, spilling to the ground. The Prussian's desperate swipes were getting closer, showing no sign of weakening. Whelan fired. Smoke and fire belched forth from somewhere in the Prussian's lower back; he toppled, and Whelan refused to let go his empty rifle, stumble-falling to the blood-soaked ground. He planted a foot on the dead Prussian and tugged the rifle loose.

Men were everywhere now, a tangled mass of clashing steel. The once dry, yellow soil was now a blood-saturated mud, and traction was difficult. No fife flitted over the wind, there were just blades on flesh, and howling. The ferocious Prussians were thinning in number, and yet for every one of them that fell, two Fusiliers paid the cost. Whelan watched as the captain shouldered his rifle and fired his last round. He watched its slow arc through the

air. As it landed, it left a red-hot smouldering hole in the back of a Prussian's helmet, face and skull bursting out through his mask.

Whelan pulled his cutlass. The closest Prussian took notice. He leapt forward, his sword held at the waist. Whelan arced his cutlass upwards and his body shuddered as blades met.

A second swing, everything he had, turned the giant blade aside a second time. A sweeping armored boot pushed Whelan's legs out from under him. He toppled into the mud. He rolled to his back, narrowly dodging the Prussian's thrust. He lashed out with a foot, kicking the giant sword from its owner's grasp.

In response, the Prussian stomped into Whelan's chest.

All wind escaped him, something wet spurting from his mouth.

The Prussian stomped again and again. Whelan could feel himself sinking into the wet soil, his eyes were watering, and his breath was in shallow gasps.

The dark clad enemy raised his leg again, and Whelan lashed out with his cutlass. The point buried itself in the soft flesh of the Prussian's inner thigh, and blood erupted, spewing like a fountain. Whelan rolled, gasping, tearing at his mask, as the Prussian fell backward, blood still spurting from between his legs.

The sounds were but a din now, the rushing blood in Whelan's ears made everything sound as though he were submerged. He coughed a red spray; his chest was on fire. He could hear a mournful sound in the distance: a horn. The Prussians were running. He could see less than ten of them making for the edge of the jungle treeline. One of the enemy stood at the edge of the trees, firing his bolt thrower one-handed while the other arm waved the black eagle, the Prussian flag. His mask had been shattered and blood ran through the cracks in his aged face; his mouth was wide open, his howling war cry echoing above the booming rifle.

From somewhere behind him, Whelan heard the captain: "COME ON MEN! WE END THIS NOW! FOR THE CROWN!"

Whelan flinched at the response; it was louder than he had anticipated: "FOR THE CROWN!"

There were more comrades left than he'd thought. Between forty and fifty souls now rushed for the treeline. A single errant magnesium bolt struck the Prussian flag-waver and he toppled backward into the brush.

Whelan was still dazed; he rose slowly to wobbling

legs. A flag bearer rolled past in full charge, nearly knocking him down again. He rocked on his heels; his breathing heavy. Soon time began to flow again, the sound of rushing water that filled his ears subsided, and all that remained was a throbbing pain at his temples. Someone stood next to him, their arm outstretched, and they called to him. The third time they tried, he heard a voice, blinked, and grabbed for the outstretched rifle.

Whelan pulled the magazine and gave it a shake. Its owner hadn't lasted long enough to fire it. He spat a gob of saliva mixed with blood and muttered to himself as he started to trot, "For the crown..."

The jungle lay ahead; it was ancient, wet, and hot. They couldn't have gone too far; the jungle had a reputation. The Fusiliers had sent a score of veterans into the jungle over the years since they'd occupied the Ishtar Terra. None returned. They gave up.

They'd heard similar stories from the Prussians; no one came out of the jungle. A few years back, Whelan had heard a story about a Prussian survivor who'd strolled into the British camp changed, horrified and babbling.

But it was only a story. None had witnessed it, but everyone knew someone who did. On paper, they'd called it 'Saltu de Silens' but one colonial captain had coined another name that stuck; they called the jungle the "Never-Come-Back".

Whelan had 527 days. He wanted to go back.

Whelan held his breath as they entered the wall of green. The canopy of trees high above

swayed lightly as shafts of sunlight drew lines in the dust. The air was thick, hard to breathe in, like standing in a chimney. It was silent, not a living thing to be heard, save for the barely present wind fingering its way through the canopy. Men glanced over shoulders at one another as they moved further inward. They couldn't have gone too far.

A man burst through the brush ahead, stumbling over himself. He ran toward the Fusiliers. He was looking over his shoulder, his helmet gone, his blonde hair streaked red, half of his armor torn from his torso, and the Prussian flag tangled about his legs. Both hands were outstretched; several men raised rifles at the sudden burst of activity.

The captain was quick to order the hold. He ran forward to meet the errant knight.

Whelan joined him; both arrived at the man as he toppled forward. Whelan flipped him over, and the captain's arms caught him. The man stared upward into their eyes, his face curled in terror.

He began to stammer in their guttural warble, "Sie sind... Sie sind... Dämonen!" His breathing was shallow, his whimper became a whisper. "Sie sind das Verhängnis von uns allen..."

He expired then, his head falling limp, blood still pumping from a large gash the length of his torso. Whelan and the captain exchanged a glance and rose to their feet. The captain waved everyone else forward. No one made a sound.

Beyond the brush, the Fusiliers entered a small clearing in the overgrowth. Whelan's jaw hung limp.

There was gore everywhere: innards, limbs, and bones protruding from the earth. The Prussians were dead, taken apart, and barely recognizable. It had happened quietly, no screams, no gunfire. A Zwiehander was protruding from a small mound at the center of the clearing.

A figure emerged from the trees, grotesque, misshapen. Several more shapes flanked it in the misty gloom. The

Fusiliers were dumbstruck. Men fumbled with rifles; the captain raised a hand, and the creatures walked forward.

They looked like giant gorillas: short legs, long arms, broad shoulders, but covered in reptilian scales. They glistened with moisture and their heads were that of giant lizards.

Their giant clawed hands were stained with blood, and a sliver of flayed human flesh hung from an Ape-Lizard's maw.

One of the mouths snapped, a tongue shot out from between jagged teeth, and the creature sniffed at the air. The Fusiliers looked on in horror: these bizarre forms, these reptilian lizard-apes were holding Prussia weaponry. One wielded a bolt-thrower like a primate would hold a club, another one of the gargantuan Prussian great-swords. The one on the end, however, was waving a gnarled branch; tied to it was a Prussia banner. The Prussian sigil was shredded, and in its place, primitive symbols and unrecognizable characters inked in deep red.

He waved his flag with purpose. He pointed it toward the shuddering men of the First Queen's Royal Fusiliers.

Whelan raised his rifle, gritted his teeth. He uttered to himself, "527 days."

The captain drew his sabre, licked at his upper lip beneath his mask.

As the men silently began to step backward, the five Lizard-Apes looked to each other. One of them opened his mouth, his jaws moved, and he hissed through clenched teeth, words snarled and grotesque, "FoR ThE CrOwN..."

Jennifer Shelby

Jennifer Shelby was born in Halifax, Nova Scotia and currently resides in Hopewell Hill, New Brunswick. She is the author of many works of short fiction, including 'Mrs. Coleman's Backyard Refugee Camp' for *Andromeda Spaceways*, and 'Toby's Alicorn Adventure' for *Cricket*.

Parachutes and Grappling Hooks

The welding arc crackled and spattered as Great-Granny Stella ran a bead of molten steel along the robot pterodactyl's sharp beak. Her phone jangled for her attention, but she set aside her welding torch, licked her thumb, and reached up to rub away a smudge on the beast's glass eye before answering it.

"Stella? Moncton RCMP again. Do you know anything about this dinosaur terrorizing the downtown?"

"I'll get back to you." A quick search on her phone showed local news sites a-twitter with reports of a T. rex making its way through the city. Stella gritted her teeth. "Hester."

Stella and Hester's rivalry began when they tied for first place in their seventh-grade science fair. Over the past seventy years, they'd both been arrested, pardoned, charged, held liable for damages, named an enemy of the Crown, exonerated, and accused of colluding with space aliens. Things were just getting exciting when Stella's beloved granddaughter up and married Hester the Horrible's grandson. Stella and Hester called a truce for the wedding, but when the union produced little Connor, the old conflict returned as they vied for his affection.

Connor turned seven tomorrow. He requested a robot dinosaur for his birthday. His two favorite dinosaurs were the pterodactyl and the Tyrannosaurus rex.

Stella hoped to give her pterodactyl a coat of copper paint to conceal its mismatched metal hide, but she'd run out of time. Tucking a grappling hook and rope into a compartment by the robot's saddle, she climbed onto the back of the beast.

"PteroConnor7.0, prepare for takeoff."

The robot stomped out of the barn. Stella hesitated; she hadn't taken a test flight. Oh well. She tugged her goggles into place and fastened her helmet. Faint hearts never won fair Connors, after all.

A quick flap of the pterodactyl's wings and they were airborne. Doomed bugs smacked into Stella's skin and smeared across her goggles.

The green countryside soon gave way to city concrete. Stella altered their course to follow a swath of destruction. They flew past crushed cars, gushing fire hydrants, glass and steel buildings with jagged bites taken from their corners. A three-story T. rex stood at the apex of destruction.

Stella rolled her eyes. Everyone knew Connor loved the Godzilla movies. Only Hester would be horrible enough to put on a live version.

"PteroConnor7.0, ready lasers." The laser mechanism shifted place. "Target robot T. rex. Fire when ready."

Stella flicked her flight goggles to shield mode as lasers shot from the pterodactyl's eyes. The tyrannosaurus' metal chest melted in the laser's beam, revealing a protected pod. Hester shook her cane at Stella from inside.

"PteroConnor7.0, fire lasers again."

The mechanism whirred, hiccupped, and failed to fire.

"Uh oh."

The T. rex opened its mouth. A cloud of flying insects

emerged and swarmed the pterodactyl. Stella plucked one from the air and realized, too late, the insects were robotic locusts. Hester must have working on them for months. The tiny machines ate away at the pterodactyl. "This is Connor's birthday present, you horrible old woman!" shouted Stella.

Hester blew her a kiss from T-rex.

Stella pulled the grappling hook and rope from their compartment. "PteroConnor7.0, circle back and come in full throttle." She tossed the grappling hook to an oncoming streetlight. The hook caught and twisted around the metal pole. "Collision course. Take out the T. rex." Stella leapt from the dinosaur, clutching the rope and swinging to the sidewalk.

She peered around to make sure no one had seen her, but everyone was watching Hester's horrible T-Rex, including Connor. Stella called to him and he came over, grinning with delight, his parents in tow. "Granny Stella, did you see the dinosaurs?"

They turned to watch PteroConnor7.0 collide with the Tyrannosaurus rex. The dinosaurs exploded into a column of flames shooting far above the city skyline.

Stella's palms grew sweaty. Hester wasn't still in there, was she? Why hadn't she installed an automatic ejector seat? Oh, that horrible Hester, how dare she get old. Her reflexes weren't as good as they used to be. Didn't she know to compensate?

"Look!" Connor pointed to a purple parachute drifting down to the street.

Stella pursed her lips.

Hester, a smug expression on her face, landed before them.

Connor ran to her. "Granny Hester, I didn't know you

could sky dive!"

Hester winked at Stella past Connor's embrace. Stella narrowed her eyes. Hester may have won this time, but Connor would have other birthdays.

Sherry D. Ramsey

Sherry D. Ramsey writes speculative fiction for both adults and young adults, and is one of the founding editors of Third Person Press. She has published over thirty short stories nationally and internationally, and her award-winning debut novel, *One's Aspect to the Sun*, launched in 2013. It was followed by two sequels, *Dark Beneath the Moon* (2015) *Beyond the Sentinel Stars* (2017).

Some of her short stories are collected in *To Unimagined Shores* (2011) and *The Cache and Other Stories* (2017).

Ramsey has co-edited six anthologies of regional short fiction with Third Person Press. A member of the Writer's Federation of Nova Scotia Writer's Council, Sherry is also a past Vice-President and Secretary-Treasurer of SF Canada and is currently SFC's website administrator.

The Swamp Cat and the Reckless Scout

Captain Stel Aurora had her magbooted feet up on the cockpit's console again, and she felt someone's disapproving glare on the back of her head. One corner of her mouth crept up in a half smile only she could see, reflected in the dark hologlass of the navigation screen. Rolling her skimchair a few centimetres to starboard, she caught Ensign Hardyp's unguarded reflection as he stood behind her.

"Ensign!" she said, not bothering to turn around. "Be a dear and fetch me a hot caffeo, would you? We'll be at the Sea Star Nebula any minute, and I don't want to miss it."

The pause before his answer was just long enough for Captain Aurora to be sure the ensign had choked back an unwise retort. "Of course, Captain," he managed, and his heavy tread retreated from the bridge.

A voice laced with amusement *tsk-tsked* from the console to her left. "Captain, you'll drive him out of the Scout-Guard altogether if you don't ease up a little."

Captain Aurora turned to grin at her second. "Why, Commander Dayne, do you have a soft spot for the new ensign? He's good-looking enough, I'll grant you, but perhaps a little young for you?"

Elise Dayne ran a hand over snow-white hair. "If I'm

going to have a May-December romance, I'll be May, thank you very much," she retorted. "I just think the boy should be encouraged a little. After all, he did manage to make it this far in the Guard, which means he has some merit. A posting to the *Reckless Scout* is no small feat, especially for a young man."

Captain Aurora flashed the older woman an affectionate smile. "He does have merit, which is partly why I test him. He thinks I'm a bad captain who doesn't have enough respect for the rules, though, which is the other reason I come down hard on him. He won't get far in the Guard if he can't take orders from a woman *or* if he doesn't know rules are—" she wiggled her fingers in the air "—bendy, out here. It's for his own good."

Before Dayne could answer, red and yellow lights flashed on the consoles in front of the two officers, and a calm, computerized voice intoned, "Captain, incoming distress call from Inderani B. The research outpost there."

Captain Aurora's casual demeanour disappeared as her boots hit the floor and she straightened in her chair. Fingers flew across the console, retrieving the data for the remote Coalition station. "Put it through, Smartz," she ordered the artificial intelligence that, if the truth were told, could probably run the ship all by itself. Fortunately, Smartz appeared to have no mutinous ambitions.

"Aye, Captain." The communications screen lit with the indistinct face of the caller. The image stuttered and shivered, a wavering mess of colour and blocky shapes. Inderani B was many light years away, and the aethercom was a relatively new technology. It wasn't perfect but utilizing threads of dark matter to piggyback comm signals was nothing to sneeze at as Coalition Space expanded.

"This is Captain Stella Aurora of the ScoutGuard ship *Reckless Scout*," Aurora said in a voice suddenly all business. "What is the nature of your emergency?"

For a moment the face on the screen resolved into that of a careworn woman, dark hair pulled back from a furrowed brow. Her eyes locked onto the transmitter as if she could clarify the connection through sheer force of will. "Captain, I'm glad to hear your voice. This is Dr. Parnika Chabra, Head of Research at Inderani Station. We're in trouble here, and I need you to come as quickly as you can."

Aurora's eyebrows rose. They could get there quickly—the spacefold drive could certainly handle it. But a diversion to Inderani would take the *Reckless Scout* considerably outside her projected mission parameters. "Dr. Chabra, what's happening? What kind of trouble are you in?" she asked again.

Dr. Chandra clamped her lips together for a moment, as if loath to explain. "It's the men," she said suddenly. "The men of the station. They're disappearing, and I have reason to believe they're being kidnapped."

"Kidnapped? From a remote science station on an uninhabited world?" Elise Dayne's voice sounded incredulous beside her.

Although Aurora was thinking the same thing, she schooled her expression as she answered this strange declaration. "I thought you were alone there. Who could be kidnapping them?"

Dr. Chandra's image wavered on the screen, breaking up like a temporarily shattered mirror before stabilizing again. "That, Captain Aurora, is precisely what I need you to figure out."

The unschooled might think of Inderani B as a 'swamp planet,' but of course there were few habitable planets in the Coalition with a single consistent ecology. One might be excused for thinking this way, though, if they knew anything about the single known habitation on Inderani B -- the Carson Research Station. It sat smack-dab in the center of a hectares-wide wetland straight out Earth's Jurassic Period—minus the dinosaurs, of course. What it lacked in prehistoric reptiles, it made up for in other exotic creatures, but all the advance probes had shown Inderani B to be devoid of what humans liked to call "intelligent life."

The probe samples, however, showed a plethora of plant life teeming with compounds, proteins, and other active ingredients that scientists couldn't wait to study more closely. And so, the Carson Research Station was born.

Now, apparently, Stel Aurora had to save it.

She brought the *Reckless Scout* in low over the western side of the swamp, entranced by the expanse of trackless, lush greenery unrolling beneath the ship's belly. Some areas of the swamp boasted thick, ropy trees whose dense mats of foliage created a rainforest-like canopy. Sunlight slanted through gaps in the upper layer of leaves to disappear into shadowy green grottos beneath. From this vantage, the habitual trails of large animals crisscrossed the soggy ground. The *Scout's* passage startled a flock of shaggy-feathered bird analogues from a blue-green pond, and once or twice the tall water grasses rippled as some large creature slunk below the level of their frondlike tips. Aurora consulted the research station's database for guesses about what it might be, but Smartz chimed in as soon as it saw what Aurora was looking up.

"The colloquially-named *swamp cat* is the largest mammal analogue so far discovered on Inderani B. These omnivorous creatures carve distinct lines of passage through the—"

"Thank you, Smartz," Aurora interrupted. "You can tell us all about it later." The AI was a fount of knowledge, but somewhat too eager to share that knowledge at length, often at inopportune times. Sometimes Aurora enjoyed the simple pleasure of looking something up on her own.

The *Reckless Scout* was fully capable of a planetside landing, but Captain Aurora noted on their first pass over the station's landing area that it could not accommodate the large ship. The station's supplies had been ferried down in runabouts from the orbital transport vessel, but Aurora was hesitant to leave her ship in orbit and come down with only a landing party. The information on what they might be dealing with here was still too sparse. She asked Elise Dayne to bring them around in an arc, find an area of the swamp with some solid footing a little distance from the station, and set them down on it.

"Some of us will hike to the station and find out what's going on," Aurora said, watching the readouts on the screen as Dayne searched for a stable landing site. "The rest can secure the ship and begin taking our own readings of the surrounding area without disturbing the scientists."

"Here we go," Elise Dayne said, and expertly settled the *Scout* into a dense patch of swamp. Although their landing made no sound they could hear through the hull, Aurora knew they'd crushed a substantial patch of greenery under the weight of the ship. She could only hope no creatures had been too slow to get out of the way.

"All right. Commander Dayne, you have the bridge. Chief Varston, Ensign Hardyp, you're with me. Get some waterproof gear and meet me at the rear airlock in ten minutes. We might have a wet slog ahead of us."

Ru Varston, Chief of Security on the *Scout*, shot Aurora a surprised glance but stifled it and turned on her heel to follow the Captain's order. Ensign Hardyp, also caught off guard, hesitated a few beats longer and then hurried after the chief.

Elise Dayne turned to look at the captain, one eyebrow cocked quizzically. "Of course you'd take Ru," she said, "but why Hardyp? One minute you're sending him for caffeo, the next you're handing him a plum off-ship assignment."

Captain Aurora winked at her commander. "Nothing like a little field test to take his measure," she said. "And I like to keep him guessing. Not much is likely to happen on this first recon, but we'll see how he handles himself."

Elise shook her head. "I can't keep up with your games, Stel."

Stel Aurora held out her hands in an innocent gesture. "No games, Elise. Just keeping my crew on its toes."

"Well, while you're doing it, make sure everyone's armed and alert," her second-in-command said. "Smartz says these swamps could be crawling with things that might like a taste of human when they can get it."

Aurora sobered. "And we have humans disappearing," she said. "I haven't forgotten that. We'll be careful. And I'll pick up FG pistols for all of us from the weapons locker."

"See that you do," Elise retorted. "I don't want to have to come looking for you. This humidity will play havoc with my hair."

"Aye, aye," Stel Aurora said, and she was still smiling when she met her two crewmates at the airlock.

Inderani B, Smartz had insisted on explaining to them as they donned their waterproof excursion suits, had a breathable atmosphere slightly richer in oxygen than Earth, with no known harmful gases or particulates. Aurora had no qualms about taking her crew members out into the swamp without helmets, but she realized the folly of that decision after five minutes of trudging through the muddy terrain. The air held one thing Smartz had neglected to mention: biting insects that demonstrated no qualms about snacking on alien flesh. Aurora, Varston, and Hardyp said little beyond "watch these vines" and "deep puddle here" and the like, but all their words were punctuated by the sound of slaps and swipes as they fought off the attacking hordes.

"Sorry," Captain Aurora said after another five minutes. "I didn't realize precisely what type of predators we should be arming ourselves against." She itched—literally—to pull out her Field Generating pistol, flip it to the heat setting and begin wildly scorching the swarms of flying creatures out of the air, but she suspected that might be an overreaction and leave her looking rather foolish. She might not mind so much in front of Ru Varston—she and the chief had been in situations both fraught and ridiculous before this—but she wouldn't let the ensign see her flinch.

The security chief and the ensign made deprecating noises as if the insects were of no consequence, but Aurora herself could feel multiple welts rising on her skin and knew the others must be suffering the same. Despite the slippery footing and clutching vegetation, some of which stretched high over their heads, she stepped up the pace, and another five minutes brought them within sight of the research station.

The cluster of buildings clung to a patch of higher, drier ground amid the expanse of squelchy wetland. They looked fragile and out-of-place in the aggressively verdant growth. Aurora knew they were fashioned from a lightweight but sturdy polymer nanofoam that "grew" into whatever configuration the researchers programmed into it, but she was glad she didn't have to sleep in one. Some sections of makeshift fencing had been cobbled together and placed around the buildings, but it was obviously an unplanned measure. The researchers had made use of whatever they had to hand. Aurora wondered if it had been in response to the disappearances. She was hesitant to call them "kidnappings" without more information.

"Let's approach carefully," she said to Varston and Hardyp. "These folks appear to be on edge, and we don't want to spook them."

"Can't you signal to them that we're here?" Ensign Hardyp asked.

Aurora resisted the urge to shoot him a repressive look. "I did contact Dr. Chabra before we left the *Scout*," she said mildly. "But I don't want to take the chance that someone didn't get the message."

Varston gave Hardyp the look Aurora had stifled. The ensign looked annoyed but said nothing more.

They needn't have worried. Dr. Chabra herself appeared at a gap in the haphazard fence and waved them in. "Captain Aurora, I'm so relieved to see you," she said.

In person, the worry lines on her face seemed more deeply engraved, and the grey streaks in her dark hair more prominent. She noticed the insect bites and welts on their faces and hands and said, "I should have warned you about the bugs. Sorry about that."

Captain Aurora waved off the apology. "We're fine. It's more important we learn more about the disappearances."

"I'll get you some special repellent we've developed," Dr. Chabra offered as she turned and led them to the smallest of the buildings. Up close, the interlocking striations of the foam lent the surface a rough texture. It had the unfortunate consequence that bits of dirt, grasses, particulates and even insects caught and stuck to the rough material. As they walked through the door Dr. Chabra held open for them, however, the cloud of insects buzzing around their heads dropped silently out of the air, peppering the doorstep with their corpses.

"Focused decontamination field," the doctor said, which was enough of an explanation for Aurora to be happy about its existence without necessarily needing to know more.

The small building's single room housed the administration of the station: three desks, only one of which was currently occupied; a scattering of screens showing various areas of the station; and a communications console. Crates, bags, boxes, and bits of equipment that apparently had no other home occupied the rest of the space.

The other occupant of the room was a man of about thirty, with sandy-blond hair and an impatient expression. He looked up when the group entered the building but said nothing, instead busying himself with the computer on his desk.

"This is Harvey Sulls," Dr. Chabra said. "He keeps us humming along here."

It was a vague job description, and Sulls didn't appear to appreciate it. He merely nodded and said, "I hope you can get to the bottom of what's happening. People are scared to go outside, and we can't function that way."

He seemed more annoyed than worried about the people who'd already gone missing, but Aurora thought that could be simply worry manifesting as anger.

"How many of your people have gone missing?" she asked Dr. Chabra. "And under what circumstances?"

"Four, now," the doctor said, her brow furrowing. "Why don't we sit and I'll explain?"

There was an awkward moment while they realized that there weren't actually enough seats to accommodate everyone. There was one at what was presumably Dr. Chabra's desk, one at the third desk, and one spare pushed up against the wall near the door.

Harvey Sulls let a pause hang too long in the air and then said in a petulant voice, "Take mine. I have to go and check on something anyway." He made a show of rising, pushing his chair out from behind the desk, and gathering up some papers from his desk before leaving the room.

Dr. Chabra gave a wan smile and a shrug while they pushed the four chairs into a crude circle. Aurora was pleased to note Ensign Hardyp take out a recording device.

"The first was one of our researchers, Barton Way," the doctor began. "We weren't worried about leaving the camp individually if we weren't going far; in the time we've been here, we haven't found any predators in the area willing to bother us. The swamp cats are the largest, but they seem to prefer smaller prey. So, I suppose we got... complacent.

"Barton went out to collect samples early one morning a week ago. He hadn't returned by evening, and by then we were worried. We'd already searched the immediate area in case he'd injured himself and couldn't reach anyone on his comm. If he'd planned to go far afield, he would have taken one of rovers, and we travel in pairs when we go that far."

She paused for a moment and took a deep breath. "We didn't find anything other than some broken vegetation that might have indicated what direction he took."

She fell silent and Varston prompted gently, "What happened after that?"

Dr. Chabra shook herself. "The next morning, I sent a rover to look further out. Fahrad Singh and Bill Tolstead went out with instructions to call in every half hour to report. We heard from them three times and they'd found nothing... and then they stopped reporting in.

"By that time, we were quite spooked," she said. "We kept the comm channel open and sent messages continuously for twenty-four hours; we were too afraid to send anyone else out looking. There are only thirty of us here to start with, so that was ten percent of our population gone missing. We sent out a survey drone to search for the rover, but weirdly, that seems to have disappeared, too. We were discussing what to do next when Mariella Stein ran into the admin building to say her husband Warren had been out in their backyard garden and vanished. That's when we sent the general distress message, and, well—you answered."

Captain Aurora asked, "The fence is new?"

Dr. Chabra nodded. "It's not much, but after Warren, some thought it would make us feel better. Captain, what do you think has happened to our people?"

Aurora shook her head slowly. "I have no idea at this point. Individually, any of the disappearances might be easily explained; an injury in the field, a rover accident that put it in water and it sank from view, an animal attack... but put them together—"

"—and they seem more deliberate," Hardyp interjected when Aurora paused.

The captain nodded. "Precisely."

"We haven't come across any predators," Dr. Chabra reiterated. "The swamp cats look intimidating, but the biggest animal we've seen them eat is about the size of a rabbit."

"I think we'll start with a flyover of the region, in one of our runabouts," Captain Aurora said, tapping one finger against her lips. "I want to get familiar with the terrain. Tell me about these swamp cats, and any other creatures you've encountered. Then I'll know if we see something out of the ordinary."

Dr. Chabra gave a slight chuckle. "We call them 'cats,' although they're really not feline," she said. "I'm not sure where the name came from, but it stuck. They're about the size of a hippopotamus—"

"A hippopotamus?" Ensign Hardyp exclaimed.

Captain Aurora forgave him the interruption, because she was taken aback as well.

Dr. Chabra continued. "Yes, and they have thick hide similar to a hippo's. But their heads and faces are very feline, and they have a striped colouration much like a tiger—if tigers were shades of green," she added with a smile. "They're omnivores who eat mainly vegetation, supplemented by small animals and bird analogues. But they don't bother us."

"Sounds like Carson Station is an interesting spot," Captain Aurora said.

"And one we thought was reasonably safe, until now," Dr. Chabra said ruefully. She stood. "Shall I show you around the rest of the station? I'll get Harvey to send you the list of fauna we've encountered or seen. Oh, and let's fetch some of that insect repellent."

"Yes, please," Aurora said. "Ensign Hardyp, would you comm the ship and ask them to get a runabout ready for us? We'll have a quick look around the station and then get into the air."

Ensign Hardyp nodded and pulled out his communicator as they followed the doctor out into the humid air and voracious insect swarms of Inderani B.

The structures comprising Carson Station hadn't been laid out with any particular design or planning Captain Aurora could discern. Living quarters, labs, and utility buildings huddled together like randomly scattered dice, now mostly penned in by the makeshift fence. Aurora met some of the other inhabitants and gave the layout of a station a quick look, but she was most anxious to get the runabout into the air and survey the scene from above. She could stand being planetside when she had to, but Stel Aurora was the first to admit that she was always most comfortable aboard a ship—any ship.

After their brief tour, the trio made their way back to the Reckless Scout, this time well-slathered with Dr. Chabra's insect repellent. It worked, although it carried a smell that was part spent fuel crystal, part citrus, and part ammonia. Aurora blinked watering eyes and wondered seriously if the insect bites weren't marginally preferable. When they arrived back at the ship, she dismissed Varston and told Hardyp he had fifteen minutes to get a quick shower before meeting her at the runabout in the docking bay. She availed herself of the same ablutions but made sure she was already seated at the runabout's pilot console before the ensign hurried in, damp dark hair beginning to curl over his forehead.

"Plot a grid around the station; let's make it four kilometres wide to start," she instructed the ensign as he clambered into the runabout beside her. "Better set the sensors to a high sensitivity for life forms and we'll see how much interference the local critters create. And set them to ping in the presence of refined metal, too, to catch the rover. We're not going to get eyes on a lot of areas because the canopy is so thick."

"Would it be better to take rovers ourselves, then?" the ensign asked. He was already programming the grid as he spoke, however.

"I'm not too keen on that idea until we have more information," Aurora said. "Not with one already vanished out here. We'll make the best job we can of this and see where it gets us."

Hardyp nodded and didn't press further, so Aurora mentally gave him some extra points.

They spent the next few hours carefully covering each section of the grid Hardyp had laid out, gradually adjusting the sensors so they weren't picking up everything from small vole-like creatures to thousand-kilogram swamp cats. Once they had them tuned to tag only bodies in the human-sized range, their search speeded up. As they flew low over the second-to-last square of their imaginary grid, however, Aurora couldn't ignore a pang of discouragement.

"I thought we'd have found them by now," she muttered.

"Me, too," Ensign Hardyp agreed. "How could they get this far from the station?"

Captain Aurora shook her head, frustrated. "We should have seen something by now. Four men and a rover can't simply disappear off the face of the planet."

"Hey, that's an idea. Do you think they could have been abducted and taken off Inderani B altogether?"

Captain Aurora frowned. "It doesn't seem likely, and why would they take the rover? But let's check." She opened a comm line to the station. The signal pinged several times before a harried-looking Dr. Chabra answered.

"Have you found something?" she asked without preamble.

Taken aback by the usually polite doctor's abruptness, Aurora said, "No. I'm just wondering if there'd been any indication of other ships orbiting or visiting Inderani B around the time the disappearances started?"

Dr. Chabra looked blank for a moment, then slowly shook her head. "No, certainly not that we noticed. I would have been suspicious immediately if there'd been anything like that. We're off the beaten path here."

"What about anything out of the ordinary—not necessarily a ship. Anything at all?"

Dr. Chabra sighed visibly and closed her eyes. She shook her head, then said. "A meteor shower... we had a meteor shower a few weeks ago. It was quite spectacular and felt very close, but not threatening."

Aurora frowned. "Anything else? Is Mr. Sulls there? Can you ask him?"

Dr. Chabra started, eyes wide. "No... did no-one tell you? No one's seen Harvey since he left the admin building earlier."

They broke the connection and Aurora and Hardyp exchanged glances. "That's five," she said through clenched teeth. "And this one was right under our noses."

She looked so fierce that Ensign Hardyp shrank back a little in his seat. "Do we start the grid again?"

Captain Stel Aurora tapped her fingers on the arm of her chair, staring out the viewscreen at the slowly unrolling tangle of vegetation below them. "No," she said finally. "We start our brains." Taking the controls again, she pushed the runabout from its canopy-skimming height up high enough that the station shrank to the size of a child's toy amidst the verdant green expanse. She set the runabout's autopilot to take them in a lazy circling pattern and switched the viewscreen to show the vista spreading below them.

"What do you see?" she asked Hardyp, peering at the screen herself.

"Er, the swamp? The station? The area we've just finished searching?"

Captain Aurora pursed her lips. "Yes, to all of those. Now let's think about what we know."

"People are disappearing from around the station and the immediate area," Hardyp said, warming to the exercise.

"Yes. And there's no visible evidence of a ship or other activity in the area by entities we don't know about."

"But it doesn't make sense that all these people could disappear on their own."

"And there was an intense meteor shower recently. A ship coming in through the atmosphere *could* have looked like just another shooting star, if anyone happened to notice it at all."

Captain Aurora stared down at the green expanse. The answer must be down there somewhere. Suddenly, not taking her eyes from the viewscreen, she reached over and gripped the ensign's arm. With her other hand, she pointed. "There. Do you see it?"

Ensign Hardyp searched where the captain pointed but saw nothing out of the ordinary. Instead of admitting that to the captain, however, he hedged. "I'm not sure…"

"The trails," Aurora said. "The swamp cat trails. Smartz," she said to the runabout's version of the AI, "what were you going to tell me about the swamp cat trails earlier?"

In a voice that seemed decidedly sulky for an AI, Smartz said, "These omnivorous creatures carve distinct lines of passage through the drier areas of the swamp, and will follow their personally-created paths to the exclusion of all others, unless external forces cause them the abandon a trail or section of trail. They—"

"That's enough," Aurora interrupted. "Invaluable information; thank you, Smartz," she added, not wanting to insult the prickly AI twice in one day. She turned her attention back to Ensign Hardyp. "See there? Some parts of the swamp cat trails are beginning to grow over—they're not being used. But they're still quite distinct, so something must have changed recently to drive them off."

Hardyp squinted at the screen. "But we went over that section earlier with the sensors," he said. "Even if there's something hidden by the canopy, the sensors didn't pick up anything human-sized in that area."

Aurora let go of the young ensign's arm and grinned, disengaging the autopilot and tapping in new commands. "Not in that area, no," she agreed. "But what about…*under* it?"

Half an hour later, Captain Aurora, Ensign Hardyp, Security Chief Varston, and Commander Dayne were in the swamp. Now liberally smeared with Dr. Chabra's high-powered insect repellent, they went unmolested by the swamp's smallest inhabitants and could concentrate on searching out some of its larger ones.

Despite their earlier flyovers, Aurora had decided that they had not necessarily lost the element of surprise. "If we approach that area on foot, with a small contingent, we might have better luck than with an all-out assault. Especially since we're still not one hundred percent certain what we're looking for." Commander Dayne had protested the plan briefly but dropped her objections when the captain invited her to be part of the ground team. Aurora knew her second-in-command well enough to be certain this was what Dayne wanted all along, despite her earlier comment about the humid air. Dayne preferred being part of the action to babysitting the *Reckless Scout*.

So they went protected from the bugs, but not the heat, the humidity, the cloying scent of decaying plant matter, or the risk of encountering some heretofore unknown unfriendly denizen of the swamp. All four carried their standard issue ScoutGuard Field Generator pistols, currently set to produce stasis fields only. If they could retrieve the missing researchers without inflicting lasting harm on the supposed kidnappers, they would; and if they were met with strong resistance, a flip of the toggle could select other, more lethal types of fields. Captain Aurora thought she detected a slight tremor in Ensign Hardyp's hand as he carefully checked the setting on his FG, but she kindly refrained from comment. Every new Scout went on their first truly dangerous mission sometime.

Stepping carefully around a particularly soggy patch of ground that could easily mask a deep sinkhole, Aurora checked their location against the coordinates on her palmscreen. "Almost there," she said over her shoulder in a low voice. "At the coordinates, we'll spread out and start looking for—"

"Captain!" Ensign Hardyp's hoarse whisper brought her up short and she turned her eyes to the path ahead again. They were following one of the swamp cat trails that would soon give way to a section that had fallen into disuse. But the owner of the trail seemed to have other ideas. Aurora stopped.

Standing squarely on the trail ahead of them, regarding their approach with an unreadable gaze, was one of the strange creatures. Sunlight dappled across its green-striped hide and pooled around it on the path. Its feline head was the size of a human's torso, and it stood almost two metres tall at the shoulder. The ears pricked forward, listening to their approach, and Aurora noted the leather fronds tufting the tips. Its liquid brown eyes were fixed on the approaching humans.

"What do we do?" Ensign Hardyp whispered. "That thing could trample all of us!"

Aurora returned the creature's stare. Although it stood in the path as if blocking their way, she sensed no defiance or aggression coming from the animal. As the swamp cat and the captain stood locked in a staring contest, a faint rumble trembled the terrain beneath their feet.

"What now?" Elise Dayne muttered.

The swamp cat shifted its feet, as if the tremor had discomfited it.

"There's something down there, all right," Aurora

said. "Whatever it is, the swamp cats don't like it."

She held out a placating hand and took two steps toward the massive creature. "We're not here to hurt you," she said in a soothing voice. "With luck, we might even get your trails back for you."

The swamp cat continued to regard her with interest but didn't seem concerned at her approach.

"Slow and easy, everyone follow me," Aurora told the others.

"Captain, I really don't think—" Ru Varston began, but the captain shook her head.

"It's all right," she said with confidence. "I think it knows we're not a threat."

She thought she heard Ensign Hardyp gulp audibly behind her, but there were no more protests. They followed her, step by careful step, up to and past the huge swamp cat as the captain kept up a steady, soothing patter. It turned its massive head to follow their progress but made no move to stop or harm them. Its warm breath ghosted across their faces, smelling oddly of lavender. Once they were past, Aurora heard a chorus of relieved sighs from her crewmates, and grinned. That would be a story they'd be telling for years to come.

Soon the trail began to show signs of encroaching overgrowth, and the Scouts moved with increased caution. Their quarry, if the captain's surmise was correct, was somewhere just beneath their feet.

And then they saw it, ahead and to the right of the path. A huge tunnel, its entrance camouflaged with carefully-arranged greenery, led underground into darkness.

Field generator pistols at the ready, two to each side of

the rough-cut passage, the four ScoutGuards descended into near-darkness. The green-shadowed light from the tunnel entrance followed them for a bit before it gradually faded, but by that time a faint glow had appeared ahead of them to guide their way. The tunnel held the acrid smell of scorched earth, and the texture of the walls hinted that an energy field had been used to dig out the passageway.

There had been another brief argument at the mouth of the tunnel, with Ru Varston strongly suggesting they should fetch more of the crew before going into the unknown. Captain Aurora, however, deemed the element of surprise more important, and decided they'd press on. "We can get in and out," Aurora reiterated. "Once everyone's safe, we can get all the researchers on board the Scout and keep them safe until Coalition forces get here to take over the situation, whatever it is."

Chief Varston pressed her lips together to hold back the insubordination evident in her eyes, held her FG pistol aloft, and nodded a grudging assent.

They'd passed several dim lightglobes attached haphazardly to the walls, and now they flanked a makeshift door—nothing more than a sheet of plasteel wedged across the tunnel. Captain Aurora had inspected the floor of the tunnel as they progressed and noted, along with tracks that could belong to the missing rover, fresh drag marks that might indicate the passage of an unwilling Harvey Sulls. Now the captain peered through the crack between the plasteel sheet and the rough wall of the tunnel and had to stifle a low whistle. She moved back a few feet and whispered, "Jackpot!" to the others.

Elise Dayne asked her question with a subtly raised eyebrow.

Aurora grinned and said, "The rover's in there. We're

in the right place. The missing men must be a little further on."

"I can try to get the rover moving," Ensign Hardyp offered. "We might be able to use it offensively, and then for a quick getaway."

Captain Aurora clapped him on the shoulder. "I like the way you think, Ensign. But we can't start it up too soon and alert them we're here. Can you hang back with the rover, and come when I call for you?"

The young ensign looked uncertain for a moment, probably at the thought of being left alone, then nodded. "Aye, Captain. Let me just make sure the keycard is in it."

It took the four of them working as noiselessly as possible, with stifled grunts and whispered admonitions, to pivot the plasteel sheet to the side and open up the tunnel. Ensign Hardyp slunk to the rover and peered inside, then gave Captain Aurora a thumbs-up; the keycard was in place. He eased inside the vehicle as Aurora, Dayne, and Varston continued along the passageway.

Aurora heard it first: the sound of muted voices up ahead. One more curve, she thought, and they'd be in sight of their quarry. She strained to make out words and realized that some of the voices spoke in a strange language she'd not encountered before. Then she grinned. Harvey Sulls' voice wafted around the corner, complaining in a petulant voice that he should be released immediately.

At a gesture from Aurora, the women retreated to Ensign Hardyp and the rover. Captain Aurora said, "All right, let's keep this simple. We rush in, blast a stasis field on anyone we don't know, and grab our people. Ensign, once we're out of sight, count to twenty, then get that rover running and back it down the tunnel towards us as fast as you can. The second we're all loaded in, get us the hell out of here."

Ensign Hardyp swallowed and nodded. His hand tightened on the FG pistol he still gripped. "I can do that."

Aurora nodded to the others. "Personal shields in place?"

Dayne and Varston nodded. Dayne's eyes sparked with excitement that mirrored Aurora's own. Varston merely looked resigned.

Aurora winked at them. "Then let's do this."

What Captain Aurora saw when she rounded the tunnel corner almost made her forget to use her FG pistol. It wasn't so much the aliens as the ostensible reason they'd kidnapped the men from Carson Station.

The aliens themselves were interesting, although not outside the realm of what the Scouts had encountered in the past. Standing a mere metre and a half tall, they sported mottled purplish skin covering slender, humanoid bodies. Their uniforms suggested either a militaristic organization or a profound lack of garment-related imagination. Upright triangular ears framed their lightly furred heads, and two front-facing eyes suggested a visual system similar to humans' own. These visages were struck with matching expressions of astonishment as Aurora and her crewmates burst into the room and blasted them to paralysis with their stasis fields. Only two of the six even had time to raise a weapon before they were frozen in place.

What gave Captain Aurora pause was the state of the kidnapped men. They appeared in good health, but their faces were desolate. One was occupied with sweeping the hard-packed floor of the secret alien lair with a rough broom, one leg shackled to a heavy weight he dragged behind him. Another had apparently been set to sorting a large pile of rocks by size, colouration, and perhaps other attributes not immediately apparent. A third man glumly folded and arranged more of the uniforms the aliens wore, while a fourth had been allowed to nap on a makeshift cot. Harvey Sulls stood near a small vehicle that looked like a hovercraft, arms folded defiantly while he ignored the bucket of suds at his feet.

When he saw Captain Aurora, he almost smiled, but managed to hang onto his pout. "Well," he huffed, once all the aliens had been incapacitated, "you took your time!"

Ensign Hardyp gunned the rover down the tunnel at that moment, saving Aurora from the retort she wanted to make to Sulls. She flipped the switch on her FG to cut the chained man loose, while Varston shook the sleeper awake and propelled him in the direction of the rover. Elise Dayne took charge of the others, although none of them needed much prompting. They ran for the sound of the rover before it was even in sight.

When she was sure everyone else was aboard the rover, Aurora swung herself up next to Ensign Hardyp and turned to him with a grin. "Let's get out of here, Ensign!"

And without another word, they roared out of the tunnel.

"What was going on in there?" Ru Varston asked one of the freed researchers.

"They were *testing* us," he said indignantly. "To see if we'd be 'useful' if they took us back to their home planet."

Varston patted his arm. "Not every species is as enlightened as humans," she reassured him. Then her voice took on a mischievous note. "But at least they didn't want you for breeding stock."

Captain Aurora bit back a laugh as Harvey Sulls harrumphed at the notion.

Outside, on the path, Ensign Hardyp slowed the vehicle. "Do you think the swamp cat is still on the path?" he asked Aurora. "I know we're in a hurry, but I don't want to hit it."

"It might be—let me go ahead," she said, and swung down from the rover to jog ahead.

"That wasn't what I—" the ensign began, but the captain was out of earshot and he let the words trail away.

From behind him, Elise Dayne said, "Don't worry, Ensign. She'll be all right. She'll have that cat talked off the trail before we ever get there."

The ensign risked a glance back at the senior officer and said, "Is she—is she always like this?"

Dayne laughed and pointed to her white hair. "She's responsible for most of this, so I'd say yes. She's a good captain—a great captain. But one reckless scout."

"Like the ship?" The ensign looked puzzled.

Dayne grinned. "Young man, who do you think the ship is named for?"

The ensign blinked and slowly returned her grin. "You know, I think I might like it aboard the Reckless Scout," he said finally. "It's not—quite—what I expected. And neither is the captain."

Ahead of them, Captain Stel Aurora came into view, earnestly speaking in a low voice as she stroked the rough armoured hide of a swamp cat, gently urging it off the path.

"That's the best compliment you could give her," Elise Dayne said, "but don't let her hear you say it. It'll only go to her head."

Ensign Hardyp grinned. The swamp cat stepped off the path. And Captain Aurora, one hand on the swamp cat's shoulder, smiled and saluted as the rover passed by, taking the kidnapped men home.

Julie Aubut Gaudet

Gaudet was born in Manitoba and currently lives in Moncton, NB.

She has published two short works, the first in the magazine *Fantascript*, 'Muerto sino Vivo' and 'L'amour véritable,' and her poetry (titled 'A Wolf of all Seasons') has been featured in a poetry anthology called *A Celebration of Young Authors- Canada 2003*.

She brings with her 'Close Encounters.'

Close Encounters

Let me tell you about the day I first met her: Captain Tristan of The Phoenix.

There were Kilntars all over our vessel, eating through both metal and passengers. Alarms were blaring, people were screaming, and smoke blew everywhere as pipes burst. The stench of the ugly Kilns permeated everything. Have you ever seen a Kilntar up close? Disgusting abominations: several black pincer-like legs and claws, a fleshy torso with multiple mouths, and eyes placed in a nonsensical matter. It's enough to make anyone lose their minds.

Anyways, we were locked down in the engine room. We could hear the crunching of metal as the Kilns chewed through the reinforced door. There was no escaping; we were done for. That's when we heard the screeches. Something was attacking the foul things. I dared to come out of my hiding spot and take a look.

There she was, her face splattered in Kiln guts, and her strange sword slicing through their thick hides like butter. Captain Tristan, of the ship *Phoenix*. She moved with impossible speed and finesse. Like a dancer, she twirled and twisted, killing one foul beast after another. It was love at first sight.

I must have been staring, frozen in place, because she

approached me and shook my shoulder. "Are you okay, man?"

I nodded.

"Are there any other survivors?"

I pointed behind me. The seven other survivors came out. She took command immediately.

"There are too many of them to fight and your ship is barely functional. You need to follow me back to *The Phoenix*."

None of us argued. Terrified as we were, we would have followed anyone who had a clue at that point. The familiar halls we walked through were covered in gore and bodies of both human and Kiln alike. I suppressed a gag. Many of the faces I knew, others were too disfigured to recognize.

We soon caught up to another of her crew, Davon, a mountain of a man with biceps bigger than my torso.

"There is no one else left; time to go."

At this point, it hit me that we were abandoning ship and all my research was going to be lost. As most people of science will tell you, losing one's research is often a worse fate than death. I interjected, "The research, we have to get the research."

She rolled her eyes at me, but Davon smiled, producing the ship's data storage box. "I ain't just a pretty face, darling."

With that we were off, jogging to the docking gate. It wasn't going to be that easy, however. The gate was swarming with Kilns. Captain Tristan activated her sword and Davon prepped his energy rifle.

That's when the creatures just exploded in front of us, sprayed with a barrage of energy blasts from the other side. A handsome man who I later learned was named

Jin, almost as tall and muscular as Davon, grinned and winked at his crewmates.

"You didn't think I'd let you have all the fun."

Davon went up ahead and kissed him. "That's my husband."

Jin gave him a tap on the ass as he passed by and waited for the remainder of us to rush through the gate. With a nod of respect to the captain, who had taken the rear, he closed the gate behind us.

Now, I know you may have heard stories of *The Phoenix* and let me tell you, they don't even come close to the real thing. Unlike most ships built for practicality, this one was built for living. Every inch was a piece of art. No bland grey everywhere. The pipes were red, gold, purple, and blue. The wiring was twisted in the most artistic ways. The ship was bright and warm. We followed the captain, doing our best to match her rushed pace.

She stopped by an open archway. I could just see the consoles beyond. She motioned for Jin and Davon to continue taking us survivors to the doctor. I wasn't injured however, and I couldn't miss this opportunity to see *The Phoenix's* crew in action.

"I would rather stay here if possible."

She sighed as she gave me a piercing look. "If you get in the way, I won't hesitate to throw you out, literally."

The others left and I stood in the corner, enraptured. Without a second thought, she turned her attention to her pilot, the only person on deck.

"Anastasia, let's get out of here."

The pilot, Anastasia, had a long side braid peeking out of her helmet. I had heard of the technology, but this was the first time I had seen it in action: intuitive flying. The helmet had a visor that went over her eyes. She wore thick gloves and a chest piece. Once given the go by the captain, the pilot smiled and clicked the gloves together, turning the device on. Bright blue light shone through the seams and she began moving with purpose, the ship following her movements.

"Captain, we have a few stragglers chewing up the hull and one of their pods is in pursuit."

"Damn it! Time for some acrobatics, girl. Hang on, newbie."

I grabbed the nearest railing, and we were soon spinning and diving at breakneck speeds. Through the widow, I could see how insane her flight path was. Strangely, inside there was only rough turbulence. Anastasia danced about, the ship mirroring perfectly. She pushed both arms forward suddenly and we rushed ahead into a space corridor.

The pilot sat back into her seat, slightly breathless. "We are clear."

"How bad is the damage?"

Anastasia was quiet for a moment. "Looks like they got to the quantum manifold."

"For f--"

"I think I can help."

They both turned to me, surprised and skeptical. I was a little surprised myself that I had the nerve to speak. However, quantum energy was my field of study and I felt reasonably certain I could help.

"I...um...know...I mean study quantum energy as well as engineering. It's kind of my...um ... specialty."

"Full of surprises, handsome, aren't you? Follow me."

I blushed at the mention of handsome, then followed Captain Tristan down to the energy chamber. The Kilns had done a number on it. Thankfully, the ship had a force shield closing the ceiling breach or we would have been truly in trouble. It was still unnerving, however, working in a room with a hole to space in the ceiling. Once I saw the quantum manifold, however, I was in my element and I went about fixing it. I couldn't see the captain, but I could hear her fixing the hull breach.

"This device is beautiful, where did you get it?"

"I made it."

"What? But how? And couldn't you have fixed it yourself then?"

"It's not that simple. When I need something, I can conceive it, build it. Once it has been created, I don't seem to be able to actually understand what I've done."

"But how... The black hole! That's not just a story. You really survived the black hole and encountered those beings from another dimension."

"Are you even concentrating on working there? How do you even know that story?"

"Ha... uh... This is a little embarrassing, but I am kind of a fan of yours. I've just read about this ship and how you've built it basically from scratch and all your adventures. I'm sorry if it's creepy that I know so much. I never thought I'd actually ever meet you."

"People certainly like to spread stories. Hope I live up to the legends."

"One more tweak and all done. Argh!"

A large glob of acidic sludge fell onto my uniform, eating away at it. I hurriedly removed my overshirt and threw it away. I was thankfully not burned, though I felt a bit silly in my tank top undershirt. Tristan was staring at me.

"What?"

She averted her gaze, but then her face twisted into a look of horror. She whispered, "Don't move."

She reached for her sword at her hip and I looked up. That was a mistake. Crawling above my head was a Kilntar.

It dropped between us, rushing Tristan. She hadn't managed to get her sword out. I don't know what I was thinking, but I just had to do something. I grabbed a serrated piece of metal that had been torn from the ship and sliced the creature from behind. It rounded on me. I looked at the small piece of metal in my hands and at its pincers and hungry mouths. I did the only thing a smart man should do and I ran... with it on my heels.

I didn't get far. Since I didn't know the ship, I ran into a dead end. I threw the metal shard like a knife, hoping it would take out one of the Kiln's eyes. Instead, it bounced harmlessly off its torso. The creature emitted a sound, I could only assume was glee, and rushed towards me. I was done for.

Then, a glowing blade came bursting through the head area, coming to a stop an inch from my own head. The creature twitched and fell to the ground. Tristan smiled at me as she put away her blade. I couldn't contain my awe for this incredible woman.

"You... are... amazing!"

She blushed slightly and gave me her hand so I could step over the large dead thing.

We were able to arrive at the nearest station without any further incidents three days later. I did my best to help with repairs and study the ship during our travels. The day we arrived Tristan called me to her private quarters.

"You have proven useful these last few days and we could use someone like you on *The Phoenix*. The pay sucks, the job is dangerous, but you won't meet a better crew of people."

I was so elated, I thought I might faint. "It would be a dream, I mean… that is… are you sure you want me?"

That's when she leaned over and kissed me. "What do you think?"

I was just about to kiss her again when Anastasia's voice rang throughout the ship.

"Captain. Kilntar incursion on Delta 1; shall I set a course?"

"Are all our passengers off?"

"Yes, ma'am."

She turned to me, smiling. "Time to party, Anastasia."

That's the day I joined the crew of The Phoenix *and kissed my wife, Tristan, for the first time.*

Corinne Lewandowski

Corinne is an award-winning poet from Halifax, Nova Scotia whose previous credits include poetry published in Loose Connections and poetry that won the Joyce Marshall Hsia Memorial Poetry Prize.

She currently lives in Lower Sackville with her wife and two cats.

Her first published prose story was 'Family Business' in *Dystopia from the Rock*.

The Final Invasion

The silver rocket glided silently towards the dock on the Alien Mother Ship.

The black void of the dock blinked into millions of points of light. The light latched on the nose of the rocket. The light swarmed in an undulating wave up over the red nose cone, past the silver edges of the front air lock and covered the round window.

Specialist Commander Tessa Kordel touched the window. The millions of points of light were little green translucent creatures. When her palm pressed against the glass, the creatures outlined her thick, gloved fingers and rippled through various shades of green.

Special Diplomat Cummings was still pompous. Still shrill.

"Do you really think you should be doing that?"

Ignoring him, Tessa turned to Space Pilot Kai. His face was full moon pale inside his bulbous glass helmet. The reflected light from the little green creatures added streaks of pale green. Moon cheese with a gaping mouth.

"Is docking complete? Did they pressurize the airlock? Check your read-outs, Space Pilot Kai," Tessa ordered.

"Ye-ye-yes, ma'am."

"Specialist Commander to you."

"Yes, Specialist Commander, ma'am, sir."

Tessa smirked. The blinking airlock indicators on the console already told her the seal was complete and the oxygen mix spot on. The boy needed directions to stay focused.

"Kordel, I am the Special Diplomat for this mission. *You* are not in charge." Cummings flailed at this safety harness trying to unclip it.

"I'd wait to do that, Special Diplomat Cummings, if I were you. Sir."

Cummings harrumphed over the mic. He whipped off his harness and floated a foot above his chair.

The Alien Mother Ship extended their gravity field to the rocket.

Cummings dropped like a meteor, slamming into his seat.

"Grav-gravity on now, sir." Space Pilot Kai was too young, too petrified, to understand how his obviousness salted Cummings' wound.

Cummings grumbled and cussed while struggling to get upright.

"Ready, gentlemen?" Tessa was standing a few feet from the air lock, her right hand resting on her hip holster where her laser gun used to be. The aliens required them to arrive unarmed. This was a formality before the end. *The Committee to Save the Earth* called them the *Last Chance for Peace Team*.

Save earth, my tushie, Tessa thought. Better to accept the defeat with grace.

"I decide when and where we are..." Cummings prattled on as he stood, with a hand from Kai.

Clunk! Clang!

The wheel on the air lock door spun fast. It was still

going when the door was slammed open. It almost hit the bulkhead, but Tessa caught it and hooked it secure.

"Specialist Commander Kordel, Special Diplomat Cummings, and Space Pilot Kai, the Queen and Mother of Our Ship welcomes you."

The greeter had folded himself and ducked his head down to fill the airlock opening.

The *Committee to Save the Earth* mentioned the alien invaders were green.

The glistening row of large, yellowish teeth going as far back as they could see never made it to the artist's rendition in the promotional materials. Earth's version was a cute elongated eyed alien that was human-like with its smile and wave.

Nothing was cute, human-like, or friendly here.

Two yellow warning bars blinked on Tessa's internal panel. The warnings indicated Kai and Cummings should consider replace their waste bags soon.

Of course. I just cleaned those. I am not scrubbing those down again. Really? Facing extinction and you're worried about getting stuck with cleaning the suits, again. Tessa snorted at herself.

"The oxygen mix is suitable for you. Spacesuits will be removed before meeting the Queen."

Two of the three *Last Chance for Peace Team* members paused and looked at each other.

Snap. Hiss. Pop.

Specialist Commander Tessa Kordel immediately removed her helmet, setting it down on a chair. Trust must be shown decisively lest their alien hosts construed their actions as discourteous. She gestured at Kai to help her unclip the rest of her suit.

The waiting room was larger than their whole rocket from red-nosed stem to silver-finned stern. Three chairs and a table had been constructed for them. The window was an entire wall.

Their red-nosed to silver-finned rocket was connected by the glowing, moving tentacles of millions little green creatures tethering it to the Alien Mother Ship. At this distance it looked like glowing rope. The Alien Mother Ship took up most of the view.

Earth hung quiet and colourful in space, small next to the Alien Mother Ship.

In forty-eight hours, everyone on Earth would be destroyed.

No need to rush the invaders' schedule and die sooner than planned by being rude.

"Thank you. We appreciate your graciousness in modifying your ship's systems for us."

The universal translators the aliens had provided were instant and very accurate. The alien linguists had studied Earth's languages for thousands of years, much to the chagrin of almost all of the historians, excepting the ones long labelled crazy conspiracy theorists.

The Greeter loomed over them and nodded acknowledgement. Or looked down so he could see the humans. Tessa couldn't tell. Clearly military from the size of the blade he carried. The blade was taller than her. It would never fit sideways in their rocket.

Special Diplomat Cummings stepped in front of Tessa to assert his authority, hastily removing his helmet.

"With greatest thanks." His awkward honourific bow didn't work in the suit and he almost bowled over.

The Committee to Save the Earth had told him it wouldn't

work.

Space Pilot Kai took position behind Special Diplomat Cummings' right shoulder, also pushing in front of Tessa. Sweat beaded down his face.

Kai was young. Last of the pilots with space experience, they said. The rest died in wave after wave of ineffectual rallies Earth had thrown against the Alien Mother Ship. Tessa really didn't think two days of war games training qualified Kai to fly or represent Earth.

The Queen required three people to be interviewed prior to the Invasion being completed.

The Committee to Save The Earth would rather a preferred third person come up. The optics for the posters would be better as per the PR consultants. Only volunteers were left for the Last Hours of Earth. Tessa didn't regret volunteering for this mission. At least she'd made the roster. She'd made sure Kai hadn't crashed them on the way up.

Tessa had been flying in space longer than Kai had been alive. Undoubtedly, he was someone's relative.

The old man, the kid, and the woman made the trip after a media circus.

Family goodbyes were done. At least she would die knowing she ensured Special Diplomat Cummings could deliver the last efforts of *The Committee to Save the Earth*.

The Committee was foolish to presume anything would prevent the inevitable.

The communities on Mars and Ganymede already discovered that.

Tessa really wanted to meet the formidable Queen who had all the power in the universe and ultimately would destroy humanity. She was pretty sure the Queen, as commander of her forces, didn't make her female underlings wear coveralls made with built-in skirts and plunging V-necklines. In pink of all colours.

Space Pilot Kai's coveralls were black and Special Diplomat Cummings were light blue. At least they had pockets.

On the brink of extinction and Tessa had nearly killed Cummings when she found out he'd spaced her sturdy, practical coveralls with pant legs and multiple pockets and replaced it with this atrocious pink thing.

"More befitting a woman," Cummings had declared.

Now all ready, the Greeter gestured they were to leave the waiting room and travel down the corridor to the Queen's Chamber.

Tessa let Cummings and Kai go ahead of her, since it calmed them when they waggled their testosterone.

Tessa swore the Greeter sounded like it was chuckling behind her. Hmmm. A scent filled the air behind her. Dear God. All the males were asserting their noxious smells and attitudes.

Tessa kept a distant pace to not bump into the men.

Click. Click. Whirrrrrr.

The slate gray corridors were lit with recessed lighting matching the human stations and ships.

A quarter of the way en-route, all surfaces started blending from gray to green translucent then smoothed into transparent. The omnipresent light dimmed and changed to two tracks of lighting in bioluminescence green matching the skin tones of the Greeter and the little green creatures.

They walked on the sky.

The depth of the dark universe lay beneath Tessa's feet and all around. Above her head, the Earth glowed with its blues, browns, whites and all the colours in between.

Atlantic Canada was lit with the band of rising eastern light. The sunrise was just hitting the edge of Nova Scotia. Martinique Beach would be splendid with all her family there.

The views of the Earth from here and from her mind's eye as if she were on the beach over lapped and seared into her memory.

Fitting.

Tessa stopped walking, full of bliss for this splendid chance to meditate on her life and loves and see the world as she never had before. It felt like she was floating in the universe.

The darker darkness for the entire right side for her vision was the Alien Mother Ship. Tessa could not see far enough to see any curve above or below of their ship.

Puking from Kai destroyed the last of the moment.

The Greeter chuckled and huffed louder.

Tessa laughed with him. Earth's last choice for a pilot couldn't handle space flight and the unexpected. Maybe she would be allowed to fly home. If they weren't killed early.

Cummings was turning shades matching the Greeter now.

"Rookies," Tessa nodded to them.

The Greeter's open maw might have been a grin. Tessa was too busy marveling again at his rows of teeth to decide.

Syncopated lights pulsed along the invisible edges of the floor lights directing the way to the Queen's Chamber.

Click. Click. Whirrrrrr.

The Greeter's sounds turned the floor opaque but left the view of Earth above.

Tessa nodded in thanks.

"Forward."

Kai didn't know if he should move or clean up the floor. Little green transparent creatures swarmed in and devoured the mess, changing colours in the process.

Tessa looked forward and start walking, as much to avoid watching the critters' visible digestive track eat Kai's spew. She'd turn sick too with that. No way that she would cave to the desires and humours of aliens.

"Diplomat Cummings?" Tessa encouraged him to move forward as he blocked everyone.

"Why would he do that to us?" his voice scraped out of his raw throat.

"He did nothing. We're still alive. Fascinating technology."

"Like playing with your food."

Tessa glanced back to the gleams of teeth coated in viscous saliva. "Oh, you have to laugh. That was funny."

Diplomat Cummings straightened up, wiggling as if adjusting himself in his suit. "Specialist Commander Tessa Kordel. I do not know how you got on this very serious mission. Or how you think that was funny,"

"Mostly my father. British comedies too."

Cummings stormed off, forgetting he'd not deactivated the magnetic sole in his interior softboot. The "storming" was the agonizingly slow *click-pop, click-pop* of his magnetic soles. He waited for Kai and Tessa to not be afraid to meet him at the sealed entry to the Queen's Chambers.

A wide semi-transparent path gently arched across the cavernous room that ended at the Queen's dais. The distant view of the Queen, her entourage and personal guards was the least daunting.

The *Last Chance for Peace Team* slowly walked up the arch. The team moved slower and slower as Special Diplomat Cummings and Space Pilot Kai looked around them.

Millions of aliens filled the room, stretched out as far as the eye could see.

Cummings and Kai ground to a full stop. Tessa nearly ran into them. Still she kept her eyes looking up and ahead, locked on the Queen.

Kai's breathing became rapid. "Be-be-below," was all he could manage.

Cummings gulped repeatedly.

"Eyes up! Respect the Queen!" Tessa whispered. "Do. Not. Look. Down."

Tessa's peripheral vision was excellent. The seething mass of limbs writhing just below the walkway was unlike any of the bipedal aliens. The "limbs" entwined, slid and pressed against the walkway, colour and shape blurred by the walkway's thickness.

The most terrifying of all aliens were right below their feet as far as Kai and Cummings knew. Tessa kept her vision fixed on the one true danger in the room.

"Move!"

The men refused to budge.

Tessa felt the presence of the Greeter's mass a hair's breadth behind her. He reached over and around her. He landed a claw on each of the men's backs and simultaneously his low voice vibrated through Tessa. "Forward!"

Kai screeched and Cummings stopped breathing, then both men practically ran towards the Queen.

Tessa waited.

The Greeter leaned away, ensuring he accidentally brushed by Tessa's skirt.

Growling, Tessa replied to his actions, without taking her eyes off the Queen. "I'm no candy ass. Touch me again and I'll have the Queen cut a piece of you off for touching her honoured guests without her permission."

The skin and the blood were different, but the Greeter's efforts at domination were no different from the tricks of her male companions.

The Greeter became so still Tessa couldn't even hear him breathe.

Tessa wasn't about to tear ass up the walkway like the men. She had studied the required protocols. The Greeter thought he could break the Queen's own protocols and the humans wouldn't know.

The end of the world was in forty-eight hours. In the pre-mission communication, the Queen had been explicit what respects would be show to each others' side. Tessa had studied every aspect of the Protocols As Gifted From The Queen front to back and sideways.

To save the Earth from losing the allotted time left, if Tessa had to pretend she was made of steel while her guts were shaking, so be it.

Cummings reached the dais with Kai on his heals. Kai stopped abruptly to prevent tripping into him.

Tessa walked at the required even, steady pace *The Committee to Save Earth* reinforced with their training and brochures on the Queen's protocols. The consequences of not following protocol was represented in a cartoon picture of a decapitated head of a fictitious member of the *Last Chance for Peace Team* on the ground. The "cute" alien stood over the head, brandishing a laser rifle.

Queen Victoria had nothing on this Queen's adherence to rule. Tessa was disappointed to not have seen single laser gun. More frightening was that which was unseen.

No one moved on the dais in the Queen's party.

Tessa heard Cummings start his greeting, even at this distance. "Your Most Honoured Majesty. We are honoured to greet you in peace." Cummings bowed deeply and smacked Kai's left arm to encourage him to start his bow.

The Queen was still staring at Tessa, never having looked at Cummings and Kai. The Queen got down from throne.

Rising, Cummings obliviously continued his introductions. "I am . . ."

The Queen walked past Cummings and Kai just as Tessa had reached her assigned position behind Cummings and Kai.

The Queen stopped in front of Tessa. "Welcome, Specialist Commander Tessa Kordel." The Queen opened both claws, palm up. "Your language is imprecise. Our translators are impeccable. Tell me. Is Specialist Commander a colloquial term for Diplomat?"

Tessa respectfully directed her eyes down and nodded her head and open hands towards Cummings. "Special Diplomat Cummings is . . ."

Cummings' face became severe. He reached out to gently touch the Queen's arm to direct her to face him. "I am the Diplo . . ."

The instant Cummings laid a finger on the Queen, tens of thousands of little green aliens whipped straight through the air from the walkway, turning a pulsing red. Instantly, they engulfed his hands while other red creatures swarmed his feet to hold him in place.

Cummings would have made a sound, but the red creatures covered his mouth.

Tessa was on a trip for biscuits. Special Diplomat Cummings had frosted the Queen. Death could well be more imminent that forty-eight hours.

"Were our protocols not clear, Special Commander Tessa Kordel," said the Queen.

Tessa lowered her head and shoulder to expose the top of her head and back of her top vertebrae to the Queen. "Infinitely clear, Your Most Nobel Majesty of the Whole Universe."

"Why is Your Male trying to touch me?

"Special Diplomat Cummings is the appointed diplomatic as decreed by the *Committee for Earth*. His motives are unknown to me. I am below his rank."

The Queen looked at Tessa, then Cummings, then back to Tessa, her eyes glazing over the youngling Kai. "Oh. Perhaps the linguists were right. How culturally backwards."

"We are learning to follow the example you have, your Majesty, where the voice of the female is heard."

A raucous snort came out of the Queen. "I am Queen. I am not any female. I have no equals."

Tessa lowered to both knees. "We are in envy of your advanced culture. We would be honoured to hear of your vast achievements, should you decree it."

Cummings was turning as red as the creatures holding him fast.

Kai turned pasty white again. Little yellow creatures supported his legs to preventing him from fainting.

The vast room was silent except for the slithering flesh made by the limbs below the walkway.

The Queen moved to stand in front of Cummings. "I hope that as Special Diplomat you will exhibit the proper grace in adhering to Our Protocols. Specialist Commander Tessa Kordel is exemplary in her actions." The Queen leaned in within millimeters of Cumming's face. "I believe in painful consequences."

Cumming's face lost colour. He was able to nod slightly in agreement.

The Queen waved a limb.

"Our honoured guests may wait in the guest room. I will start the private interviews with Special Diplomat Cummings."

The Greeter approached to escort Tessa and Kai away from the Queen.

Little red creatures whipped out of the air. The Greeter's neck was encased in a mass of red creatures cinching down hard. The Greeter gurgled and wheezed.

"Never again let any creature outperform your ability to follow The Protocols! Especially an alien! A million wait to replace you."

The Greeter dropped to prone and exposed his back to the Queen.

"Good." The Queen faced Tessa and smiled. "Do please enjoy the refreshments and sustenance. We made everything special for you."

The Greeter stayed on the other side of the door and kept staring Tess until the door closed and locked.

Tessa finally let her breath out. Still alive by some miracle.

Hot tea, cold drinks and little triangular sandwiches filled a table. Cookies shapes like the aliens in the *Committee to Save the Earth*'s brochures stacked a plate.

Tessa almost spit out her orange pekoe tea.

"What happened out there?" Kai burst out. Loudest the kid had ever been. He paced the room and physically shook while little green and yellow aliens followed him back and forth, trying to attend his needs.

"We survived a near death experience. Cummings nearly killed us all and shortened the clock for Earth. Cool it! Don't follow bad examples 'cause we don't want to lose the pinks to our ride home."

"We might die here!"

Tessa stared at him and laughed. "Eureka! You have determined the threat level of the Queen and the Alien Mother Ship."

Tessa plunked down in a chair. It adjusted itself to follow her shape. The singular most comfortable thing she had ever sat on. The female version of her jumpsuit's miniskirt and plunging neckline was giving her goosebumps. Or perhaps the near-death experience. The chair warmed up, adjusting to her needs. If only someone had invented chairs like this back home, they'd make a mint. Instead, it was chrome this, plastic that. No one made good old fashioned comfortable wooden chairs anymore.

"Or you could have read page two from The Committee to Save The Earth's brochure on what the risks were to this mission." Tessa skipped page one. It was propaganda rhetoric about the Earth's last attempts to save everyone.

A shadow hovered over Tessa. Kai stood swaying over her. "We could have died."

"Yes, you've mentioned. We will die. It's just a matter of when." Tessa would never tire of the view of Earth from above. The tea was just right.

"I... I wanted to let you know. In case... we die sooner," Kai ran a hand through his hair, puffing up his chest with Space Pilot muster. "I think you have a classy chassis."

Tessa took a deep breath. "Let me explain in a way you'll understand." Tessa leapt out of the chair and stood up in his face. "My chassis doesn't park in your garage. Cool it! Act like a professional, Space Pilot Kai. Now enjoy the guar-an-teed once in your lifetime view!"

It was hard for Tessa to truly be mad at Kai. Kid was pushed through graduation and training. Probably never kissed a girl. Now he was afraid he'd never make it back for one last chance to find someone.

Tessa was not *his* someone.

Heading for the third cookie, Tessa finally noticed a fresh pressed stack of coveralls with each of their names on them. Their hosts thought of everything.

"Hold this!" She passed her tea and half a cookie to Kai.

Her uniform had pant legs and pockets!

Tessa started whipping off her cover-nones and started pulling on the proper coveralls. Kai squeaked and turned his back to her to give her privacy.

Funny that.

"Ahhhhhhhh!" The pockets were deep and useful. It was good to be alive.

"Thank you for taking the time to meet with me."

Tessa bowed her head deeply, being sure to remove her hands from the gloriously deep pockets of her coveralls. "You Honour Us with Your Presence and Consideration."

The Queen had chosen to interview Tessa in a training centre area of some kind.

"May I?"

The Queen extended a claw out. Tessa held her palm out. The yellow pearls that encircled the Queen's joint turned into the yellow glowing creatures. They trailed from the Queen to Tessa's wrist and gently connected and hung there like a bracelet.

Tessa knew to accept all the Queen's offers, no matter how unusual. The tickle of the creatures made her smile.

As they walked along the high arch training areas, Tessa could see countless aliens of various sizes working on different projects. Everything from schematics to floating mathematics to ship maintenance were being taught.

The Queen touched the creatures on Tessa's wrist.

"By accepting My gift, you can comprehend what you see instead of waiting for verbal language to be translated."

The tour continued. Tessa marveled at the levels of skills and abilities the aliens demonstrated. One group was designing a sphere hovering over the table. The sphere twinkled with stars. A marvel.

"Each sphere represented each of the species we've conquered." The Queen started listing names so unusual, the translators had no English to represent the sounds and syllables. As the sphere was released, it rose in a controlled path to a dark point on the high domed ceiling.

Tessa gasped. It looked like the all the stars in the universe in one place. More than she had ever seen any time Tessa lay on beach blankets on Martinique Beach.

"All our soldiers could be gone in an instant. We'd have a thousand times more to replace them. I always get what I want."

"An impressive amount of citizens."

The Queen stopped walking. "Citizens? They are my children."

Tess let out a low whistle. "All of them?"

"Yes, a Queen has two duties. Lead the Invasions and Create all the Children."

The quiet industriousness washed over them for a while.

"Hmmm. Not much time for hobbies of your own choosing."

"I am Queen. I create and rule all! I do not have to choose!"

Tess winced. The children below had stopped milling about with their structured activities. The Queen's echo rippled throughout the dome. "Have you no children?"

"Not of my own nor of my partner's."

"It is the Great Purpose in Life."

"We have full lives with many family members, friends, and their children. We teach others. We enjoy our desires and our hobbies to the fullest."

Tessa remembered the time her partner had added a plant's worth of mint to the first butter cream cake icing she had made. Everyone politely said how wonderful it was. The house smelled like mint for days.

"What do you do with these hobbies?"

"Cooking, photography, writing, walking on the beach or yard sales. Read. Sleep in. Cuddle and talk."

"Cuddle and talk?"

"Yes. Perhaps embrace translates better."

"I do this as Queen. I talk to the other lesser females, dominantly embrace them and speak to them."

Tessa shrugged. "Isn't it wonderful to be able to do that for as long as you want, whenever you want? I can speak and be free in the company of my partner from all the worries of the world."

"Well, no. Not like that." A noise emanated from the Queen.

"Oh, I misspoke." The Queen sounded strange. "I did not mean to offend."

"No offense taken."

"I thought you were Queen."

"I AM QUEEN."

Tessa lifted her hands palm out and backed up. The little yellow creatures were heading toward an orange-red shade and spreading up her wrist.

"My Most Humble Apologies. I merely meant as Queen, you can do as you please."

"I can do . . ." the Queen's voice faded as the Greeter, or his twin, suddenly came up close to the Queen.

"Your Majesty, these tasks need immediate attention." Greeter Two handed the Queen a claw-sized device.

". . . what I want."

The Queen was clicking icon after icon of one duty after another on the screen. "Um. When I want."

Click. Click. Scroll.

"As I desire."

"I see." Tessa politely took a few steps back to give the Queen privacy as she reviewed her agenda. She swore she caught a glimpse of an image of Earth with a big red line through it at the top of the list.

"Whenever I desire."

"Again! What did she say? What did you say? Exactly!" Cummings hovered over Tessa as she leaned back, letting the alien chair conform to her body.

Kai stood, shaking a little from standing too long. He was still too afraid to sit on something with moving little creatures in it.

Tessa stared out the window in guest area with another cup of hot tea. Fitting it was a wonderfully nutty Japanese brown rice tea. Sunrise in Japan now. "I've told you everything. Look."

"Look. Look. Look. Earth's fate rests in the hands of conversations about hobbies and your personal life!"

"No, I mean look." Tessa reached up, grabbed his elbow and made him look out the window. "Show some appreciation. Be grateful for that! Or at least pant legs."

"Appreciation? What? Pantlegs? Now, we're all really doomed because of a *woman*."

Tessa laughed.

"We were always doomed. Do you not understand this is the Queen's routine before every termination?"

Cummings face burst into fire-engine red. "How dare you speak with the Queen of your own volition. You have no idea what she is doing. It is my task to . . ."

"I didn't."

Cummings stopped only after huffing and sputtering out a few more words before he registered what Tessa said. "How do you know this then?"

Tessa kept her eyes locked on Earth. "She told me."

The Greeter stood watching them. Clicking and whirling in his odd way. Apparently, she wasn't the only one who didn't trust Cummings. He stayed by the door as the Queen had directed him.

Tessa ticked off the list on her fingers. "Observe. Intimidate. Outlast attacks. Invade. Interview species. Kill and preserve the population for food. Rinse and repeat. Apparently, her children are voracious in their appetites."

Tessa felt the goosebumps, sure she could feel the Greeter's eyes in her back.

Cummings approached the Greeter, with less bluster. Clearly afraid of him but not enough to prevent pestering him with a rapid fire of questions.

"Kai, sit," Tessa ordered.

"Ngggg. I dunno..."

"Sit!"

Kai plunked on a chair. The creatures in the chair turned different colours by his low back and calves, their glow a stark contrast against his black jumpsuit.

"I don't know if this is safe... ohhhhh. I don't even care if I get cooties."

Tessa chuckle. Kai's eyes were half closed as the chair stimulated his sore muscles.

"SIT!" Greeter boomed, closing in on Cummings.

Cummings dropped like a rock and sat on the floor. A concentration of little green critters congregated underneath, turning yellow. They made quick work returning the dark blue spot on his pant leg to a dry light blue. Cummings bit down and swallowed his distress and refused to move. Afraid and embarrassed.

Finally, it was quiet.

All they could do was wait for the Queen and have more cookies and tea.

The interview data was like thousands before.

The Queen rolled the yellow creatures in her cupped claws like thousands of tiny marbles. She found she could hear theirs stories and see their images better if she touched them.

The thoughts of the aliens rolled through her mind.

She reviewed Kai's thoughts first.

Space Pilot Kai the youngling thinking only of reproducing before he died. Wondering if he was going to get eaten before being allowed to return home for the last few hours. At this lack of maturity, her own children would not even be allowed to watch over the incubators, let alone fly a ship.

The Queen's clicking was rapid sounding as monotonous as she felt bored.

Special Diplomat Cummings was as all the other diplomats and politicians she had defeated across the universe. In every corner. Convinced Only He Could Save The Planet with His Cunning Diplomacy. The Queen Would Bow to His Mastery of Her.

Cummings thought little of the Queen and even less because she was female.

Only for her own Protocols, did the Queen not eat him there and then upon their first encounter. She had developed her ironclad Protocols for a reason.

Tessa was a curious creature. Every fibre of Tessa respected the Queen. She knew the Queen was superior and had bested the Earth even before When The Invasion Began. The woman appreciated that alien culture reflected a female with such incredible powers over the Universe. A place where women were revered and in control. Tessa was humbled by the powers of the Queen, knowing only she could but enjoy the graciousness of such a hostess for a short while.

The little yellow creatures rolled around the Queen's limbs.

Tessa's only regret was there was not enough time to truly appreciate the Queen. For the rest of humanity to not have witnessed and learned of the Queen's great advances in science and the incredible opportunities, was one of Tessa's regret.

The second was that her partner would not be able to see what she had seen.

Those thoughts were quite interesting. Oh my.

Tessa could hear the Queen scolding the Greeter over the helmet's headpiece as Greeter Two helped by carrying Kai' floppy body.

The Greeter's high frequency response popped Tessa's ears a little.

"Your Majesty this, Your Majesty that. I have other things to do."

Greeter sounded almost forlorn as Tessa and Greeter Two settled Kai into his seat.

"What will you eat? I am always getting food for you. Look! Look what you wasted. That was perfectly good Martian. I do not care if you do not like the crunchy inside bits."

The Queen shouted, "Enough! There are too many of you. Go ask your siblings. Fight it out for all I care. I'll be housing with the females. They are far more engaging in conversation than you lot."

Tessa started turning down her mic volume.

"No. I am not conquering Alpha Centauri."

The Queen's last line echoed in Tessa's helmet. Greeter Two left the spaceship but lingered as if he wouldn't mind missing his ride.

"I am QUEEN! I will do as I please for once. I am going to cuddle and catch up on a few thousand planets worth of reading. Now pick up your Martian and finish it, you wasteful child."

"Closssssse eyes minute then... flllllllyyyyy."

Kai lolled his helmeted head again before Tessa finishing securing his safety harness.

The Queen ensured Kai was given a sedative to prevent disrupting Tessa's piloting.

The peace and quiet was the one of the last gifts the Queen had given her.

The mothership turned the rocket to align with the best re-entry angle. Tessa was on autopilot for a spell of time.

"Comms on. Come in, Canso Space Port! Come in, Canso! Specialist Commander Tessa Kordel reporting for Special Diplomatic Team!"

"You're alive! Did you..."

"We are successful. Earth is safe. We have been gifted life and treasures of advanced technology."

The rocket smoothly transitioned into the re-entry arc for Canso Space Port.

"Our congratulations to Special Diplomat Cummings! Put him on!"

"Special Diplomat Cummings chose to stay with the Alien Mothership to explore their culture and secure our peace treaty."

"He? Oh."

"Space Pilot Kai..."

"Is asleep."

"Congratulations Specialist Commander Tessa Kordel for being a team member that saved Earth. Are you in any condition to fly?"

"Yes."

"Prepare for re-entry at 0600. Canso Space Port, out."

Tessa dimmed all unnecessary lighting. The view of Earth, whole and hale, filled her port hole. The blues, browns, and deep greens of a hale and whole Earth filled her port hole.

Inside, the only strong light came from the glass

sphere Tessa had duct taped in a console nook. Thousands of green translucent creatures swirled and pulsed in the glass.

Tessa pulled out the smallest computer she had ever seen in her life. The Queen had taught her how to do something called "coding" to teach the green creatures what to do when they got to Earth. The Queen advised the best replication conditions for the creatures was a brine liquid.

Holding the palm-sized computer a breath away from her lips, she activated her custom program. "Queen's Treaty. Program One. Commence."

The green creatures turned ocean blue.

Tessa adjusted her flight.

"Specialist Commander Kordel, your flight has deviated. Correct."

"Unable to correct due to technical failure, Canso."

"Advise your landing will be a wet one off the coast of Louisbourg."

"Roger." Tessa leaned back and smiled.

"Cummings, you are 1134582."

"My name is Cummings."

"You are 1134582."

The green little creatures danced and undulated in a thin around Cumming's neck and extended into a pyramid shape on the back of his head. The colours turned ocean blue.

"I am... 1134582."

1134582 shuffled along with immature alien males and cleaned the creche area, redirecting the waste for repurposing.

"I am 1134582. I work and live for the Queen."

Daniel Windeler

Daniel Windeler hails from Happy Valley Goose Bay, and is a biologist and storyteller.

He brings with him his first published tale: 'Freeson's Leap.'

Freeson's Leap

"The humans are here!" Halvie leaned through the bar door and bellowed out. Halvie's race, the Naanth could be mistaken for a ferret if he wasn't nearly five feet tall with an extra set of paws. That, and the fact that he was wearing a pressure suit and speaking fluent *ascended* perfectly. His vermin eyes narrowed as he peered into the shaded bar, finally locking onto Nathan Doshi sitting at a barstool. "Come on, you can greet the locals later."

Nate turned back to the Herriot who was trying to charm him. Of all the alien races at the station, the Herriots had the most "human" appearance: two arms, two legs, two eyes, a mouth; all the essentials. A protruding nose and actual ears weren't really essential in Nate's opinion, but living amongst the stars gave him more of an open mind, or that's what he told himself. Flashing his ID band to pay for his drinks, he gave the drunk Herriot a slap on the shoulder and leaned in for the traditional shoulder bump before sliding off the stool. Nate could feel the drunk's gaze bore into his back, grey eyes narrowed in annoyed wanting. He sauntered outside and matched his little friend's swift pace down the 'street'.

It was the middle of the day in the domed residential floor of the station on the edge of the Sol System. While it had a long number designation for the astrological catalogue, the locals dubbed it "Sol Watch" since it was the closest to the human dominion. Nate looked up through the dome to the docking stations visible on its edge; the large silver-shined vessel of the Earthlings was docked at the biggest one. Many of the local populace had their eyes on the vessel, and all the talk in the 'streets' was about them finally arriving.

"I can't believe we'll get to see a human, after 150 years!" Halvie chuckled. For a species that looked like a mascot of a vid-cartoon, Halvie had a deep baritone voice, which used to surprise Nate when their partnership began nearly a decade ago.

"What do you mean see a human – I'm a human!" Nate waved his hands over his thin honey face, dark blue eyes narrowing on his business partner. He was a bit short for the average Earthling human, and had never actually been in the Sol System, but he still had all right parts.

"Yeah, but I mean a real human, a Sol human. Not like you guys."

"I take offence to that, Halvie." Nate raised a pencil thin eyebrow to the Naanth.

"Nate, you called me a cat last week, and I don't even know what that is." Halvie's shoulder's shrugged and his lower paws waved a little in the air. "Look, nothing against you Freesons, but I'd like to see a Sol human before they go off to the big government parties and diplomatic trips. Let the little guys wave before they shoot off again. Other than some high government birds and Herriot Generals, no one has seen one in over a century!"

Halvie was right about that, no one outside the highest authority had seen a Sol Human, let alone spoke to one. 150 years ago, Humanity finally developed faster-than-light travel and shot their way out of their system, only to come across the sixty-seven military vessels waiting for them (the 'welcoming party' as it would later be referred to). The universal government of nearly a hundred alien races, calling itself "The Risen", put its proclamation out: if humanity wanted to fly out to the stars with the rest of them, then they'd need 150 years of general peace to prove itself worthy of joining. This was common practice amongst the Risen, and they made sure Humanity knew it wasn't playing around. So the Sol System worked to better itself, joining together to show all the aliens they could play nice. Now, 150 years later, the embargo was lifted and they were sending their best and brightest to greet their new universal allies. Humanity was finally allowed to venture out into the stars.

But Nate was walking, talking proof that humans might have already broken that rule.

He reached for his ID band to pull up a vid screen; he had the newest article on the human delegates on file for the last few weeks, and had been looking over all the senior officers on the diplomatic ship *Kota*. He flicked his finger through the various officers and their vid pictures. Officially the names, backgrounds, and photos of the crew were supposed to be a government-kept secret, but such things didn't stay secret for long. For the last year, names like Captain Vihaan Sanyal and Second Officer Marcus Peck were common among the public.

Nate flicked through the pictures, seeing all the different nationalities and ethnicities of the Sol humans. Some of them had a few similarities to him, but none really seemed to have the same mix of his honey-shine skin and dark blue eyes. He wasn't really surprised; his ethnic background was commonly referred to as the Freesons:

humans born and bred out in space. While the embargo was mostly successful in keeping humanity in its little star system, small bands of nomads and colonists slipped past the welcoming party. Honestly, humans had been out on stations and vessels for almost as long as the embargo was in place. Nate felt a swell of pride that his people could get past the most rigid universal law to make a name for themselves in the universe. Due to the smaller gene pool of the travellers and the disconnection from the Mother Sol, the Freesons developed into a whole new group of people, ethnically and socially. While they were humans in all rights, they understood the universe that Sol humans were just venturing into; in his opinion, that could be an advantage for his far-off cousins from Earth.

One picture caught his eye in the article, one he found a few weeks ago that he kept coming back to: Dr. Amelia Crawford. The photo they chose for her was from a classified report sent to the higher-ups back in someplace called India. She was standing next to a large aquarium, a computer pad in hand, looking at one of the cetacean Navigators that was sent to Earth nearly fifty years ago. The photo of the dolphin-like alien didn't do it justice, the luminescent markings on its dorsal side looking dull in the photo, unlike the real thing. But the glow was there all the same, and the Navigator's four eyes were locked on Dr. Crawford, who stood just outside the glass. The Navigator clearly enjoyed the beautiful woman's presence, some of its markings trying to mimic the colour of her shoulder length hair, a nice lush blonde, or her dashing cerulean eyes. A smile lit up the doctor's face as she looked at her subject. Since Dr. Crawford was one of the leading marine biologists on Earth in the field of the Navigators, she was chosen to come along for the diplomatic run, tending to the *Kota's* personal Navigator.

While this photo was supposed to be classified, someone had gotten a hold of it and it was now the poster shot of humanity's willingness to collaborate with the stars. The doctor had become an intergalactic celebrity in a matter of months.

Nate looked over the photo and her bio as they walked down the street. The streets, as they were referred to, were mezzanines that jutted out from the station's walls under the clear dome, making the layers like a bowl so every street could get a view of the expanse. As Nate and Halvie made their way to the upper ring, more and more onlookers were joining the pilgrimage. Aliens big and small were making their way to the upper floors, trying to get as close as they could to look at the docks. Whole Naanth families scampered by; Nate saw a father with three of his litter climbing over his back and head. Herriots from the lower class trying to shoulder their way through, only for the lumbering Jaxr (an eight foot tall armored biped that could be best described as an armadillo with an extra set of eyes) to push back. Even a group of Freesons, skin colours from pale white to dark obsidian tried to rush by to get a look at their lost brethren. There were view screens all over the domes to give a better view of Earth's diplomatic party, but no matter the resolution of the cameras, people wanted to see them in person. Decades after this event, people would tell their friends and children of the day they saw the Earthlings exit their vessel and join the rest of the universe; it was through two domes and across empty space, but they saw them with their own eyes!

The pilgrims made their way to the edge of the dome, faces raised to the stars to get a look at the docking bay outside. There was already a crowd there, heads bobbing back and forth from the docking bay down to the view screens on the wall. The screen's audio was cranked up to hear the Earthlings as they made their way in front of the cameras and the diplomats. One of the Naanth cubs, specifically the one sitting on his father's head, had a personal screen out with the newest article open, pointing to each human and saying their name and occupation. The constant drone of whispered voices and questions was white noise compared to the view screen.

"Look, it's the captain! His face has fur on it!"

"It's called a beard, Earthlings got hair on their mouths."

"How does he fit it all in his helmet?"

"Poorly, that's why Freesons cut it."

"Look, it's Dr. Williams! He sounds funny, what's he speaking?"

"It's called Britain, it's a language from Earth. They have a bunch of languages there; English, France, Britain, Japanese, to name a few."

Nate eavesdropped on the crowd as he looked to the docking bay, eyes darting to the nearest screen to watch each Earthling step out from their ship, looking over the crowds cheering in various languages. He finally saw who he was looking for: Dr. Crawford stepped out onto the stage built in the docking bay, beautiful blue eyes bulging with surprise. A professional like her was prepared to see the crowd of aliens on the station; what she wasn't prepared for was the signs. The crowd of aliens around the stage had personally made signs and painted their pressure suits with various Earthling colours. Three Herriots at the front of the crowd had the Union Jack painted over their blue faces. Her name was the only thing she could pick out on signs covered in alien languages she didn't understand. Dr. Crawford was expecting aliens, she wasn't ready for fans.

"I think we should go meet her," Nate spoke without taking his eyes off the view screen.

"Excuse me?" Halvie looked up to his friend.

"I think we should go meet them, the Earthlings I mean. They should know that there are other humans out here; they need a man on the inside." He waved to the screens at the Risen officials bowing and shaking hands. "That crowd probably got every Freeson out of the docking bay and government dome so the Earthlings don't know about other humans. I think we should introduce ourselves so the Earthlings will have some equal footing in space."

Halvie listened to Nate's speech with a frown of disbelief, gaze darting from the screen to his friend. When he recognized Dr. Crawford, his eyes narrowed.

"That's the only reason, to help the humans. The only reason, *no other reason*?"

"What other reason would there be?"

"You can't think of any other reason to see the humans? Any other reason to meet Crawford. *No other reason at all?*"

"Stop saying reason, Halvie."

"Stop feeding me lies, Nathan."

Nate just shrugged and tried to look unconcerned, but the Naanth wasn't buying it. Halvie looked back at the vid screen, which was now a close-up view of the biologist. His ermine-like nose flared and let out a snort.

"You got to be crazy, thinking you're getting anywhere near the Earthlings. Someone like us can't get clearance to the soirees and if you show up at the front door every sentry there will tackle you." Halvie listed all the problems on each finger of his lower paws, the upper set waving around to emphasize the idiocy of the notion.

"I have a plan to get in," Nate said so casually it made Halvie's ears flatten in bottled rage.

"Oh, do you now?!"

"Yes. It's not that hard either, we're already halfway done." Before the Naanth could protest, Nate took hold of his friend's shoulder and turned him around, jostling through the crowd who didn't seem to notice their presence. Once they were away from the crowd, they skirted into one of the side passages between the barracks. There, Nate pulled out what looked to be an ID band.

"Wha-" Halvie took the band and looked it over, one finger rubbing past the screen until a name came up. "Tonnis G'cha… You stole that drunk's ID band?!" Halvie's deep voice went up an octave before Nate grabbed his muzzle and shushed him.

"Why don't you tell the whole bloody district? Or maybe a few sentries!"

"I very well should! Stealing an officer's ID band is not just some fine, Nate! You could be sent to one of the penal colonies for a year! And may very well drag me there too!" Halvie grabbed Nate's shirt with all four paws. "You may find a bunch of Freeson buddies up there in jail, but I don't know how many Naanths will be there! I'll be the littlest guy in jail!"

"Oh, come now, like the Naanth are angels. Half of your lot are space faring hoodlums."

"I don't know what an angel is."

"Whatever! We're getting off topic. Look, I have his ID band, and he's so drunk he'll be out for the rest of the day and well into the night. By the time he figures out it's gone, we'll be done. I'll even bring it back, Freeson's honour." Nate ran two fingers across his chest and lifted them in the air. Halvie just rolled his eyes.

"Yeah, yeah, you got the ID band but I don't really think you'll pass as a Herriot. But I might be a cynic." Halvie reached up and grabbed hold of Nate's nose. The Freeson let out a snort and stood up.

"I have that covered too, come back to the ship, I'll explain everything." And with that Nate gave a wink and slipped the ID band back into his suit.

"This plan is stupid, we are so screwed…." Halvie's voice came through the helmet's speaker into Nate's left ear.

"Come now, we have all the gear, no one is the wiser." Nate was marching through the upper dome that belonged to the station's top officials and officers, wearing a suit of Herriot Sentry armor. With the helmet and the obscuring face mask, he looked like any other Herriot, albeit a short one. It wasn't very difficult procuring the armor; they were pretty cheap on the under market at the station. It even came with the standard electro baton. "They can't tell who I am, and as long as I keep my pants on no one will know."

"A consistent problem for you if I recall." Halvie snickered on the speaker; Nate just ignored it. He was marching up to the new gate placed at the upper residential dome where the top station officials' quarters were located. There were three-storey complexes with lawns and a mansion-like community centre where the station held diplomatic events and parties. Since the Earthlings were attending for the first time, half of the dome was cordoned off. Sentries stood by the gates holding back the crowd of civilians with signs and fan paint. Just out of throwing distance from the sentries were booths built from debris and loose tiles from the lower quarters that had probably been put up in the span of minutes. They were selling "authentic Earthling paraphernalia", which consisted of flags, tower souvenirs, and bobble heads of some queen.

The crowd instinctively widened for Nate in the armor, allowing him to walk up to the nearest gate. Nate flashed his ID band to the guard, who pulled out a gun-like sensor and pointed it at Nate's wrist. With a click Tonnis G'cha's information appeared on the screen. The Herriot grunted under his helmet.

"You're not supposed to be on shift tonight."

"They called me in early, the lot of us are coming in for extra security. There'll be more in a few hours." Nate slouched his shoulders and gave a fake exhale. "Orders from the Risen council themselves; can't do much about it." The guard swore under his breath but let Nate pass. Nate tapped him on the shoulder, a sign of comradery amongst the Herriots, and marched off past the gate.

"Wow, didn't think that would work," Halvie muttered through the speaker. Nate turned to look back as he marched. Looking up at the edge of the upper residential dome, if he squinted hard enough, he could just make out a lump on the roof of a building. Nate knew Halvie was lying down on the roof, binoculars to his eyes and a com link to his ear. "All the diplomats are heading through the front. It's being guarded and it doesn't look like any of the sentries are moving there so I don't advise trying to meet her there. From what I can see, there's a service entrance for the staff, on the east side of the complex."

"Meet *them*, you mean," Nate corrected, scanning the front of the complex for the service entrance, seeing a pair of sentries on the side watching the door. He marched up and saluted to the guards before heading inside. Even on the side of the complex, he could hear music and chatter from the party. The service hall was empty so Nate speed walked through.

"No, I think I was right the first time." Nate could hear the thick sass through the speaker. He didn't have a rebuttal so kept his mouth shut; he still needed his friend to watch the entrance for any problems.

Further into the complex, the decorations became more frivolous and flashy; in the main hallway holographic galaxies and stars flashed over the ceiling, with names and coordinates appearing occasionally. The names changed between Ascended, English, Herriot, and Hindi. Planets flashed various colours to show the spread of Risen through the centuries. Over at the entrance of the main hall, the Sol System was overgrown and flashing a luminescent blue, changing to a magnificent silver to exemplify it joining the Risen.

Back in the public eye, Nate fell into the march, appearing to make his rounds of the hall as the party goers drank and mused over delicacies. Slipping past a crowd of diplomats, Nate stepped into the large ball room and pressed himself against the wall, looking across extravagant room slowly.

Speckles of green could be seen through the crowd of aliens; all the Earthlings wore a dark green dress uniform to the party, the glint of golden embroidery glittered on the left breast in the light. The embroidery was of the Sol System's star and at the bottom was a silver planet that was supposed to be Earth. The Earthling's dress uniforms seemed drab compared to the diplomats of the Risen, who wore flashy robes and pressure suits, looking like magnificent peacocks rather than officials. The only other group wearing anything conservative were the Herriot Generals, whose dress uniforms looked more along the lines of battle armor.

Nate kept his eye out for Dr. Crawford, mumbling the names of the various officers as he spotted them. Captain Sanyal could be easily picked out from the bright crimson turban he wore, along with the service medals on his chest. He was sitting at the main table with a Jaxr diplomat, his second officer keeping an eye on the party goers while Sanyal made small talk. Throughout the ball room the aliens seem to congregate around the Earthlings, being polite but asking dozens of questions to each officer. Most of the Earthlings took it all in stride, but a few looked a bit overwhelmed, trying to speak in Risen while being questioned on all sides.

Suddenly a flash of blonde caught Nate's eye, and he turned to see Dr. Crawford coming into the room from the entrance on the opposite side. A Naanth elder was with her, explaining something, and Dr. Crawford nodded occasionally before asking her own questions. She almost bumped into a few diplomats as she spoke to the Naanth, so transfixed on whatever topic they were discussing that they could have been in an empty room for all they cared.

Nate gently pushed off the wall, heading into the crowd of party goers, with such subtly that a few diplomats turned to look at the sentry leaving their post. He hadn't thought of how he was going to get Dr. Crawford's attention, or how he was going to take his helmet off in the middle of a crowd. Honestly, Nate's plans usually never had an ending; he found that once a scheme was in motion, variables and coincidences always made a mess of a well thought out plan. So after he figured out how to initiate it he just winged the rest, which made his skill for improvisation and thinking on his feet all the better.

But now he was walking up to a woman he had never actually met but felt he knew so much about because of her articles. He didn't know what to say without sounding like a stalker, so as he walked across the ball room, his pace slowed, and his mind was a jumble. He'd come up with something before he reached the pair.

"Yes? Is something wrong, sentry?" the Naanth elder asked, pulling her attention away from Crawford.

"Umm... Dr. Crawford?" Nate asked, ignoring the Naanth's question.

"Yes? May I help you?" Dr. Crawford turned to look at Nate's face, which was hidden behind the helmet, crystal blue eyes sparkling in the light. Nate just looked at her, getting lost in her brilliant gaze and soft demeanor. He blanked, couldn't think of any way to go about this properly. He let out a sigh and pressed the lock on the side of the helmet, releasing the skin tight clips so he could take off his helmet. Crawford looked a little perplexed but waited for the sentry to speak.

"Nate! You got to leave now!" Halvie's voice cut through the tension, snapping Nate out of his awkward fumbling. He turned around and spoke through the helmet in a hushed whisper.

"What's wrong? I'm right in front of her!" Nate complained but was relieved to be given a few extra seconds to think of something to say, not that it would matter.

"Your drunk Herriot friend came to the gate and is yelling at the officer in the front. Even I can tell he's screaming about his stolen ID band. Soldiers are running to the complex, they know you're a fake!" Halvie's voice was crackling through the speaker, clearing cutting in and out because he's yelling directly into the mic.

"Is everything alright?" Dr. Crawford reached up and touched his shoulder. Nate felt flustered; she was gentle in getting his attention, just a little pat to get his attention, but not too pushy seeing as he was talking on the helmet radio.

"Umm… got to go, Doctor!" Nate noticed sentries coming into the ballroom, looking around, one saw him near Crawford and pointed to him. The sentry and his compatriots began to slip into the crowd, trying to get to him as quickly as possible without stirring up the diplomats. Nate turned and looked at Crawford. "Talk to you later!"

Before Crawford could say anything, Nate sped-walked through the crowd in the opposite direction. When he made it to the hallway he started to sprint, making his way to the nearest service exit. He couldn't go back the way he came and he didn't know what was on this side of the complex.

"Halvie, where's the exit on this side of the building?" Nate growled through the mic, taking a turn down a side hallway before he came upon a pair of sentries. Nate edged back and rushed for the nearest room, heading inside to see it was some office.

"What other exit? All I can see is the main door and the service entrance you came in before. What other entrance?"

"A place this big can't have only two doors!"

"Well, try the back! I can't see anything from this vantage point; you didn't look this place up beforehand?"

"I didn't have time!" Nate swore and quietly opened the door a crack, enough to peer out, hoping the sentries had already passed. Looking through the crack he couldn't see anyone, but there was a commotion coming from the main hall. Slipping out, he rushed down the hall, opening doors as he went. Everything in that wing of the complex was offices, one after the other.

After coming upon half a dozen private rooms, Nate opened a door to find a stairwell. All he could hope for at this point would be to go up a floor and make his way back to the service entrance. From there he'd have to find a way to skirt past the gate or find another exit out of the dome. But that was a plan for later, getting out of the complex will be hard enough.

"Hey! Stop, soldier!" someone called down the hall.

Nate turned to see a sentry running toward him. He swore and pushed the door open, running up the stairs as fast as he could. He could hear the sentry gain up on him, and Nate took the stairs three at a time, running past the second floor entrance.

Before he could reach the third floor, he felt a hand wrap around his ankle and pull it away. Nate turned to see the sentry had caught up to him on the stairs; clearly he had taken the stairs four at a time. The bigger soldier pulled him down and let go of his ankle, letting Nate tumble down the stairs towards the second floor entrance. Nate tried to break his fall by rolling, but slammed into the metal wall hard, his shoulder and arm getting caught under his body and his head hitting the side of the door. Pain sprouted throughout his body as he rolled over, groaning as stars and lights sparked into view. A heavy weight slammed down onto his chest; thankfully the sentry body armour kept his ribs from caving in. The sentry had pinned him down with one foot and leaned over to grab Nate's helmet with both hands. Nate felt the helmet get roughly pulled off and flung to the ground.

"What the-?" The sentry pulled back in shock, not expecting to find a human in the armour. Luckily this gave Nate an opening. Using his free hand, he grabbed for the baton magnetically strapped to his side. When his fingers wrapped around the handle, the magnet released and the baton extended to its full length, a faint buzzing noise echoed from the tip.

Before the sentry could react, Nate swung out and slammed the tip into his attacker's chest. The sentry's body locked up and started to seizure, the electricity travelling through his body caused him to stagger back, foot sliding off Nate's chest. Nate rolled forward onto his knees, using his bad shoulder to slam into the sentry's abdomen; a wave of pain blossomed but he shoved hard. The sentry fell back and tumbled down the stairs to the first floor, hitting the door with a hard smack.

Nate got to his feet and gripped the rail for support, looking down at his attacker. The realization that he just attacked an officer of the law and threw him down the stairs started to dawn on him as he looked down to the limp, silent body. Nate's lip quivered as he realized that they could add "murder" to the list of charges when they caught him. He was thinking about going to down check on him when the sentry let out a pained groan.

"Oh, thank God he's alive!" Nate shuddered, stepping back and opening the door to the second floor, only to see three more sentries running his way.

"Stop right there, Freeson!" one yelled as Nate slammed the door and ran up past the third floor. He wasn't thinking at this point, just running on adrenaline and regret, running to the last door on the stairs and swinging it open. Nate found himself on the roof of the complex, frantically searching to find any way to get out of there. In the middle was a large glass dome, the lights of the ball room ascending out into the starry sky. He skirted around the dome, looking down to see most of the guests were seated at this point; one of the Risen top diplomats was standing, giving a dry speech to all those assembled.

Nate's head darted the way he came: the door had swung open and the three sentries had rushed out onto the roof, spreading out and quickly descending upon him. Nate looked across the roof; his face lit up when he saw a second roof entrance on the other side. If he could just make it there, he could rush to the first floor and back to the side entrance, find a place to take off the suit and make it back to Halvie, then they could head back to the other domes and stay low for a few days. All he needed to do was get back to the ground floor!

He was running at full speed now, listening to the sentries call out to him as they made to surround him, but he'd reach the other door before them, and then just glide down the stairs and out door.

But Nate felt his heart drop as the door opened thirty feet ahead of him to reveal four more sentries who stepped out onto the roof and spread out. Nate took a hard turn on his feet and found the glass dome in front of him, with soldiers on all sides and closing in. Nate's chest was heaving, eyes darting to look for any space between his assailants but could find none. There were sentries everywhere except the glass dome in front of him. He looked at the ever-shrinking circle of angry soldiers with batons and did the math. If he could get across the dome, it was a straight path right to the door, while the soldiers took the long route around it, he could make it in time.

Nate took a deep breath and darted; the soldiers were

less than ten feet from him when his foot reached the glass. As batons were raised and swung down, Nate took a leap, legs splayed out in the open air as he jumped as far as he could out onto the dome. He looked down at the party below, three stories and a sheet of glass between him and the floor. If the Risen could build fully functional, self-sustaining space stations to keep out of the void of space, surely they could construct a layer of glass that held the weight of a single Freeson.

Nate's front foot stepped onto the glass and took the rest of his weight a heartbeat later. It was a few seconds of silence, and Nate smiled triumphantly as the rest of his back leg pulled in to make a second leap. But it was only a few seconds until the silence was broken when a spider-web of cracks blossomed across the glass.

His back leg didn't even touch the glass before it all crumbled below him. Nate turned to look back as his body began to fall through the new hole, meeting the shielded faces of the sentries behind him. A few reached out, having dropped their batons and spread their hands to grab for something, any part of Nate. The Freeson reached out as well, but he was already too far gone for it to do any good. More glass started to shatter around him; the air was filled with the light shimmer of fragments dancing their way to the ground, and Nate, the belle of that deadly ball, twisting in the air. He could hear gasps and screams coming from below as he plummeted, legs flailing and arms out wide to grab for something to slow him down. There was nothing within reach, but Nate kept grabbing at the empty air as he fell closer and closer to the ground.

Something finally slowed him down, and the Freeson hit one of the tables before he hit the ground. He tried to curl up in a ball to protect his head, hoping the sentry armour would take most of the impact, but Nate hit so hard it knocked the wind out of him, and the table broke under his weight. Waves of pain spread throughout his body and Nate cried out, gasping as he tried to breathe. He felt his head crack against a plate of food, debris and food flew everywhere as he lay atop the broken table.

All Nate could see was black spots in the corner of his vision and the blinding lights of the party. Voices and yelling broke through the pain, making it all the harder for him to compose himself and figure out how broken his body really was. He could feel a few spears of white-hot pain in his chest; he knew he broke a few ribs on the fall, and one leg felt out of place. A crowd was forming around him but he couldn't make out a single face in all the pain.

But then a lock of blonde hair caught his eye. With great struggle, Nate turned his head to see a familiar face right above him. The beautiful blue eyes of Dr. Crawford were wide with shock, her face looking paler from what it did in their first meeting. Nate pulled his hand out of a mash of what used to be a cake and lifted it, extending his hand in what he hoped looked like a formal greeting.

"Hey Dr. Crawford, welcome to-" Nate's greeting was rudely cut short when the bottom of a wine bottle slammed into the top of his face. If the fall and the bottle didn't knock him out, the three electro batons that followed sure as hell did.

Nate was lying down in the cell when Halvie was flung inside, having been told by the prison doctor it would take a few hours for the Risen nano-gel to work on mending his broken ribs and leg. It wasn't a nice experience, so he called out a greeting but didn't move. His friend didn't speak, just got off the floor and climbed up onto the second bunk. Nate caught a glimpse of his face before he disappeared onto the bed; one ear was covered in a bandage and his snout was puffy and bruised. Clearly when the sentries found his hiding spot, the Naanth didn't go down quietly.

The two prisoners spent the night in silence. Nate tried to ask his friend what happened, but no matter what he said Halvie wouldn't speak. So Nate gave up and tried to sleep through the mending pains. It took a while but he finally passed out, only to be woken up when Halvie dropped the breakfast tray on his chest in the morning.

Nate swore through the pain and sat up, just grabbing his tray before it tumbled over. While he was still sore as hell, the nano-gel had done its job. Halvie hopped up onto Nate's bunk and ate his slop, not making eye contact with his comrade.

"Hey bud…. So sorry about--"

"About dragging me into your idiotic plan as lookout? About getting my tail flung into jail and probably sent off to the nearest penal colony out in the sticks of space? Or about getting me in the position to get tazed and roughed up by Herriot sentries, who are tall to you, so they're *gigantic* compared to me!"

"I never told you to fight back-"

"They weren't really looking for a quiet surrender by that point!" Halvie's snarl made Nate jump, almost spilling his slop on the floor. It looked like Halvie's list of regrets could have gone on longer if they weren't interrupted by the noise of the sliding door. Both prisoners fell silent as they heard two pairs of footsteps make their way to the cell. The first was a sentry, who plugged in the code for the cell's see-through barrier, which slid up with only a quiet *hiss*.

The second newcomer made both prisoners stand up in shock, Dr. Amelia Crawford stepped out from behind the sentry. She was now wearing the regular uniform of the Earth crew, made of the same green material but without the gold fringes, and a pale blue band across both shoulders that designated her as a Science Officer. Out of the ballroom Crawford's hair was pulled up into a practical bun. She gave a flick of her wrist and revealed an ID band, the holographic view screen appeared and she looked it over.

"Mr. Doshi, I presume, and…?" She looked over Halvie, who stood at attention almost militaristically. Nate raised an eyebrow at his friend's newfound formality.

"Halvie Scorz ma'am, originally from the Scorz-Mallo colony fleet," Halvie introduced himself and gave a little bow.

"Ah yes, thank you, my contact information was only on Mr. Doshi, but I was informed that he had an accomplice. My apologies for my crew's lack of data."

"No apology needed, ma'am, he is the one with the stiffer charges." Halvie's eyes darted to Nate for a second before going back to Crawford.

"Yes, that is apparent to all of us. I could list them all if you like: trespassing, impersonation of a sentry officer, assault-" Crawford read them out in a calm, apathetic voice, as if she was reading off the menu of a restaurant.

"But not murder, right?" Nate asked meekly, the lump of regret forming in his gut about shoving that Herriot down the stairs.

"No, the sentry you threw down the stairs will make a full recovery. I'm not an expert on Herriot biology but from what I gather he had their version of a concussion and a minor burn from the electro baton. But nothing too serious." The holographic screen disappeared. "But the list is long enough to send both of you away for a very long time. If it wasn't for the community service deal...."

"Community service?!" Nate and Halvie stepped forward, wanting to press her more on the possibility of not rotting away in a penal colony. But the second they moved towards Crawford, the sentry whipped out his baton and stepped into a menacing stance. The two prisoners jumped back with their hands up, but Crawford placed her hand on the sentry's baton arm and lowered it.

"Yes. It was quite a surprise to have a human tumble out of the sky in the middle of the soirees, especially since we were supposed to be the only humans on the space station. Captain Sanyal demanded an explanation after that, and we were all the more shocked to find out there is an entire civilization of humans living out in space."

"That's why I was trying to meet you, doctor!" Nate spoke up, Crawford gave him a perplexed look, and Nate could feel the glare Halvie was drilling into the back of his head. But Nate just smiled at Crawford and waited for her response.

"Whatever the reason for breaking into a private venue and throwing yourself off the roof, the captain finds the act a little admirable."

"Really?" Halvie snorted. Nate turned and shot a glare right back at him but did no more. Crawford's first impression of him wasn't the best, and he didn't want her seeing him give Halvie's ear a smack.

"Yes, not the whole assault and running from the authorities, but the fact that you risked your life to tell your fellow humans that the Risen are keeping secrets from us. And then the captain said, '*If they are keeping these Freesons out of view, what else are they hiding?'"* Crawford turned a gaze to the sentry, who had been silent up to this point, then the Herriot gave a little cough and looked away. "So the captain proposed the idea of community service for you. We have quite a few Risen guides on board now, but he would like someone on board who isn't controlled by the Risen, someone who has humanity's best interest at heart."

"That's me, ma'am, I'm your man!" Nate stomped a boot and gave a salute. He was hoping it looked somewhat respectable, but Crawford's scowl said otherwise.

"Yes, well, at the very least we paid your bail and debated with the Risen to have you both on board our vessel. I feel Mr. Scorz will give more level-headed advice on our journey."

"You're right about that..." Halvie snorted.

The two companions left the cell and followed the doctor down the hall, giving a fiendish grin to the silent sentry as they passed. "But not to sound rude of anything, ma'am, but I do have one question. Why were you sent down to pick us up? You must have more responsibilities then dragging us out of jail." With that Crawford seemed to fluster, she frowned and looked away. Nate and Halvie waited for her response, surprised to see such a professional person look embarrassed.

"Well, seeing as we will be working together for the rest of the journey, the captain felt it would be better for me to come down and apologize for striking Mr. Doshi with the wine bottle at the soirees." Crawford's gaze was focused entirely on the door in front of them, trying her best to not look either of them in the face.

"That was you?!"

"Yes. You fell from the sky and all Earthling officers

are trained in basic combat, to protect ourselves in case of a possible threat. At the time you were a possible threat."

"But with a wine bottle…"

"Anything can be used as a weapon. That said, I apologize that you put us in a situation that led to me hitting you."

"That's not much of an apology…"

"That's all you'll get. Now come along, we have a whole orientation to get through before you're ready for the vessel." And with that, Crawford marched through the door.

Nate watched her leave, a smile growing across his face. He leaned over and whispered in his companion's ear, "So my plan worked!" He winked and watched Halvie's fur bristle.

"Like hell you're taking credit for all this! You got us thrown in jail and beaten up by sentries!"

"Yeah, but the plan still worked, we're going to go work with the humans, aren't we?" Nate waited for his friend to rebuke his statement, but the Naanth just growled and stomped out through the door.

Nate chuckled, wincing at his sore ribs, and limped out the door. All in all, the plan was a leap of faith, and to a Freeson that's all you need to make it in this galaxy. Nate Doshi followed Dr. Crawford out of prison that day, whistling an old Earth tune as if the whole night was nothing more than a skip down to the docking bay.

JRH Lawless

J.R.H. Lawless writes Science Fiction full of dark humour and hope.

Lawless is a multiple award-winning Canadian SF author who blends comedy with political themes — drawing heavily, in both cases, on his experience as a lawyer and as Secretary General of a Parliamentary group at the French National Assembly.

A member of SFWA and Codex Writers, his short fiction has been published in professional venues, and most recently in the Third Flatiron Press *Terra! Tara! Terror!* anthology, to great reviews, placement as 2018 Recommended Reading, and an award for Best Positive Future Story 2018.

Lawless is also a craft article contributor to the SFWA blog, the SFWA Bulletin, and Tor.com.

Lawless' tale recounts the story of *L'Oiseau Blanc*, a historically famous lost plane.

His first novel, *Always Greener,* was released in February 2020.

Breaking the Ice

[Original, unedited TransSER Expedition Log #72 6f 6d 65 6f – Start
Timestamp: 04/21/2531, 07:12 Standard
Reporting Agent: Ja'far Beidegger]

The damn green recording light flashes in my HUD while I'm projectile vomiting sticky blue cryogenic fluid. Great. The lenses chose the perfect time to start the mission log. An awesome start to this historic mission.

I close my eyes, retch some more, and offer a silent prayer to whatever gods might be listening out here, around Gamma Leonis. At least I remembered to put the bucket next to the cryo bed before setting out from Regulus — nearly fifty light-years away.

When I've finally got the last of the sour, blood-tasting fluid out of my stomach, I open my bleary eyes. Pulling up an augmented reality overlay to cover the ugly machinery of my tiny, window-less control room, I take in the view from outside the Lightway shuttle. And there they are, like I've always pictured them: the twin stars of Gamma Leonis.

Massive as they are, both local stars are dwarfed by

the creamy orange monstrosity of a gas giant in front of the shuttle — that is, if you give in to instinct and call the lightsails at the rear as the "back", and the opposite, the direction of propulsion when the laser thrust beam hits the lightsails, the "front".

Gamma Leonis b is an absolute beast of a planet. Roughly the same size as Jupiter back around Sol, but denser than lead, giving it the look of a peach-coloured, heavy metal marble.

But my real destination hangs above me, and I crane my head to get a good first look at what will, I hope and dream, be the crowning achievement of a long career in service of TransSER — that's Transbody Space Executive Reporter, for the uninitiated — and its imperative mission: finding intelligent life in the cosmos that humankind can sit down with and have a meaningful exchange of ideas.

Gamma Leonis b's single moon glitters above me like a diamond tucked away by some cosmic jewel smuggler. The TransSER probes confirmed the presence of advanced biological life signs and technology in the liquid water ocean beneath the moon's icy shell. And now, as a result, here I am, for the manned first contact mission. Like they say, there's no replacement for the human touch. They tried to use probes to make first contact with the sentients around Denebola, a century or two ago, and failed. They still haven't managed to sort out the resulting confusion with the natives.

Speaking of probes, I trigger another button in my AR display and watch as the little ion propulsion constructor probes set off to collect bits of interplanetary dust. They'll soon have the Lightway laser thrust station up and running at the nearest local Lagrange point. My ticket back to home base at Regulus.

With that final pre-mission task ticked off my checklist, I power down the AR projection. I fight back a twinge of disappointment as the glorious starscape disappears, revealing the drab, functional confines of my Lightway shuttle.

There's nothing left to do but to suit up and head on over to the target.

This is my chance to make history. What I've sacrificed my friends and my family for, as well as any chance at a normal life.

And yet, all I feel is numbness. Even if I do discover yet another intelligent species down there, will it mean anything, in the vastness of space? Can it really change anything? Even for a single person amidst the hundreds of billions of variform humans spread out across a thousand solar systems?

I shrug off my musings and get on with climbing into the exo-suit set into the hull of the shuttle. I didn't come all this way to sit here and eff around with the ineffable. On with the show.

The ice-encased world zooms up with all the inevitability of an income tax deadline. My jets cut off just in time to allow me to spin and make a crunching landing that barely destroys my kneecaps at all. There's a good bit more gravity here than I expected.

Limping somewhat, I take humanity's first steps on Gamma Leonis b1. This designation is a mouthful, so I decide to use the momentous occasion to name the moon — at least until we can find out what the natives call it.

"Globie," I say into the confines of my bulky exo-suit helmet, for the benefit of the official log recording my senses and thoughts. "I shall call you Globie."

Globie doesn't seem to care particularly much. Its outer shell shines blindingly bright, reflecting all its giant sun's brilliance. Only the maze of deep fissures and cracks under the constant stress of heat and freeze, of tidal push and pull, give the landscape any sort of depth. And I'm well aware that those cracks are barely skin deep; a mere blemish on the surface of the kilometre-thick icy shell beneath my boots.

I set down my little transport crate full of scientific equipment with a sigh. It's going to be long, hard work getting any kind of a reading through this much ice. And even if the probe readings are right and there is technology down there in the dark, how can I get any sort of reaction from them with remote signals?

Such a waste of time. If only TransSER guidelines weren't so cautious, I could skip the months of waiting around and just drill down into the ice to meet whatever's down there. But no, life can never be as simple as you wish.

And with perfect ironic timing, that's when the Universe decides to teach me a lesson about being careful what you wish for. A terrific rumble vibrates up my legs in the soundless environment, and the ice splits and fractures, a mere fifty metres sunwards from my landing spot.

The rumble grows to a fever pitch, and it's all I can do to keep my footing on the ice. Then it stops, and shards of ice fly up into the vacuum, shimmering in the Gamma Leonis glare. The blinding light reveals a monstrous sight, a vision straight out of a nightmare: sharp, tentacular metal claws emerging from the ice, gripping onto the icy crust of the moon and pulling, as if dragging a heavy weight up to the surface.

Before the thought of fleeing can even form in my mind, I soon see what the claws are lifting, and curiosity erases any potential thought of leaving. At the centre of a sea urchin-like mass of tentacular metal limbs, still dripping with the water of the world-sea below, lies what I can only describe as a form-fitting, oily rubber suit, encasing some sort of giant, rugged shell creature, not entirely unlike a giant clam back in humanity's neck of the galaxy.

The sight is so unexpected that it takes me a moment to come to grips with what I'm seeing. And at first, it's the smallest details that capture my attention, like how the gripping metallic claws seem to have little gooey apertures, like membranes, all along their length. They use these to probe at the ice and even at the vacuum around them, as if searching tentatively as they pull the central mass forwards.

Then my own thoughts catch up with me and I realise that, whatever this fearsome apparition is, one thing is certain: it's moving straight for me.

Eyes still rivetted to the creature, I take an instinctive step back, bump into the crate of measuring equipment, and fall straight onto my heavy-suited rump. The suit and I hit the ice with a helmet-rattling clunk, and I watch in fascination as the Globite — for this must be one of the native lifeforms in the hardened flesh — fixes immediately on my position, and charges forwards with new vigour, all hesitation gone.

Some sort of tremor sense? It would explain how it located me in the first place, with the impact of my landing, but I have no further time for speculation before the thing is upon me. With my back pinned against the ice, my jets would rip my suit apart, and the massive creature beats my struggling arms out of the way with no effort at all.

I scream inside my helmet and brace myself for the hiss of decompression as it tears into my suit and I die, alone and cut off from the rest of humanity, who will never even get to see my mission log. But that moment never comes, and I soon realise that the Globite is being surprisingly careful. Gentle, even.

It prods my exo-suit all over, yes, with special attention to the seals and the oxygen tank connectors. But it never breaks or pierces the suit, which must be extremely difficult, given how sharp those tentacle limbs are... and how easily they tore through the icy shell of the moon.

Just as I'm observing it, the Globite is clearly analysing me, with whatever unknowable senses and thought processes govern its decisions. It doesn't have any eyes I can identify, or any orifices at all, as far as I can tell.

It's been a long, long time since my core xenobiology classes. And that's not even taking into account the fifty years in cryo. But from where I lay, pinned beneath the weight of the handsy shell-creature, my best guess is that those membrane-like apertures in the metal tentacles play some sort of sensory role. Some kind of touch-based perception, perhaps?

And that's when I get a much closer look at those membranes than I ever wanted to. The creature clearly reaches some sort of decision about me, as it flexes half of its tentacles and wraps them around me, engulfing my exo-suit and holding me tightly in place. The other half of the appendages act as octopi's legs to move the two of us back over to the hole drilled up out of the ice.

I'm none too proud of the scream of horror that echoes in the confines of my helmet as the creature plunges down the hole, taking me along with it, powerless and captive, into the depths below.

My new quarters are roughly the same size as the cabin back on the Lightway shuttle and nearly as ugly.

When the creature finished dragging me through the dark ocean depths and arrived in some sort of laboratory, I was almost relieved. At least there was some wavering, chemical light here. It illuminated a bank of various-sized vats, some underwater, some with bubbling air, and all filled with a dizzying array of organic life.

My relief was very short-lived, however, since the creature proceeded to slit my exo-suit down the middle with one sharp metal claw, and I promptly started drowning in water that felt strangely warm and comfortable.

Surprised, yet sensing my distress, my captor hurried to shove me into an airlock-style mechanism, which then cycled and dumped me out into a mass of black spiky fungus growths in what has since been my pungent new prison cell down here, under the ice of the far too cutely-named Globie, with my implants severed from any connection with the outside Universe.

There is no doubt that I'm being held, in nothing more than my regulation TransSER undergarments, in some sort of aerobic life storage vat in the biology laboratory of my captor. In the gloom of their own natural habitat, the Globites are even more reminiscent of giant clams: large, craggy shells, with anywhere between two and six mechanical limbs manipulated by any of the dozens of porous, flexing membranes spread across their thick defences.

There are many individuals who come and go in the lab, which is clearly an active workplace. The only sounds are deep booming echoes that resonate everywhere, plus the local buzz of machinery, so I try to learn what I can from the glimpses I get at the edge of the bioluminescence in my vat. Some of the shells are spikier than others, and all have some pattern of external growths, usually in drab browns and blacks barely distinguishable from the shell itself. The one exception is my captor, whose bright purple patterns are burned into my memory from when it nearly drowned me.

In fact, the patterns remind me of nothing less than the beautiful coral reefs colonists sometimes grow on terraformed planets. Out of some subconscious bias, the patterns and the colour make me start thinking about my captor as "her" instead of "it". I highly doubt my perception of my captor's gender is of any importance under the circumstances, but in my own mind, I decide to name her Coral. A vain attempt at asserting some control of the situation, no doubt, but the name sticks.

The Globites all come over to my vat every now and again, to manipulate the machinery with their mechanical prosthesis. Sometimes there's a pumping noise, and a feeling of suction which leads me to believe that some of the air has been drawn out of the chamber. At other times, one of the Globite appendages enters the chamber, like a manipulator in a containment field. Sensor membranes flexing and tasting the air, it snakes towards the one of the pulsating growths covering the nutrient solution on the vat floor, before snipping off a clump or a stem and promptly pulling it back out into the water, for unfathomable purposes.

I soon stop being scared of the sharp, intruding limbs. There's little I could do if they decided to do me harm, and there's even less hope of escape. I'm far, far deeper down than I could possibly hold my breath, and with my exo-suit still laying slashed open in a corner of the laboratory, the only thing waiting for me at the other end of the drill hole is the vacuum of space. Assuming I could even find the damn thing again.

So instead, if only in an attempt to remain sane, I focus my efforts on learning about my captors. And especially Coral, who seems to be spending an inordinate amount of time trying to learn about me as well. For starters, she's the only one who notices that I don't just take root or suck on the nutrient fluids running along the floor of the vat in a steady flow.

It takes some trial and error, since hand gestures, body language, and spoken words seem absolutely unable to convey the message that no, I can't eat the rocks or the soapy substances she shoves through a sealed flap in the vat for me. The biggest reaction I get from her is when, exhausted from gesticulating and shouting, I flop panting on top of what looks like a tree stump, and try to catch my breath.

Coral's manipulator arm drops the blessedly edible piece of seaweed-like growth my exertions have finally earned me, and suddenly perks up, membranes flaring. Snaking over towards me, it wavers through the air beside my head and my torso, as if intrigued. As nervous as the sharp metal hovering near my face is making me, I make a conscious effort to calm my body and centre myself, using the meditation techniques they taught us in the TransSER mission prep classes, one deep breath after another.

Just as I feel calm and control wash over me, it's broken by a sudden, surprised jerk from Coral, who retracts her arm in a rush and floats off, somewhat erratically it seems to me. She pauses over by the slashed ruins of my exo-suit, takes a tentative step back towards the vat, then turns and hurries out of the lab altogether.

I don't see Coral again on that first day of my imprisonment under the ice of the Globi moon, which gives me plenty of time to reflect on what must, somehow, have been some form of successful communication, and to plan the next steps.

I eventually fall asleep, struggling to ignore how gross and foul-smelling my fellow vat-mates are, and trying to get my head around these odd beings, how they think, and how to communicate with them, as if my life depended on it — I strongly suspect it does. I wake up to the sound of Coral floating there and working the chamber controls, which is a welcome sight. Especially since, as opposed to yesterday, she seems to be the only Globite in the lab today.

Is it just the clammy equivalent of the weekend, or a bank holiday? Or did Coral specifically take steps in order to be alone with me today?

I soon come to suspect the latter, since the first thing Coral does is struggle into the same airlock mechanism she shoved me into yesterday and emerge into the chamber, in all her purple-patterned glory.

Climbing to my soggy, socked feet, I peer at her up close and in person for the first time, just as she seems to be doing the same to me, not so much with her feelers as with the myriad membranes set directly into her shell.

This is it. This is my chance. Everything in Coral's behaviour has led me to believe that she's a curious creature. Kind, even. If that's false, then none of it matters. But if it's true, that means my life depends on this moment, on managing to convince her that I'm a thinking, intelligent being. One that shouldn't be kept in a vat with the mushrooms and the plants. And that means finding a way to speak her language.

Eyes and vocal chords are useless here, so I do my best to unlearn over three billion years of evolution, and think like a Globite.

I know I don't have long, either. Coral's shell is pulled very tight, which must be the Globite equivalent of holding your breath to dive underwater. She's going way out of her comfort zone here physically and, most likely, psychologically and socially. Why else would she only come in here today, when the lab is empty?

She's going out on a limb here for me. And even if it is a deadly sharp, puckered metal limb, even if she's the one who kidnapped me and dragged me here in the first place, I'm genuinely grateful.

On the off-chance, I bundle that feeling of gratitude up into a tight ball in my mind, and focus on exuding it towards her, with every pore in my grime-covered skin.

I'll never be sure exactly how much of what I was feeling carried through, and how much was lost in translation, but Coral's reaction is unquestionable. She dives on top of me once again — the second time in two days. This time around, her warm metal limbs aren't the only thing caressing my skin; the entire bulk of her shell lowers down on top of me, and with a quiver of excitement I wish I hadn't perceived quite so clearly, the little membranes along the bottom of her shell push against me, sampling the sweat at my neck and the air her crushing weight forces out of my mouth.

Chemoreception, that must be how the Globites communicate, how they perceive the world, how they think! The same way Earth-grown life uses pheromones, but on a far grander scale, completely replacing sight and sound as the dominant forces of evolution and the shapers of intelligent thought.

But with more pressing matters to attend to, I try to bundle together a sense of flattery but also of eagerness to leave, to return home. No small task, especially since chemical signals tend to be very species-specific — let alone planet-specific.

And yet, Coral lifts her crushing weight from me, and I sit up, smiling in triumph and lifting my arms in the air. I did it! I'm on my way back to the shuttle!

But my hope is short-lived, as Coral exists the vat through the airlock, only to return a few moments later with another wad of the foul-tasting seaweed-like substance.

Ah. So, we've found something close to the Globite chemical word for hunger.

This could take some work.

I've got to admire Coral's tenacity. I don't have any choice in the matter, but she could be anywhere. Instead, she chooses to remain in the vat with me for as long as she can hold her breath, which my connection-less HUD clock tracks as roughly half an hour.

It's slow going, but I think we've worked out a few basic signals. It must sound like baby-talk to her, at best, but on top of "hunger", I've found that a series of rapid exhalations, on the edge of hyperventilation, gets a reaction from Coral that feels similar to calling out to someone, and that the meditating trick from earlier makes Coral relax her mechanical limbs as well, as if among friends.

Even more fascinating to me, I start to get some sense

of her chemical messages as well, wafting through the air. It's incredibly vague, especially since the Globites have clearly evolved to communicate through water, but there's a sharp tang on the air which I find stimulating and can't help but associate with curiosity. And there's a floral note too, which arrives most sharply when Coral taps a limb to her shell. I half fancy that's the Globite equivalent of her name, and I can't deny that I think it's quite lovely.

It seems clear we'll probably never reach a level of communication that would let us talk about the specifics of anything, either about her world and view of the Universe, or about humanity and our life spread across hundreds of systems. Hell, I can't even ask her what her favourite colour is, because the notion probably doesn't even exist for Globites. But it's a start, which was more than I had when I woke up this morning.

She doesn't get quite so heavy-handed again with the physical contact, and I'm grateful for that, too. I certainly don't begrudge her the occasional gentle pat of a tentacular appendage at the nape of my neck, or even under my arm, tickling me. I keep telling myself it's the Globite equivalent of an intent stare and take it as a compliment. Hell, under the present circumstances, I'll take any gesture of affection I can get.

And so, it's mid-caress, with Coral in the vat with me, arms extended, that a grey, craggy-shelled Globite enters the laboratory through the cavern at the far end, and pauses, limbs tense.

Coral pulls her arms back, speeds over to the airlock, and rushes over to the clearly shocked intruder. Even pressing up against the transparent vat wall, I can barely see them through the water and with the dim light that makes my implants strain.

But, even among alien clam-creatures, there's no mistaking a row between office co-workers, when one has walked in on the other doing something completely unauthorised, and probably morally repugnant to boot.

Coral lowers down on her limbs and adopts a clearly subservient position. I could almost imagine her begging. She even opens up her shell, and I get my first surprised glimpse at the inside. It isn't at all the muscular, clam-like innards I had, foolishly, come to expect. Instead, the brief bit I see looks more like a writhing colony structure, like an aquatic beehive or anthill, or possibly a microbial mat.

For all her pleading, the newcomer does not seem to back down, and it turns towards the far exit from the room. A minute later, three more Globites appear, these ones with a collection of sharp spikes extruding from their shells. They "listen" for a moment, then two of them huddle around Coral, looking for all the Universe like security officers monitoring a felon. The third follows the original intruder over to a small, open-bottomed aerobic tank, which they pull out of storage and start clam-handling over to my vat.

I don't like where this is going, but I decide that resistance would probably be very unwise right now. So, exuding as much compliance as I can, I let the metal arms herd me through the airlock and into the tiny, mobile air bubble.

The chamber they take me to is the largest I've yet to see beneath the ice of the Globi moon. Row upon row of hard-shelled Globites line its walls in rising tiers, like an ancient amphitheatre. Many have craggy shells, some have spikes, some display colourful patterns that are nearly as beautiful as Coral's, who is nowhere to be seen in the feeble bioluminescence of my tiny cage-like vat, no matter how hard I peer into the murky water to catch a glimpse of her.

My sharp-shelled captors drag my vat, none too gently, into the centre of the vast, open chamber, where they hold it tightly. Beneath the open water hole at the bottom of my little bubble of air, the porous, sponge-like floor seems so close I could touch it.

Fearing the worst, I brace myself, waiting for something to happen, for one of the Globites to approach. But the minutes drag on into eternity, and not a single member of the assembly moves. I watch them through the clear crystal-like window at the front of my new prison, but I see nothing, no gestures, no movement whatsoever. They simply float in judgement, glaring at me without eyes as I wait in the centre of what is clearly some sort of hearing or deliberation chamber.

The water laps gently, invitingly even, at the bottom of the prison. Soon enough, boredom and curiosity join forces and get the best of me. Tentatively, I dip a finger into the water, which feels lovely and warm. Then I dare to plunge my hand in entirely, and I get confirmation of what I suspected. The water is churned by competing currents that sweep hot and cold waves against my skin. Since there's nothing else here to explain such currents, I can only conclude that they're coming from the Globites themselves, to convey what must be a raging chemoperceptive debate in terms unfathomable to us humans.

But I must try, regardless. Since I'm in the centre of the chamber, the debate must be about me, and my life is clearly on the line one way or another. If only I could understand what they are saying.

Pulling my hand out of the water, I lift my wet fingers to my nostrils, close my eyes, and smell deeply. There's definitely something there, a rich chemical tang that reminds me of the Lightway shuttle docking bays back home, on the Denebola disk habitat.

It confirms my theory, but it's hardly going to get me out of this place and back up to the shuttle in orbit. Damnit, I haven't travelled 120 light-years from home just to die down here.

Desperate, I plunge both hands down into the water, until it's lapping at my chest. The guards holding the vat twitch — finally some sort of movement, even if it's not exactly what I was hoping for — and start lifting their jagged claw arms.

Damn, those things look deadly, gleaming in the weak light of my little vat. But I force myself to push all thought of them aside and focus on my fledgling Globite vocabulary. "Hungry" isn't going to cut it here, so I take a deep breath, try to ignore everything around me, my fears, my hopes, and enter a state of collected relaxation.

A few funk-filled breaths later, both my arms still seem intact, so I risk opening my eyes while trying to hold on to that sense of balance. The guards have turned to face me, insofar as a clamshell can be considered to have a face, and their metal appendages are floating in the water, halfway to my arms.

And even more significantly, the temperature of the rival currents against my bare skin seems to have evened out, with a pause in the clash between hot and cold. Whatever I just said in Globite, I've certainly got their attention.

Now, I just need to figure out what to do with it. And that was the only signal of any value I know how to send.

Panic rises within me, and that's the last thing I want to be broadcasting. But just as I'm about to give up, pull my arms back out of the water, and resign myself to whatever fate the Globites may decide for me, a curious, floral scent comes to mind.

That's right. If I can't speak for myself, I need someone to speak for me. And there's one person who could possibly do that.

Without pausing to question my sudden use of the word "person" to refer to a Globite, I focus on the flowery zing of Coral's name-scent — even though scent is only the start of it. I don't know if the human body can possibly produce anything remotely like that chemical combination, let alone at will. But it's the only shot I have left. I have to try. Humanity needs my report, needs to know what I've discovered here. This is so much bigger than me — and I want to live to see the results!

I take all that need, all that desperation, and picture pushing it down my extended arms, and out into the water, in the shape of a call to Coral, the only Globite who can possibly save me now. The blossoming shape of her chemical signature fills my mind, and I lose myself in the moment, focused entirely on my body, my knowledge of its workings, and my training to control it.

I'll never know for sure whether I truly did succeed in forcing my body to use senses our evolutionary tree branched away from aeons ago, or if it was just coincidence. But either way, I strongly suspect I'll never again know the joy that fills me when I open my eyes and see Coral's purple-patterned shell charging forwards, to half stand, half float next to my little bubble of air.

Her specific chemical note fills the water next around

the vat, and I can only wish I had learned enough to listen to what must be an impassioned speech. If only we weren't so alien one to the other and understanding at that level were even possible.

A minute or so later, a metal appendage snakes its way through the water towards my extended hands, and I almost pull away in fear. But then I realise it isn't one of the guards, but Coral herself reaching out towards me, gentle and comforting. I smile, and reach my hand out to meet her, clasping her pulsating membranes against my wet skin.

That's when the temperature of the water suddenly plummets, and Coral whisks her metal appendage out of my hand, in such a rush that she slices my palm. I cry out — not that anyone here will even register the sound — and yank my arms out of the water. The cut is only shallow, but the swirling chemical mix in the water burns the wound something fierce.

But none of it hurts anywhere near as much as the sight of Coral backing away as the guards surge forwards, grab my vat, and drag me unceremoniously out of the chamber. Hurt, confused, alone, and unquestionably doomed.

In my new confines, I have plenty of time to reflect on how unintentionally cruel fate can be. It makes sense that this prison would be the deepest, darkest dungeon to a Globite mind. The most hostile and undesirable of environments.

But for me, the little series of cells attached to the bottom of the moon-encasing ice shell is a tease, a constant torture. To think that light and humanity are just on the other side of that kilometre of ice. So close, yet still hopelessly far away.

The only visitor to my little air-tight box is the rib-shelled Globite guard who shows up twice a day, regular as clockwork, to thrust a sealed tub of the soggy, sour seaweed-like food into the cell's airlock, and to take away the previous one.

I know prison guards aren't renowned as great conversationalists, and that's probably the same for humans and Globites alike. I would have enjoyed at least being able to make a snide comment, to shout, rattle the walls, anything that might have been at least perceived by the guard or gotten some kind of reaction. But I don't even have that small satisfaction to look forwards to here. Just endless icky nutrient solution on tap, and seaweed mush, day after day. The Globites are keeping me alive for purposes of their own, in complete and utter isolation.

After just four days, I can already feel my sanity slipping away. So when the mid-morning cycle feed guard starts tapping at the observation window, my first thought is that I've completely lost it.

But the tapping is damn insistent, for a figment of a tortured mind. I look up, and there's Coral, a vision in grey and purple, with a splash of some sort of black ichor covering the appendage tapping at the crystal windowpane. In her other metallic arms, she's carrying a, even more welcome sight: my exo-suit, floating in the aquatic breeze, with a seam of rubbery material down the entire length of the slash Coral herself cut into the material when she pulled me out, what feels like years ago.

The airlock mechanism cycles, and I rush over to grab my exo-suit with a cheering whoop. I don't think I've ever hauled a suit on so fast, but at least the seal seems to hold, all systems read green in my display, and the oxygen supply is still intact.

There's a tense moment while I try to jam my bulky exo-suit and myself into the cramped airlock, then wait for Coral to trigger the release. But then I'm out! And free to move, for the first time in forever!

Coral seems slightly hesitant as she reaches out a metal tentacle towards me, but I waste no time in grabbing it by the least pokey bit and swimming out and up, towards the ice.

My Globite friend seems of a like mind, as she pulls me up and off towards a side where, in the distance, I can see diffused, blessed natural light, from what can only be the bottom of Coral's drilled well. The one that goes straight up to the surface.

As she drags me off towards freedom with amazing — and perhaps a touch frantic — speed, it hits me how brave Coral is to have helped me. And how much personal risk she's taking.

I mean, I'm no Globite doctor, but as an exobiologist, I know that whoever that ichor stain on Coral's appendage belongs to isn't reporting in for work tomorrow. Or ever again, considering how carefully the Globites guard their squishy, colony-like innards.

So, she's killed, or at least severely wounded, one of her own. Just to save me. To get me out of that hole and out to freedom, to the rest of humanity. To my future.

That level of personal sacrifice is nothing less than amazing. I gaze at her beautiful, purple-patterned shell swimming ahead of me, and the nobility of it is boggling.

Did she do it out of principle? Because she knows I'm just as intelligent as the Globites, and she believes intelligent life shouldn't be locked up like that? Even if that means killing another intelligent creature, one of her own?

Even if it means defying the inescapably clear decision of that assembly, or tribunal, or whatever happened in that chamber down there in the black depths of the Globi world-ocean?

They'll know it was her. It couldn't possibly be anybody else. Has she only traded her life and her freedom for my own? And could any rational, intelligent being make that kind of sacrifice for another, for an alien, just to stick to their beliefs, however strong?

Or could this be something even greater, in Coral's chemosensitive eyes?

The light grows stronger around us and, finally, we pull up to the round mouth of the bore hole up through the icy shell. There, Coral pauses, and I swim around to face her — which doesn't make any sense, I know. But it feels right, like looking someone in the eyes when speaking to them.

Still holding tight onto Coral's arm, I start swimming up towards the bore hole. It's freezing up again around the edges, but still plenty big enough. Yet Coral doesn't move, holding me back. I turn back to face her, and even if we can't communicate, I sense her thoughts, her feelings, clear as a Gamma Leonis sunrise.

The ice shell must be terrifying to her, like all Globites. The freezing cold would kill chemical transmission. That would make them blind, even destroy their own internal processes. And that's nothing compared to the cosmic horror of the chemical-less void beyond, which is even more hostile and alien for them than it is for us. At least humans can see in space.

And whatever plans Coral made to free me, they didn't allow for securing another one of those rubberised space suits of theirs. She's come this far, but she can't possibly go any further.

With all this clearly in mind, I swim closer, stroking Coral's metallic hand with my suited fingers. A little shiver rushes down her arm and through her bare shell. A smile on my face, I swim closer still, and spread my arms to embrace her rugged shell.

There's the briefest moment's hesitation, and then she rushes forwards to meet me, nearly driving the breath from my chest, exo-suit and all. Her metallic appendages go limp, forgotten tools, as I hold her shell tight in my arms, my suit rubbing against the manipulator and sensory ganglions covering the rugged, purple-veined surface.

There's a bubbling exhalation, and despite the cold, responding to some deep, biological urge, Coral relaxes her clam-shell protection ever so slightly, exposing the fragile, colony-organs within.

And that's precisely what I was waiting for to flick my eyes in the AR display, triggering the suit's jets to propel both Coral and I straight up the bore hole, through a kilometre of freezing water, and up to the void of space.

Held tight in my arms, Coral bucks and shudders, but I'm not letting go of my prize anytime soon. There's a split second where I fear she might figure it out and slash at me with those sharp claws, but as expected, her entire system goes into shock as innards are exposed to the freezing temperatures inside the bore shaft.

I grip Coral's motionless shell and smile within my helmet as we jet through the icy crust of her lunar world. Nobody's going to be able to say Ja'far Bidegger sacrificed years of his life for nothing, that's for sure! Wait until they see this, a perfectly preserved and documented example of the most technologically advanced sentients ever discovered in the Leonids!

Some people might object, of course. I'll have to make up some cover story. Something tragic about how she died accompanying me to the ice. About how her own people drove her to it, chasing her for what she did to save me, maybe. That's close enough to the truth, and it'll be easy to edit the recording logs to support the story, as long as nobody has cause to check the report too closely.

At least she died painlessly, as far as I can tell. I can't help but feel I owe her that much, even if it's a lot better than the long, tortured death of the mind her people were going to give me, as a direct result of her interfering with my mission and dragging me down there in the first place.

This way, everyone's a winner, when you think about it. With a sample like this, humanity will be able to learn all about her people, and we'll be ready to communicate with them properly the next time TransSER sends someone out this way. Thanks to her sacrifice, both of our species will profit. Lord knows we're the ones who are going to have to do the work. The Globites certainly show no inclination to learn our ways or to meet us halfway.

And I'll be set up for life, a legend in my own time. The man who came back with the modern-day Rosetta Stone. Hell, the story rights alone will be worth a fortune, let alone the scientific fame.

Everyone's a winner. Even Coral, who was doomed anyway, after what she did to help me. Better a quick, relatively painless death. It's the least I could do for her.

The light around us gets brighter, and then, without warning, I burst through the far end of the bore hole, in a spray of glittering, half-frozen crystals that shimmer like tears in the impossibly bright Gamma Leonis light.

I signal the shuttle to plot a rendezvous trajectory as soon as the signal goes live again, and I've never been more grateful to see an icon go green in my display.

Almost as an afterthought, I also ping the shuttle to prepare a cryo storage unit for my Globite friend. The intricate purple patterns on her shell glisten in the unnaturally bright sunlight, but I don't know how well they'll keep during the fifty-year trip back to Regulus.

It's a shame, really. But it's all for the greater good. And I've never been that fond of seafood anyway.

[Original, unedited TransSER Expedition Log #72 6f 6d 65 6f – END

Timestamp: 04/25/2531, 11:33 Standard

Reporting Agent: Ja'far Beidegger

Status — ON PAROLE, Wanted for Questioning]

Jon Dobbin

A native to the St. John's metro region, Dobbin tied for first place in the 2017 *48-Hour Writing Marathon*. He describes himself as "the father of three, the husband to an amazing wife, an educator, and a tattoo and beard enthusiast."

He has been featured in both *Chillers from the Rock* and *Dystopia from the Rock* before this.

His first novel, *The Starving*, was released in May 2019 from Engen Books.

His second novel, *The Broken Spire*, is set for a December 2020 release.

On Mission

1

Gunfire thundered through the thick rainforest, and the shouts of men followed under the sharp crack of branches breaking and trees falling before all noise died in the hesitant air.

"Where the hell is Mercer?" a strong voice rose above the echoing silence.

"Dead," was the answer. The silence roared.

Ross McCutchen used the butt of his rifle to help him stand. Sweat and grime streaked his face. He ran his hand over his eyes, and it came away red.

"You hurt?" It was the professor, Goodbrey. The man's thick grey beard framed his ruddy face, his dark eyes focused on McCutchen's open hand.

"I'm good, Albert. Must be from shrapnel."

"Or it's Mercer's blood." Carl Abner untangled himself from the jungle and checked the loading mechanism of his rifle. "Are you sure he's dead, boss?" Wet, green eyes probed McCutchen's face.

"He's dead, Carl. I saw it." McCutchen loaded up his own gun, shaking his head.

Goodbrey put one thick hand on McCutchen's shoulder, his other hand and scrutinizing eyes studying the wounded man's face. "Nothing serious, a few scrapes."

McCutchen pushed the professor away and moved further into the jungle.

"Time to move, we're losing daylight."

Slowly, the foreign sounds of the unfamiliar forest returned and engulfed them and their boot falls in chirps, creaks, and ululating of unknown animals. McCutchen kept his rifle at the ready, slung across his chest, his eyes scanning the vegetation as he hacked a path through the jungle. It'd been one full cycle since their ride went down into the overgrown rainforest. Four of them walked away from the wreckage with as many supplies as they could manage, but it wasn't much. Water, rations, scattered medical supplies, and ammo. Sparse, he thought. Sparse.

McCutchen knew little of the mission, other than that it was meant to be glorified babysitting. His unit was assigned to Goodbrey and his team, keep them safe while they squinted over artifacts or some such. It was supposed to be easy. Sounded easy enough to get his team off rec leave; easy money. Then it all went down the toilet.

"You sure it's this way?" Abner called from the back; his movements were jerky, and he jumped at each sound.

"Take it easy, Carl," McCutchen grunted as he cut through another layer of jungle.

"I believe so, Mr. Abner," Goodbrey cut in, swallowing a mouth full of air. "The site in question was supposed to be due north. Judging by my instruments," McCutchen could hear the older man rustling through his bags, "we're heading in the right direction. More or less."

"Great," Abner said, his voice raising. "More or less? That's great, man. Just great. And how long will that take?"

"Easy, Corporal." McCutchen halted his progress and tried to get a look at the only remaining member of his team. Goodbrey followed suit.

"I would say about another day and a half worth of walking," the professor said as he stroked his beard, "depending on how much sleep we want to get."

"Great." Abner struck out at a low hanging leaf, desperation crawled over his brow and his eyes glinted in the bright sun. "So, how many of those things are we going to run into on the way? There's only three of us, man. Three. Mercer's dead, damn it!"

McCutchen pushed his way past Goodbrey and grabbed Abner's flak vest. "Get it together, Corporal." McCutchen was in his face, could feel the heat rolling off of him. Abner was a head taller than McCutchen, his bared arms laced in muscle and tattoos. He was made tough from off planet training in low oxygen and heavy gravity. He'd been with McCutchen on ten missions without a hitch, though he often had been a little too mouthy for McCutchen's liking. Still, his results spoke louder than his comments.

"We are on mission until we aren't." McCutchen spoke slow, making sure Abner caught each syllable. "Now, get to the front of the line and chop us a path. Get your energy out." He pushed Abner ahead, passed the professor.

"Yes, sir," Abner said, hanging his head and grumbling as he slung his rifle and unsheathed his machete.

"Is he all..." the professor said, his eyes turned down, focusing on packing up his things.

"Don't engage him," McCutchen cut in, eyes watching Abner as he began to cut through the vines blocking their way. The chopping sound echoed off the trees.

"I'm sorry, what…" The professor peered over his glasses, eyebrows raised above an involuntary grimace. His hands stopped their probing, mid-movement.

"Don't engage. From now on, all conversation goes through me. I'm commanding officer."

"Yes, but…"

"No buts, Professor. That's how it is. Understood?" McCutchen stared at the scientist, trying to remain impassive.

"Yes," Goodbrey said and finished packing away his things.

They moved to follow Abner and his slashing machete.

As night fell, they huddled into a small clearing Abner and McCutchen had opened up with their blades. A small fire was stoked in the centre of them all, though the heat of the sun still clung to them in the harsh grip of sweat about their brows. The fire merely served as a light, its smoke an insect repellent. That was a fresh horror that McCutchen preferred not to think about.

"Why don't we know much about this place?" Abner's sunken eyes stared across from the dancing flames. He was leaning his cheek on the barrel of his rifle, cradling it like a child.

"Too dense," Goodbrey said after getting an obligatory nod from McCutchen. "Sensors' readings weren't reliable."

Abner nodded his head slowly. "And those things?" He let his mouth hand agape, licking the corners of his mouth with his tongue.

Goodbrey searched McCutchen's face for a moment.

The lieutenant shrugged.

"Well," Goodbrey said, turning back to Abner. "W-we knew that there were some aggressive species here, but we couldn't be..."

"Aggressive?" Abner was on his feet, rifle held in his hand like a club; his thickly corded arms quivering in the firelight. "Yeah, I'd say they were pretty fuc..."

"Stow it," McCutchen's voice was quiet, but it carried within the small space. He too had stood and was now facing the corporal across the embers that floated above the fire.

Abner's eyes were wild, his mouth fell into a deep grimace, and he took a step towards the fire. "I don't know what your problem is, sir, but you got to see how messed up this all is. They just sent us into a meat grinder. It's bull..."

A loud crack sounded from the trees to Abner's left, and a blur of motion exploded from there. Abner went down with a loud, shrill scream. Blood spattered the fire with a crackle.

It took McCutchen just a moment to react, his rifle drawn to his shoulder, his eye at the sight, as he spun around the fire toward Abner and the creature.

It had the massive body of a feline. McCutchen hadn't seen any up close, but he'd seen a picture of a lion once and that's what the creature reminded him of: large, agile, and powerful. Each paw held spring loaded claws, three inches in length that now scraped the soft dirt around Abner's struggling body. The beast's face was decidedly not feline. It was split down the middle, now popped apart revealing a long, fleshy, vine-like tongue that was wrapped around Abner's neck and drawing him into the few, but large teeth that stood open in anticipation.

Abner's rifle had been lost somewhere in the darkness, but his augmented muscles and off-world training had taken over, and he was able to keep the creature off of him, for the moment. The beast's tongue worked against Abner's conditioning; it drew him in.

McCutchen brought his rifle to bear and squeezed off six rounds, the rifle bucked against his shoulder with each launched projectile. Four of the shots landed centre mass, big hand-ball sized holes appearing on its tawny fur, bubbling with dark maroon blood. The creature let out an ear-splitting scream and jumped away from Abner to face McCutchen, its claws dragging across Abner's torso as it went.

Blood leaked from the corporal's chest and shoulder, his face reddened, and his hands gripped the creature's twisting tongue in hopes of prying it from his throat. The creature whined, but its luminescent yellow eyes were focused on McCutchen with a steady determination. Its tongue began to drag Abner towards it once more.

McCutchen cursed and lined up his aim. One more shot caused the rifle to impact against his shoulder, a friendly reminder of the violence to come. The bullet passed through the two open flaps of his face, striking the central skull-like area that hid within. A loud crunch was heard as the bone splintered and cracked, a gout of blood poured from it for good measure and the beast went limp on the ground. Dead.

2

"My guts are spilling out," Abner wailed. McCutchen had the corporal's arm wrapped around his shoulders. He had gripped the other man's belt and proceeded to drag him in slow staggering steps across the jungle floor. "I can feel 'em, L.T. Feel 'em slipping out." Abner had his free arm tight to his wounded side, a bloody hand in a death grip with his stomach.

"You'll be all right, Carl. Just hold out until we reach the target. Extraction should be en-route," McCutchen said as he watched Goodbrey struggle to cut through the thick vegetation with his borrowed machete.

It had been like that all night. Abner crying out with pain, McCutchen tending to him, and Goodbrey looking on, wiping the sweat from his forehead with a cloth. The jungle was thick with heat and sweat stung McCutchen's eyes. His arms strained carrying the larger man who could only move his legs every second or third step. Even then it did little to help. McCutchen could feel the carbon fiber tendrils pulling on his muscles and tendons, his upgrades grinding against his flesh and blood. He couldn't do this forever.

"Albert," McCutchen called to the dumpy scientist who'd managed to distance from them some. "I'm due a break," he said and propped Abner against a fallen tree to a cacophony of expletives. Goodbrey collapsed close by, the machete falling to the wayside, and he sucked air as he wiped his face with his shirt.

"You're making good headway," McCutchen said with a nod towards the hacked jungle.

"I'm afraid you gentlemen make it look easier than it actually is," Goodbrey said. "How's Mr. Abner doing?" he said in a whisper.

McCutchen just shook his head.

"I'm out," Abner said and tossed his canteen off to the side with a groan.

Goodbrey sipped from his own canteen and shook it with a dubious look. McCutchen hefted his from his pack.

It was light.

"Take it easy on the water," he said, his voice a slow grumble from his chest.

"Did we take Mercer's?" Abner said through a pained grimace.

"Couldn't get it. Here, let me check." McCutchen produced two more canteens from his pack and shook each next to his ear. "That's all we have left from the wreckage. The rest were with Mercer. It's not much."

"How the hell are we going to survive in a place like this with no water?" Abner's eyes had widened, their full attention now on McCutchen.

"We take it easy on the water, Corporal." McCutchen didn't break eye contact, but he could feel the tension surging toward him from Abner. McCutchen figured there were two kinds of people in the world when they get hurt: the type to curl into a ball and suffer, or the type to lash out trying to spread their pain around. Abner seemed to be the latter; if anything, his injury had made him more erratic.

"I guess I better get back at it," Goodbrey said "I'd like us to make some more progress before night falls again."

"Good thinking, Professor," McCutchen said as he and Abner broke their stare with some hesitance.

With a slight nod, Goodbrey hefted the machete once more and headed into the trees. The callous sounds of chopping started up again, leaving McCutchen and Abner to ponder on their situation once more.

"Damn it," Goodbrey said and the thwoking of machete through branch and vine came to an abrupt halt.

McCutchen put Abner on the ground, a squeal of pain

exiting the large man as he adjusted himself and pointed his rifle in Goodbrey's direction. McCutchen did the same and plodded forward.

"Goodbrey?" McCutchen said, his cheek against the slick metal of his gun, his eye trained in its sight, ready to take aim.

The professor was bent forward clutching at his arm, the machete stuck out of the ground next to his feet. A layer of debris was scattered around Goodbrey, tree limbs, leaves, and vegetation of all kinds wilting, dead.

"Goodbrey, what is it?" McCutchen scanned the tree line, squinting to see any movement that didn't involve the professor. Nothing.

"Oh," Goodbrey said finally. "I'm... I'm fine. One of the vines pricked me is all. Hurts like hell." He turned to face McCutchen and held out his wrist towards him, a thin trickle of blood ran down his forearm, a pained look on Goodbrey's face.

McCutchen suppressed his initial reaction to curse and throttle the old professor but settled instead for a long sigh as he stowed his rifle and took a closer look at Goodbrey's arm. The wound was small, but red lines had started to dart out from it. Little tendrils creeping away from their origin. A hint of brown surfaced from the cut. "I think you may have a thorn in there," he managed after a moment.

"Oh, yes," Goodbrey said, taking a closer look at his wound. His face paled some as he worked his fingers around the abrasion. It wasn't long before he pulled out the thorn. Thick and brown, it was sharp and hooked like the talon of some sort of bird of prey. "Nasty little bugger," Goodbrey said between clenched teeth.

"Everything okay?" Abner's voice rose from the path

behind them. The large man was lying where McCutchen had left him, his hand wrapped around the handle of his rifle though the barrell now rested on the ground.

"All good," McCutchen said and gave Abner a curt wave.

A foul odour hit McCutchen as he turned back to Goodbrey. A reeking stench that made him cover his nose and mouth. "Do you smell…"

The professor had fallen to his knees, his hand placed firmly over the cut on his arm. "I believe this may be more serious than it appears," he said and took his hand away from his injury. It was a bright red now, as if a light had been inserted beneath the skin, and it pulsated with an apparent fever. The tendrils McCutchen had observed before were longer now and stretched to his wrist. As he approached Goodbrey, he could feel the heat radiating from the arm. A heat that even overpowered the nearly suffocating temperature of the surrounding jungle.

"Damn," McCutchen said and fished through his pack.

"I don't suppose you have any antibiotics in there, would you?"

"No, but I do have this," McCutchen held up a small white bottle and worked the cap off.

"Alcohol?"

"Something like that," McCutchen said and cleaned off the wound and poured the clear liquid onto Goodbrey's arm. The older man sucked his breath through his teeth, his face even more pale than before.

"We used up most of what we had on Abner, and I'm keeping some aside to clean his wounds again later. But, we have enough to do a small patch job. How are you feeling?" McCutchen watched the professor as he tended the man's wound. It wasn't good. None of this was. McCutchen had never seen an infection develop and spread that fast.

"I'm a little weak, a little thirsty, but I'm fine. I'll be fine," Goodbrey said. McCutchen was sure that the last bit hadn't been directed towards him.

"Drink." McCutchen handed the professor a canteen. "But take it easy. We'll need water to clean up Abner and yourself. Hopefully extraction comes soon rather than later."

"I'm afraid I have been keeping something from you." Goodbrey fell back to his backside, his short legs gathered in front of him. He reminded McCutchen of a child, his red face and blank expression like that of a toddler, tired after a day of playing.

"And what would that be?"

"I wasn't completely honest with you when you were first contacted for this mission." Goodbrey's expression turned serious. "You see, this isn't necessarily a sanctioned foray into the unknown."

"That doesn't make sense. Your department can't make the call to deploy us."

"Well, no, we can't. But then again, computers really do control most everything. Not many people are going to bat an eye at a well-placed command, especially if it appears to come from a high enough rank."

"You hacked the system?"

"Yes, I suppose we did."

"But why? Something like that brings heavy sanctions, criminal charges, even death."

"It's important, Lieutenant. If what we suspect to be here is actually here, it could open so many avenues. It could change how we view our lives, our species. It could change everything." Goodbrey adjusted his glasses, a pained grin apparent on his bearded face.

"Why are you telling me this now?" McCutchen said, his heart beating fast in his chest.

"There isn't going to be any extraction. There never was an extraction plan aside from flying ourselves out of here. And that is out of the question now."

It was McCutchen's turn to fall on his ass.

"You dropped us into a meat grinder," he whispered rubbing one calloused hand over his face. No extraction. They were dead. Dead men walking. If the jungle or the beasts didn't kill them, the lack of food and water would. "No extraction," he said, shaking his head.

"What?" It was the low, calm voice of Abner that turned McCutchen, tightening his grip on his rifle once more.

"No extraction, is it?" Abner stood before them, one hand gripping his injured side, the other his machete. His torso was covered in the plant life Goodbrey had meticulously shorn, long green blades of grass, brown twigs, and leaves of all colours. His face was pale and covered in beads of sweat, his eyes wide and manic.

A trail of blood and gear lay in his wake. He crawled most of the way, McCutcthen thought, thankful that Abner's pack and rifle had been left along the path.

"Or perhaps you meant no extraction for me. Is that it?" Abner accentuated his words with the dull thud of his fist slamming into his thigh.

"Take it easy, Abner." McCutchen stood slowly, one placating hand extended before him.

"No." Abner's wild eyes flashed towards McCutchen in a brief flicker of anger, but they didn't stay on him. No, Abner was focused on Goodbrey.

"Corporal, you need to stand down," McCutchen said, his finger lighting on the trigger of his rifle.

"It's his fault, L.T. Him and his squad of boffins. They pulled us out here, and for what? To crash us in this godforsaken jungle with nothing but hope and a prayer that we'd be able to leave. And you know what I think? I think it was all for nothing. Where's this miraculous find? How could anything survive in this hell hole? It was all a waste." Abner took a stuttering step forward.

"Easy, Corporal." McCutchen raised the barrel of his gun to kneecap level.

"Mercer, Whitman, Price, Haddad, Martin. Dead, L.T. They're dead. Good soldiers, good men, and this asshole got them killed. I say we return the favour." A grim smile stretched across Abner's face and he took another step forward.

"Don't make me shoot you, Abner. Last warning."

Abner moved fast, faster than his condition should have warranted. McCutchen had a chance to fire off three rounds, but Abner had struck his rifle with his machete and knocked it off course. McCutchen hit nothing.

With size on his side and his built-up momentum, Abner knocked McCutchen back to the ground. He pushed forward, machete raised, and a strange squeal erupting from his gullet.

Looking back on it later, McCutchen couldn't tell if Goodbrey had accepted his fate in that moment or was just too scared to do much about it, but he didn't move. Instead, he sat there with a small grin on his face, held his injured arm, and watched the maniacal Abner run over the short distance between them.

Two shots put Abner down, though McCutchen had fired at least ten more. The large man fell flat on his face just inches from Goodbrey's feet, his side weeping blood.

McCutchen let out a long sigh. "I thought you might have let him... well, you know."

The professor was still smiling when McCutchen dug his fist into his jaw and knocked him out cold. He stood over the bodies of what was left of his crew and chanced a sip of water from his canteen.

"No extraction," he said and looked into the endless maw of the jungle before him.

3

"Do you see that?" Goodbrey said pointing one thick finger into the horizon. "Do you see that there?"

Goodbrey had woken up not long after McCutchen had cold cocked him. It was just enough time for McCutchen to dispose of Abner's body and scour his pack for any supplies. He had nothing of any real use: some field rations, extra ammo, and illicit painkillers and performance enhancers. No wonder he'd gone off at the end, McCutchen thought, and slung the rest of the pack into the trees.

They spent a quiet night with a small fire after that. The only voice rose through the night after Abner had fallen asleep. A fevered conversation that he had with himself that made little sense. McCutchen listened to the professor all night and stared up at the stars.

"I see it," he said, chopping down another layer of vegetation as they pushed through the oppressive tree line. Just over the horizon something had caught the sun, a flash of reflected light that spoke of something unnatural. Something that didn't fit the jungle.

"It looks like it's on a hill of some sort. Standing above the trees as it is." Goodbrey's injury hadn't bothered him since he woke that morning, or, if it did, he didn't let McCutchen know.

McCutchen grunted and put his weight behind the swinging machete. He didn't much like the idea of cutting through the jungle and climbing a hill at the same time, but the mission was the mission -- no matter how it had been presented to him. *Besides,* McCutchen thought, slashing out again, *what else am I going to do?* Stuck in an uncharted jungle with no radio, supplies dwindling, and with no hope of escape, McCutchen figured he might as well satisfy his curiosity. What the professor had described to him was incredible if it was possible, McCutchen mused. And a reflection being cast from a hilltop didn't exactly instill confidence in him that there was something so life-altering that it warranted a risk of life and limb to discover. A flash of Abner falling to the jungle floor pushed him forward, his machete striking faster and faster.

They had settled into another silent break, taking short sips from their depleting water. McCutchen couldn't tell the exact time of day, but he estimated that it was sometime after midday. He supposed he could have asked Goodbrey. The professor seemed like the type of man who would be able to tell you the time of day just from the position of the sun in the sky. Then again, there were two suns in the sky overhead and possibly a moon.

"Looks like the land slopes up from here on out," McCutchen said. The break in the silence made Goodbrey jump.

"We're at the hill then?"

"Seems so. The jungle has receded as well. We may not even need these to make a path," McCutchen held out his machete for emphasis and dug then slid it back into its sheath on his belt.

"Small blessings." Goodbrey allowed himself a grin, but he didn't have anything to put into it, so it slid from his face as quickly as it had come. He rubbed at his arm.

"How's the arm?"

"I... I don't know. I'm trying to ignore it," Goodbrey said and cupped his hands together, his fingers turned a violent white.

McCutchen shook his head and said through a frown, "Let me see it. Bandages need to be changed anyway."

Goodbrey cringed away from McCutchen, his arms raised in an inadvertent defensive response. McCutchen could see a bruise forming through the professor's beard and frowned.

Goodbrey stared up at him a moment longer before he cleared his throat and lowered his defense, another emotionless grin slipped into place as he averted his eyes from McCutchen.

"Easy there, teach. I'm just going to take a look." McCutchen eased Goodbrey's arm into view. The dressing was stained through with the dark maroon of blood and something else too. An evil looking green seemed to pierce the centre of the stain and it made McCutchen remember the smell.

With a deep breath, McCutchen peeled back the bandage. The stench hit him once again. The distinct odour of decomposition, of rot and death. He reeled back, his eyes tearing up as his hand covered his nose and mouth. And still, even above the stink was the heat. McCutchen pulled his hand away as though it were a hot stove.

"It's not good," Goodbrey said. His voice was distant, droning.

No, it's not good, McCutchen thought. Not good at all. With some effort, McCutchen managed to force himself to look at Goodbrey's arm. The wound was bigger than he remembered. A tear shape opening about the size of a high caliber bullet stared back at him crusted over with black blood and yellow pus. McCutchen grimaced and poured some of the sterilizing alcohol over it. Goodbrey bit his lip and grunted through it.

It wasn't the noise that alerted McCutchen that something was amiss, because there wasn't any. It wasn't Goodbrey's widening, fearful eyes, because McCutchen had been too focused on the other man's wounds. It was the creature's breath, hot on the nape of McCutchen's neck that warned him that something was terribly wrong, if a little too late.

McCutchen made a dive to his right and towards his rifle, but he was caught. Something large and sharp impacted on his ribs and sent him flying in the opposite direction. He rolled to his knees, breath coming in large gulps.

It was the beast, but larger than before, and it had a long mane that fell around its neck like feathers or grass. Its alien face split open in a silent roar.

"Sh*t," McCutchen said and reached for his machete, but the beast was on him. Its vine-like tongue lashed out like a whip and wrapped around his throat. Its razor-like claws ventured toward his arms, chest, and groin, but it was too large and couldn't get the right angle; his flak vest took most of the damage.

He clamped his hands on either side of the creature's split snout and pushed himself away from its mouth, but the vine-like tongue pulled against him and it tightened around his throat.

Darkness seeped in around his vision, tentacles of shadow that grew and multiplied. McCutchen's hearing became muffled, his breathing a faraway wheeze. The strength was leaving his arms and he could feel the pull of the creature's tongue; its strength.

McCutchen became vaguely aware of a bang that went off somewhere in the distance. It echoed in his head and he forced his eyes open. The creature was still standing over him, its tongue had loosened some, but there was no doubt he was still in its grip.

His fingers began to tingle with the return of feeling, and pain creeped in with it. Pain around his throat, and a sharp sickening feeling on his legs.

The creatures head was turned, its body moving around with it, and McCutchen thought of what had happened to Abner just a day before. Would his guts soon be spilling out?

Goodbrey shouted something but McCutchen couldn't quite understand it. The creature's entire body was now facing his feet, distracted by something. Another bang. Closer now, not as muted. The beast flinched, its tongue loosening some more.

McCutchen snaked his hand down his torso and ripped his machete out of its sheath. In one swift motion, the constriction around his neck faded, the darkness at the edge of his vision had fully subsided.

The creature was flailing over him, crying out in its silent voice. McCutchen took his chance and rolled away, pain shooting through his leg and hips.

The scene he took in was chaos. Goodbrey stood to the side, McCutchen's rifle held awkwardly in his doughy arms. The older man's face was ashen and frozen in a shocked grimace. The creature shook its head, still recovering from the pain of its severed tongue, but its focus was coming around to the two men once again, its talons scraped along the ground.

"Here," McCutchen said and waved his arm towards Goodbrey. "Throw it here."

Goodbrey's head snapped towards McCutchen but it was a blank, frenzied stare; there was no recognition in it.

"The gun," McCuthchen pointed. "Toss me the gun."

With a slow nod, Goodbrey threw the rifle. It wasn't a far distance, but the gun seemed to move in slow motion as it sliced through the air. McCutchen rose to meet it, his arm extended out toward it, his thoughts already turning toward what he needed to do with the automatic weapon. He could picture the beast flailing with each successful hit, could see it fall in its death throes like the beast that had attacked Abner before it.

And with the gentle feel of a breath on his neck, McCutchen knew none of that would transpire.

The beast hit him front on with its powerful frame to send him sprawling over the ground until he came to a sudden stop by way of tree. He groaned. He'd never been hit by a truck before, but he was sure this was what it would feel like.

Consciousness threatened to leave him once more, but he fought through it. His carbon fibre implants pushed his limbs to move, to get up despite the pain. McCutchen was sure he had several broken bones, but his modifications wouldn't let that stop him, not with adrenaline pushing them to their limits.

The beast came on, its mouth agape, a green liquid

oozing from its severed tongue. McCutchen was up on his knee before the creature struck. It lashed out with one large paw, but McCutchen was already moving away, and its claws scraped against his flak vest, finally tearing it asunder.

McCutchen was in the vegetation, flailing desperately to see the beast before it attacked again. A quick roll and he almost fell face first into a strange looking plant, its one thin, straight stalk sticking out of the ground. It was covered in brown, hooked thorns. He grabbed it at its base and pulled it free.

The creature slashed through the brush, an empty snarl on its trembling lips. McCutchen could feel it shred through his flak vest again and bite into his skin. He fell forward but lashed out with the thorny stalk as he fell. The thorns found a home in the beast's snout; McCutchen could feel their bite sink into the creature's thick hide.

A noise finally came from the beast, something akin to the creak from a rusty hinge. The creature jumped back; its paws rubbed at its snout. McCutchen pursued it, whipping it with the thorny switch, drawing more green blood and renewed squeals.

Whether in a frenzy of rage or pain or fear, McCutchen couldn't tell, but the creature retreated. It bounded through the brush and disappeared into the thick jungle where he hoped it would die a long and painful death. Still brandishing the thorned plant, McCutchen sank to the ground and let unconsciousness take him.

4

The hill was steep and neither man was in the shape to climb it. The beast had done severe damage to McCutchen's leg and back, and they'd been forced to use the remaining bandages to keep him in one piece; his shirt was sacrificed to the cause as well. Goodbrey, on the other hand, had been vomiting a thick stream of grey bile every couple of hours. His skin had the darkening pallor of a gravestone, and one of his eyes had developed a layer of milky white over the pupil and iris. Goodbrey was dying.

Neither man had given in, and with a silent acquiescence they trudged on. It didn't matter that McCutchen had to crawl at times, dragging his leg behind him as his thick fingers dug into the dirt and pulled him forward. Nor did it matter that Goodbrey had to stop every so often to heave a viscous mess on the increasingly rocky ground. They were gaining on the hill, approaching the top.

McCutchen wasn't sure how long it took them, but they had made the top, a plateau so flat that he initially thought it had to be manmade. Lying there, staring at a sky free from the tall trees of the recently escaped rainforest, McCutchen was certain that he'd passed out on more than one occasion up the hill. Even doing so, Goodbrey was never too far away. The older man was always just ahead, patting his forehead dry with a cloth. A bewildered smile set McCutchen's teeth on edge.

"We're here, Lieutenant," Goodbrey said, using his handkerchief to wipe the back of his neck. "Can you feel it? It's just within our grasp." The professor's voice was coarse, and his speech was broken up by phlegmy coughing fits.

"Let's go." McCutchen pulled himself to standing and began to limp forward motioning for the professor to follow. Goodbrey raised his one good eyebrow.

"I'll be damned if I witness this from my belly." McCutchen smiled and moved on.

They fell into the wreckage. Goodbrey had tripped over a rock dislodged from the ancient crash and pulled McCutchen down with him. Adding more bruises and scrapes to their long list of injuries, both men laughed where they fell, true laughter that bubbled up from the gut and spilled out. It ended when Goodbrey broke into a coughing fit that lead to another session of vomiting.

"Well, Professor, what are we looking at?"

Goodbrey chuckled, a deep, rolling laugh that bubbled up from his chest. "I'm afraid I can't say."

A flame of anger licked at McCutchen's sore body, a flame that was turned back by sheer exhaustion. "What do you mean?"

"I mean to say that, as you may be able to see, I cannot." The old man pointed to his eyes, both of which had turned an aged white with no hint of the dark brown that had inhabited that space just a few hours before. Goodbrey laughed again, a short bark without any mirth in it. It startled McCutchen.

"It's wrecked," McCutchen said. "The impact with which it hit broke it apart so that even if we wanted to, we'd never find all the piece."

Goodbrey turned his sightless eyes on McCutchen, his face slack but he nodded for McCutchen to continue.

"There is a large white dish that lead me to believe this may have been a satellite of some kind."

"Astonishing," Goodbrey murmured.

"The body doesn't seem to be intact, though I can see a golden disc affixed to its side. I'd say we found our reflection culprit."

Goodbrey nodded, his hands moved quickly in front

of him. More, more they seemed to say.

"I don't know what else I can tell you, Professor," McCutchen said finally and used a piece of the wreck to stand up.

"Thank you, Lieutenant. You did what you could," Goodbrey said and lay on his side as a small, stifled cough erupted from his lips. "We made it."

"We did make it, Albert. Mission accomplished."

They sat in silence for some time. Each of them pondering the find in their own way.

The jungle sounds soon reached their ears from below.

It won't be long until it catches up with us, McCutchen thought, and climbed up on the satellite dish to get a better view of the rainforest that surrounded them. A word was emblazoned on the white surface of the dish, not large enough to catch his eye before but obvious enough now that McCutchen couldn't believe that he missed it. It was in a language he couldn't understand, so he didn't realize that it said Voyager-1 as he wiped it off in order to rest his injured leg.

The suns set in the strange sky, and unfamiliar stars blinked into existence. McCutchen lay back on the satellite dish and wondered if anyone was looking back.

Jeff Slade

A resident of Salmon Cove, Slade is a prize-winning author and avid reader who enjoys both making and hearing puns, playing the guitar, and cats.

Slade has previously been featured in 2018's *Chillers from the Rock* with his short story 'The Culling,' in 2019's *Dystopia from the Rock* with his story 'Anchored,' and in *Flights from the Rock* with his story 'Flight of the Puffin.'

His award-winning story, *Extinguished*, was featured in *Kit Sora: The Artobiography*.

The Daring Mid-flight Heist on the Moonbeam Express

The moon loomed large in the foreground, the same silent titan that stood guard in his bedroom window every night when he was a child. Quiet and unmoving, cold as a tombstone and the same ashen shade.

Jace raised one hand and squinted, trying to cover it with his thumb. Another childhood habit of his. This time it was too big and getting bigger still.

I guess you do outgrow some things, he thought, then turned his attention back to the task at hand.

The sleek silver maglev train on which he stood whistled through space, as soundless as its lunar destination as it soared farther and farther from Earth. He checked the chronometer on his wrist; he had two minutes before they hit another launch loop that'd push them on to the next link in their path to the moon.

I'd best get back inside.

Jace looked back at the long chain of coach class cars behind him. He'd hacked an unmanned airlock, unpacked and donned his space suit, then slipped outside when no one had been paying attention. Given the conditions in coach, no one was ever paying attention. Those cars were full of the poor and sick looking to immigrate to the moon in hopes of a better life; likely a life of labour on the newly settled dark side of the moon, but at least they'd have a roof over their heads and food in their bellies.

He'd boarded the *Moonbeam Express* in hope of a better life himself, though in a slightly different way. Somewhere on board, his girlfriend, Ava, was being held hostage. A mean bastard with a grudge named Holt had kidnapped her several days ago, leaving Jace for dead in the process.

It was a long story, longer than Jace cared to remember. His focus was on reaching Ava and rescuing her.

With that in mind, he took one careful footstep after another, switching off the magnetics in each boot only once the other was firmly turned on and attached. He loved space, but he didn't exactly want to float around in it aimlessly forever, rebreather in his suit or not.

He reached the end of the coaches and looked ahead at the next car. It appeared to be a freight car, likely full of the luggage and belongings of the first class passengers up ahead. Jace peered through the rear door window to try and catch a glimpse inside.

He didn't expect to see another face staring back at him.

The other man, clad in thick metallic armour with his helmet off, yelled something, though it was impossible to hear exactly what was being said from outside. Jace taunted him by raising a hand to one ear and an eyebrow from behind his visor.

The guard stepped back, unslung a weapon strapped over his shoulder, and lifted his helmet over his head. Before he could finish, however, Jace reached out and tapped the window. The guard paused, then leaned in closer and frowned as Jace lifted one foot up and placed it on the glass.

The frown disappeared behind a smear of blood and

broken teeth once Jace activated his high-power magnetic sole, which slammed the guard's face against the plasteel window with bone-crunching force.

He slowly slid down into a heap of limbs while Jace entered the freight car's airlock and hacked the terminal to gain entry. Once the chamber had decompressed, Jace took off his helmet, shook loose his mousy brown hair, then entered the freight car. He stepped over the unconscious guard, stopping long enough to pick up his assault rifle.

Could come in handy later, I reckon.

He poked and prodded at various boxes and crates, curious to see what they contained. One large crate that dominated the middle of the room, nearly as tall as his six-foot frame, caught the bulk of his attention before he remembered he had a job to do. Ava would be in one of the cars ahead, and he had to keep his wits about him.

His watch beeped, a pre-set reminder that the *Moonbeam Express* was about to enter the next launch loop. The train shook ever so slightly as it passed through the maglev station, getting another magnetic boost to push it towards its destination. There was about an hour left in the five-hour trip, so he had to get a move on.

Jace leaned against the entrance to the next car, peeking through its window to inspect its interior. A pair of guards sat at a table, wearing the same garb as the previous one, but it was otherwise empty. They were playing cards and not paying attention to either door, but once he entered, they'd surely notice.

He looked down at the gun, then slid its safety switch into the 'off' position. *Looks like it'll be sooner rather than later.*

Bursting through the door, Jace fired a spray of bullets at each guard. His aim was true on the first shot, but he missed the second guard with his second attack. In the moments it took him to unleash another salvo into the remaining guard he heard the guard's panicked voice requesting back-up.

Dammit.

He positioned himself behind the table on which the now deceased guards had been playing cards, flipping it up and praying it was made of the same strong material as the train itself.

Three more armoured guards poured into the car from the one ahead of him, guns out and hot. The table held against their weapons, and Jace was nearly deafened by the loud pings and pangs of bullets reflecting off its metal surface.

In a mix of inspiration and panic, Jace summoned all of his strength and lifted the table, holding it in front of him and ducking down as he charged at the three newcomers. He managed to bowl all of them over, and he raked gunfire over their prone bodies before he released the table.

"Piece of cake," he panted out loud to no one in particular. He struggled to catch his breath before he realized a red siren was flashing in the corner of the car, paired with a loud klaxon announcing his arrival.

Ava. He dropped his rifle for one of the fresher ones and charged ahead. He burst through into the next car, which was also empty, its three previous inhabitants bleeding out in the car behind him.

No passengers here either, he realized. *Someone knew I was coming.*

He came to a screeching halt as he opened the next door. Inside stood Holt, equal in height to Jace, clad in the same armour as his guards, and, in his arms, Ava. He had a firearm in one hand, raised and pointed in Jace's direction, and his other was wrapped around Ava's neck, pulling her shorter frame close to him.

"'Bout time you showed up," Holt snarled, a twisted smirk sliding across his stubbled face.

Jace's watch beeped again, indicating another launch loop was imminent. He gripped the assault rifle in his hands. If he timed it just right, just so, he should be able to hit Holt before the other man shot, though there was always the risk of hitting Ava -

Before he could act, the train shuddered and Ava acted first. She kicked one of Holt's shins with the back of her heel, then spun and jabbed something at him before either man could react.

When she pulled back, Jace saw a small hypodermic needle sticking out of Holt's neck. The man's eyes rolled back deeply, and he collapsed onto the floor as Ava stepped out of the way.

"What the -" Jace started.

"You almost screwed it up," Ava complained. She shook both Holt's limp, lifeless body off of her and her head at Jace at the same time.

"Beg your pardon? I mean, I presume you meant to say thank you, Jace, for saving me." He walked over and kicked the gun out of Holt's hand, just in case. "You're welcome, by the way."

Ava dashed over to a large computer desk, her scarlet ponytail whipping into the air behind her. Well-manicured fingers flew across a keyboard terminal. A moment later the flashing lights and klaxons stopped just as quickly as they'd begun.

"It was a trap, stupid. Which you walked into and sprung, lock, stock, and barrel." Ava sighed and picked up Holt's handgun, tucking it into the back of her pants. "And now the whole train knows what's going on."

"Well it's a good thing I've taken care of the guards then, isn't it?" Jace gestured back to the way he'd came and the body trail throughout the same.

Ava pointed to the door at the front of their current car. "There are a few more cars ahead of us, boss." She drawled out the last word, something she knew bugged him.

As if on cue, a pair of angry faces appeared in the window. They couldn't get in; Jace reckoned that Ava had locked the doors along with whatever she'd done to terminate the alarms.

"We don't have much time though, come on," she said, tugging on his arm as she ran past him toward the other doorway.

"Ain't nothin' out there but a few guns, though I guess we'll need all the help we can get," he replied. He swallowed the lump in his throat. It'd be a hell of a firefight, but they weren't going down without one.

"Forget the guns, I've already got a plan," Ava said.

"Wait, what plan?" He followed behind her, closing the car door behind him. It'd buy them a few seconds at least, once Holt's remaining guards broke through. "Also, how do you know I didn't have a plan?"

"The one you're in the process of messin' up. Also, see exhibits A through E," she answered, kicking at the dead and dying guards he'd strewn across the cars. "And F, which - Jesus, Jace, what'd you do to this guy?" Ava grimaced as she found the first guard with the obliterated face.

"I did so have a plan, I just... I just thought there were less guards, is all." Jace toed the dead guard with his boot.

"An' he had it comin'."

"Fewer," she corrected as she moved boxes and crates off the largest one in the middle of the room. "Now give me a hand, would ya'?"

"Less, fewer, whatever." He helped her clear the crate, then helped pry it open once she started doing the same. "I was gonna rescue you, that was the plan."

"Then what?" Ava pried one wooden lid off at the same time as he removed another.

"Then... then the train would land on the moon and we'd disappear into the crowd. I dunno," he confessed. "What in tarnation is this?" he asked, peering into the now open crate.

"My plan." She removed a space suit of her own and slipped into it while he finished taking the sides of the crate down. "I was waitin' until we were close enough, then I was gonna take care of Holt and, well. Voila." Ava splayed her fingers out before her, revealing the crate's contents.

Inside was a large piece of machinery, complete with a cockpit and a set of vertical take-off and landing thrusters. On its side was a label with a series of initials on it.

"Well I'll be," he said. "I haven't seen a High Orbit Recreational Space Explorer in quite some time."

"They're antique, to be sure," Ava said, putting on her own suit which she'd also stashed inside the crate. "But we can reminisce later. For now, get in the back, cowboy." She opened the cockpit and then moved to the terminal Jace had previously used, her fingers quickly clacking against keys once again.

"A two-seater, huh?" Jace grinned as he begrudgingly got inside the back. She'd had her own plan, it was true, but he was still glad to see there'd been room for him in her plans, just in case.

A loud bang sounded from a few cars down. Ava jumped in and sealed the cockpit just as the remaining guards swarmed inside the freight car.

Which was horrible timing for them; Ava had hacked the airlock to open above them, and not just the one-man entrance Jace had used, but the entirety of the freight car. It was how large items were loaded inside, including their escape vehicle.

Various crates and guards alike whooshed out along with the oxygen, spilling out into the void. Once there was ample room, she fired up the H.O.R.S.E.'s engines and exited the car, veering away from the *Moonbeam Express*.

"So, where to now?" Jace said. There was no way a vehicle this size could re-enter the Earth's atmosphere, so he already had a pretty good idea of their general destination.

"I figure we might as well help settle some new territory, don't you?" Ava replied. "'Sides, I think we've kinda outgrown our old home."

Jace looked over his shoulder at the big blue marble that'd been home all of his life up until then. He raised a hand and squinted. This time his thumb covered his target entirely, and it continued to slowly shrink in the distance.

"I couldn't have said it any better myself."

Nicole Little

Nicole Little is an award-winning short story author from St. John's, Newfoundland. Her previous writing credit, "Sweet Sixteen," won the June 2018 Kit Sora prize. She has also placed in the Writer's Alliance of Newfoundland and Labrador "A Nightmare on Water Street" contest, October 2018.

She was featured heavily in both *Dystopia from the Rock* and *Flights from the Rock* in 2019.

She has appeared in six anthologies from Australian publisher Black Hare Press, including *Eerie Christmas, Apocalypse, Storming Area 51, Monsters, Beyond,* and *Bad Romance.*

She is a mother of two.

Squid Wars

"Delivery for Edward Allen Farris." The message flashed in bright red letters.

"That's me!"

Ed placed his palm on the scanner where the delivery-bot indicated and grabbed the small cardboard box when it dropped from the slot. He hadn't ordered anything, and he didn't often receive unsolicited mail, but he did like surprises! He turned it over and over in his hands and gave it a light shake. A muffled rattle from within piqued his curiosity.

There was no return address.

He closed the door, grabbed scissors from the junk drawer in the kitchen, and deftly sliced through the tape. He pawed through the sea of trappings in search of buried treasure.

"What the flip?" he muttered under his breath. *GROW A FRIEND!* declared the retro, overly bright, child-centric packaging. Mystified, he read aloud from the instructions on the back: *"Place your egg in water and watch it hatch! Within 24 hours, you will have a new best friend! Add more water as necessary."*

Ed laughed mirthlessly. This was a joke right? Who in the world would send such a thing to a forty-year-old man? He tossed the toy on the counter and stalked out of the room, disappointed and oddly irritated. He sat at his desk and tried to concentrate.

But his attention waned.

It was 11PM; Ed stood at the kitchen sink, rinsing an empty wine glass. Finally, admitting defeat, he got down on his knees to rummage through the cupboards. He emerged, triumphant, with a large bowl in hand. Seconds later he was standing at the counter observing the opalescent-toned egg as it wobbled and bobbed in its incubator of tepid tap water. He was embarrassed to admit it, even to himself, but he was intrigued; a certain childish curiosity had overtaken him. He sighed in resignation and went to bed.

Ed sat straight up in bed, his heart beating a wild tattoo beneath his chest; his legs tangled tightly in a twisted sheet. Flipping on the lamp next to his bed, he strained to hear what had woken him. It had not been a dream. It had been much too loud, echoing even now above the rush of blood in his ears. As the minutes languidly ticked past, Ed, mustering courage, crept from the bed to the doorway. Met with silence there, he tiptoed stealthily down the hall. No burglars or boogiemen greeted him in the small lounge, so he continued into the kitchen.

Dappled in moonlight, the alabaster bowl upon the counter immediately drew Ed's attention. *Needs more water,* he thought. Mechanically he filled a measuring cup with liquid from the tap, poured it carefully into the bowl and watched the egg weave, dip, and dive in its replenished fluids. Within minutes, he was back in bed, his breathing slow and deep. Asleep.

Whether or not he noticed the long crack running the length of the shell is anyone's guess.

Bleary eyes blinked tiredly over the rim of a chipped blue coffee mug emblazoned with the proverb *Edit or Regret It*. Ed's internal clock would not allow him to sleep past 615am even though it was a Saturday; even though he felt strangely exhausted. It was as though he hadn't slept well at all. He yawned widely, ran a hand over his chin stubble; the entire day stretched out ahead of him and he wondered, idly, if it was worth shaving for. He tossed the dregs of his coffee into a potted plant beside him (a plant that somehow seemed to thrive despite his indifference) and, leaving the mug on a side table, he meandered upstairs to get dressed. He was spitting toothpaste into the sink when he heard the muffled sound of glass breaking. He wiped his chin hurriedly and fled the bathroom.

The mug, his favorite, lay in jagged shards on the floor.

"What in the world?" he sputtered.

There was no draft of wind, no mischievous pet to knock it over; he was sure he hadn't left the mug near the edge. He sighed, took a knee, and began to pick up the broken pieces, cursing elaborately under his breath. He wasn't paying much mind to anything other than the task at hand. So when the oily black tentacle whipped out from beneath the recliner and wrapped itself around Ed's wrist, well, let's just say, it definitely got his attention.

Ed had finally met his new best friend.

"What's the word, Sook?"

Roxy Buckles sashayed her way into the office. It was 10am and she reeked of scotch and late-night shenanigans.

Suki Kwan, who'd been fielding irate calls all morning, wrinkled her nose in distaste. "You need a shower, Roxy."

Roxy sniffed an armpit. "I didn't have time to go home last night... or this morning. Either way, I'll freshen up before my first meeting." She stopped mid stride. "When is my first meeting again?"

"Two hours ago," Suki responded with wide eyed innocence.

Roxy cringed.

Suki grinned. "You can relax. I moved all your appointments. Ethel-Beth Lester will be here in ..." she glanced at the time, "... twenty minutes. Her husband ran off a Witchlet again. She's afraid they'll eat him this time. Go spray yourself with something. There's a coffee on your desk."

Roxy ran a hand through her golden halo of curls and flashed Suki a grateful grin. "Thanks, Sook. What would I do without you?"

"Die probably," Suki muttered as Roxy slammed the door of the inner office.

Suki was feeding handwritten notes into the Transcripto Scanner when she heard an alarm reverberate throughout the room. She froze for a few seconds before glancing around to make sure she wasn't imagining things. It wasn't a sound she heard often in the office. Oh, yes they received thousands of alerts a year but *never* on *that* line.

Suki smashed the acknowledge button, printed the specs, then wheeled frantically to the inner office door. Bursting in, Suki caught Roxy as she was just about to spritz herself with a can of Shower-On-The-Go. The can hit the floor and rolled beneath the desk.

"Jeepers, Suki! You scared the life out of me!"

"Rox. There's a problem … um … *over there*." She widened her eyes dramatically. There was only one *over there*.

"Earth?! Really? Shoot. What is it?"

"Here." Suki handed Roxy the small paper printout.

"Flunk me dead! It's a LanQuid! This is … this is extinction level!" Roxy bent to grab the can of Shower-On-The-Go and called over her shoulder to Suki, her voice hard and resolute: "Cancel my appointments, Sook, and fire up the Zip Ship. "

Suki sighed in resignation, thinking mournfully of the calendar she'd only just rearranged. She began transmitting instructions to the Bots down in transport. The Zip Ship, used for short interstellar jaunts, would be prepped and ready to go whenever Roxy was.

Within minutes, Roxy was on the tarmac. She climbed up and settled herself into the pilot seat of the Zip Ship, pleased but not surprised, to see that Suki had already programmed the coordinates into the navigation system. She quickly did her pre-flight checks and secured her safety harness. Satisfied that everything was as it should be, she took a deep breath: it was go time.

Urging the Zip Ship onward at top speed, Roxy mentally reviewed everything she knew about LanQuids. Greedy as they were for anything liquid, they'd driven their home planet into an irreversible drought. Intercepted before they could travel to other solar systems, they'd been ordered to remain in situ by the Planetary Regulation Committee. They'd eventually died off.

Or so everyone thought.

A LanQuid on Earth would be utterly disastrous.

Eventually Ed stopped screaming.

The tentacle had retreated back beneath the chair. Ed wondered – hoped that maybe he'd imagined the whole thing?

He took a deep breath. Then: "Hello?"

A small squeak in reply.

"Can... can you come out where I can see you? What *are* you?"

Silence. No movement. But then, slowly, something that Ed could never have imagined in his wildest dreams scuttled out from beneath his favorite recliner. It resembled a small squid; if that squid had been drenched in motor oil. It was obsidian-black, aqueous in appearance and many-tentacled. It twitched and writhed in constant movement, as though furiously seeking... something. Two large moist eyes, centered perfectly upon its countenance, peered curiously out at Ed from above a small, sharp beak-like protuberance. It squawked and Ed felt his bladder tremble.

"What do you want?!" Ed finally croaked.

A sound which might have been a cough emanated from behind the beak and suddenly Ed knew. "Water?"

The gleeful noise that followed was all the answer he needed.

Ed's new friend was splashing ecstatically around the bathtub; the bathroom floor was splattered. As was Ed for that matter. And if Ed's eyes didn't deceive him, it had grown at least a few inches. It *had* consumed a considerable amount of bath water though.

Ed hated calling it *It*.

"We need a name for you, little buddy." Two large liquid eyes blinked at him quizzically. Ed thought for a minute. "What about Inky? Wait… Cal! That one's short for Calamari!" Ed chuckled to himself. The creature didn't seem to find it very funny. "Okay, Cal it is!"

Ed turned on the tap, adjusted the temperature. Cal squealed loudly in delight. "Wow. You sure do like water, hey?! I'll fill it back up for you then!"

It had been a very long time since Roxy had navigated through Earth's atmosphere. Sweat ran down the sides of her face as she felt the craft vibrate and shudder beneath her hands; she breathed an audible sigh of relief when the Zip Ship finally touched down on terra firma. Night had fallen over the small town of Port Sebastian. There was little chance of getting lost but Roxy grabbed her map-nav anyways before exiting the craft. Leaning against the Zip, her breath forming a mist in front of her lips, she studied it closely, using her intuition to narrow down the areas she suspected that the LanQuid might target. She memorized the street names and jammed the device into her pocket. She set off at a steady pace.

The sound of Roxy's combat boots scuffing against the asphalt echoed loudly on the otherwise silent thoroughfare of Ripley Avenue. She ambled down Ripley, then left onto Connor; eyes constantly scanning the houses, cloaked though they were in darkness; sleepy and still at this time of night – not even a curtain twitched. Roxy stuffed her hands in her pockets, her fingers brushing the map-nav; she suppressed a small shiver. The jacket she was wearing, though perfect for the year-round balmy weather on Aurora, was wildly inadequate in this chilly autumn breeze.

Thus far, Earth wasn't living up to the hype.

Rounding the corner onto Leonard, Roxy was beginning to doubt her instincts. There should have been some sign by now surely… unless she was wrong. It didn't happen often but, though she was loathed to admit it, it wasn't entirely outside the realm of possibility.

The screech that split the night air had Roxy reaching for her weapon – a multifunctional tool that, with a simple spin of a dial, could adapt and challenge any hostile being large or small. Roxy fell into a crouch, her senses on alert. Another scream pierced the silence. Loud enough that Roxy could pinpoint its location: 14 Leonard Way. A blue, nondescript house with a tidy front yard complete with white picket fence. Roxy crept closer, read the name printed on the mailbox: *Farris*.

A thunderous crash. The upstairs light went out.

Bingo.

Ed returned from a day out running errands. Night came early this time of year; he flicked the lights on as he walked through the house, not particularly concerned with his carbon footprint. He was tired and hungry. He wanted a sandwich and a beer in front of the TV followed by an early night.

You know what they say about best laid plans.

Yawning enormously, Ed plodded up the stairs, a small bag of shrimp in hand. He'd grabbed some earlier at the supermarket, thinking it might be a nice treat for his new mate Cal. He strolled distractedly into the guest bathroom and stopped short. The bathtub was empty. And completely dry. A few hours beforehand it had been filled nearly to the brim and had contained one tiny squid-like creature. Absurdly, the toilet bowl was also empty. Ed stood there for a few moments, blinking stupidly, his mind processing the scene; the forgotten bag drooped limply by his side.

A deafening shriek made the floor beneath his feet tremble. The bag of seafood tumbled onto the bathroom rug as Ed flinched and covered his ears. Sprinting from the bathroom, Ed soon found himself face to face with Cal. A grown up Cal. A rather large, rather menacing Cal.

It towered over Ed by at least two feet and was nearly four times as wide. Spittle dripped from its beak as it squawked and sputtered, slithering slowly down the hall toward Ed, its girth brushing against the framed photos on the walls. A picture of an elder Farris hit the floor and smashed. An antique side table had much the same fate. But Cal did not slow. The beast's bulbous ebony head swayed gelatinously as it moved, its red-tinged eyes squinted but remained focused in the bright of the light spilling out of the bathroom.

It charged.

Ed screamed.

And that's when all hell broke loose.

"Who the hell are you?" Ed screamed.

"Roxy Buckles: Intergalactic Exterminator. And I'm here to save your ass!"

The woman, who had seemed to appear out of nowhere in Ed's upstairs hallway, was holding a weapon that his brain just could not comprehend. She moved with a fluidity he associated with dancers or perhaps swimmers, dodging wild swiping tentacles without blinking an eye. She fell to one knee and took aim at the creature formerly known as Cal.

"Get down!!" she ordered. Ed hit the ground and rolled through the still open doorway of the bathroom.

From the hallway came the classic sounds of a tussle: grunting, and flesh pounding flesh. Ed cringed as the din reached a crescendo: glass shattered and a torrent of curses reached his ears. Under different circumstances, Ed might have blushed over such colorful language. Then, a peculiar whirring noise erupted, like thousands of bees had descended on Leonard Way.

"Cover your eyes!"

Ed barely heard the warning over the cacophony of noise but did not hesitate to do as he was told. A superhuman wail filled the house and the hair on the back of Ed's neck stood on end. A violent shudder and he felt the floor ripple beneath his trembling body… and everything went black.

"Hey! Can you hear me?"

The softly spoken words penetrated his subconscious and Ed's eyes blinked open. "Am I dead?"

She chuckled softly. "No, Mr. Farris, I think you'll be okay. You're safe now. Though you'll need to do some renovations. And also probably take a shower."

Ed raised a hand in front of his face. It was covered in a thick black gore. Raising himself slightly on his elbows, wincing as his lower back protested, he saw that his entire self was covered in the sludge. And the walls. And the floor.

And also the woman crouched next to him. She looked like *Carrie* at the prom… if they'd dumped motor oil on her instead of blood. She ran a hand across her mouth, turned her head to the side and spat.

"Gosh, this stuff gets everywhere."

"Um. What exactly is this *stuff*? Is this ... is this *Cal*?"

"Cal?" she questioned. "This is the ichor from the LanQuid I just blasted to smithereens out there in your hallway."

"Lan... Quid?"

"Yes. That's what I said. An invasive species. We thought they were extinct!" She seemed delighted, given the circumstances.

"But he was so tiny this morning."

"Let me guess, you gave it water?"

"Of course. He seemed to really love it!"

"They sure do, Mr. Farris, sure do. It's absolutely gluttonous when it comes to liquid. The more it drinks, the bigger it gets. It can decimate an entire planet in *days*. Especially a planet like this one."

Ed felt a little twinge of sadness. So much for a new best friend.

"Sorry, in all the chaos I missed it. What did you say your name was?"

"Roxy Buckles." She extended a hand and pulled Ed to his feet.

"And you, hunt things, kill them? Things like Cal? I mean, the LanQuid?"

"That's my job!"

"I can't thank you enough! You saved my life!"

"All in a day's work, Mr. Farris." She smiled and glanced down at a small device on her left wrist that was emitting an insistent beep. She grabbed a towel off the rack – it seemed to have escaped the worst of the slaughter -- and swiped at the face of the electronic. "Sorry to cut this short, but I have a meeting about a Witchlet that I cannot miss."

Before Ed could react, she was gone out the door.

It had been the wildest day of Ed's entire life.

He'd stayed at a hotel for a few days while the cleaners came in. Thankfully they didn't ask a lot of questions. Ed didn't have a lot of answers anyways. It would take a while longer to repair the walls and floor upstairs, but the house was habitable enough.

He was sitting at the kitchen table, drinking a cup of coffee when the doorbell rang.

"Delivery for Edward Allen Farris."

"That's me!"

Ed placed his palm on the scanner where the deliverybot indicated and grabbed the small cardboard box when it dropped from the slot.

He already had the bowl ready on the kitchen counter.

But maybe not so much water this time.

Chantal Boudreau

A Toronto native currently living in Sambro, Nova Scotia, Boudreau is an avid and prolific author with over sixty credits to her name. She is the author of the Fervor series of novels, as well as the *Masters & Renegades* series and *The Snowy Barrens Trilogy*.

Boudreau is likely best known for her work in short fiction, and the anthologies she has appeared in have been shortlisted for both the Bram Stoker award and the Aurora award.

Her extensive short-fiction bibliography includes fantasy, dark fantasy, and horror.

A Sticky Situation

As Captain Sybil Daniels collected the gear for the away mission, she could sense Glenda Fields fidgeting from across the room. It made the veteran spacefarer irritable.

"Permission to speak, Captain?"

Captain Daniels had earned the reputation of being a curmudgeon, and she wasn't about to degrade it. She gave the ensign a steely-eyed stare with a hint of lip curl. "If you have something to say, just say it. I don't have patience for people who have to ask me if they can ask me something." She cursed as the zipper jammed on the pack she was readying.

Fields jumped a little at the sudden outburst, always on edge around her captain. "Are you sure we should be going?" she asked. "The manual says we should have a minimum of four people per landing party. Considering my lack of experience..."

"We all have to muddy our feet at some point, Ensign Fields. The manual doesn't account for the remainder of the crew coming down with Pardovian flu. Nobody else is fit to join us." With an annoyed grunt, she hoisted the pack over her shoulder and headed for the next one. She didn't trust the ensign to check her own kit.

"I know, but maybe we should postpone until someone else is, per regulations."

Daniels rolled her eyes. Rookies always clung to the regulations.

"No time. We've delayed as long as we can. We have to leave here by tomorrow morning to make sure we make the rendezvous point as scheduled. All we're missing are a few soil samples and I'm not leaving the planet without them. We don't have to go that far -- just find a spot with some mud, scoop it into the jars, and we're done. We don't need four people for that."

Fields bit her lip, brushing a few sandy strands that had escaped her tightly bound ponytail away from her face. "There are safety considerations."

Captain Daniels ran a hand through her shortly cropped silver hair and sighed. "Look -- if you're that scared, you can stay here with Mother and try to make the folks in sick bay comfortable. I'll go get those soil samples on my own. We need them -- leaving without them would make the whole trip rather pointless."

Mother was the ship's AI, currently focusing her efforts on the doc-bot treating the worst of the flu victims. She controlled other areas of the ship as well, making sure things like life support, engines, and the weapon systems were online and properly maintained.

"Not entirely pointless. We have the core rock samples. That's why we're here, right?"

"No, Ensign Fields. This was an exploratory mission for population sustainability as well as resource study. All of the information we were hired to bring back will allow our employers to determine how they will approach their mining process on the planet. They need those details to help them decide things like colonization potential, the best equipment type for planetary conditions, storage options, and much more. If we're missing anything, they'll have to send another ship down and that will mean a severe dock in pay. I'm not willing to make that sacrifice for the sake of one lousy set of soil samples. So, like I said, if you're so hell bent on following protocol, you do what you need to do. I'm going out there."

"Oh." Fields pursed her lips, her green eyes wide. "Oh no, I can't let you go out there alone. That would be even more dangerous."

The captain gave her an icy look, trying to appear menacing. "You're not honestly going to try to stop me. Because if you're up for a brawl..."

"No -- no, of course not! I meant I'll come with you. I guess we can make an exception to policy under exceptional circumstances."

The captain gave her a hint of a smile -- the most encouragement her superior was willing to offer. It was the first one Fields could recall ever seeing from her captain.

Within the hour, they had finished kitting up and made their way out of the ship. Fields had her scanner out, taking readings, while Captain Daniels plunged forward through the brush, not trying to hide her haste.

The greenery about them yielded like rubber to the touch, slick with humidity. The broad leaves shuddered as Daniels forced her way past, shedding water droplets. Hung with ropey vines, it reminded the ensign of a cartoonish version of a jungle, but one with an alien edge.

Several minutes in, she reviewed the results on her scanner. "There's a higher level of humidity present today then there has been in the last two weeks," Ensign Fields informed the captain.

"Good -- that ought to make a patch of mud an easier

thing to find. Like that one right over there."

The captain gestured towards a somewhat exposed tract of soil: swampy looking, but easy to access. She altered her trajectory slightly and pressed on, reaching for one of the sample jars. Fields stepped more lightly, wary of her footing. She continued her survey of the area.

"You might want to be careful," Fields warned. "The scanner indicates that patch has a greater than normal water content along with a high density of sediment. It's not just mud, but more like wet clay. You could get..."

Captain Daniels roared a string of curse words that were partially obscured by the slurpy, suction sound of trying to withdraw a boot from the cloying sediment... and failing.

"...Stuck."

The older woman's weathered face reddened. She stood upright with a huff. "Fine. I guess this is as good a place as any."

Securing the sample jar in her slippery envirosuit glove, she fumbled with it until successfully removing its cap. The captain then leaned down and started scooping the muck into it. She paused only long enough to toss another jar to Fields.

"Get some of the drier soil along the periphery. I don't want them to get the impression that it's all sludge. When you're done, give me a hand out."

By the time the ensign had gathered the sample, her captain had sunk a few more centimeters into the mud. Fields took her hand and pulled ferociously, but to no avail. Their struggles to free Captain Daniels only seemed to have the opposite effect, and by the time they gave up, she was already knee deep. The curse words poured out of the older woman in a steady stream.

Fields flushed. "I'm sorry, Captain, but I can't do this on my own. Perhaps we really did need those other two crew members."

"We're just doing it wrong, is all," the captain insisted. "Time for some alternative tactics."

She tried everything she could think of: wriggling out backwards, splaying herself forward to reduce any gravitational effect, trying to lever herself out with the planet's equivalence to a large tree branch... None of it had the desired effect. The attempt just added to her already massive frustration.

And she was now mid-thigh deep.

"I'm going to get help," Ensign Fields proposed.

"Help? What help? All of the flu sufferers are as weak as kittens. How do you expect them to help? There's nobody else on planet and nobody nearby off planet."

The younger woman shrugged; her features drawn with despair. "Maybe someone else on the ship will have an idea, even if they can't physically help. I'll come up with something, somehow, but I'm not doing you any good standing around here. It won't be much longer until nightfall; and then what?"

"Most of them are barely conscious and some are delirious," the captain growled. She waved the younger woman off. "Go then, but don't take too long or I may be totally submerged by the time you get back."

She watched Fields disappear into the foliage before shouting one parting thought: "Remember to secure those samples on board the ship!"

Captain Daniels felt the ensign's absence almost immediately. The alien environment surrounding her trilled, squeaked, and clicked with unseen life, giving her what her Uncle Clive would have described as "the willies."

There might not be any actual threat beyond her patch of mud, but Daniels hadn't survived as long as she had without some level of paranoia. Always being a little on edge had kept her from being shot more than once, helped her avoid mines and pitfalls, and even prevented a near devouring or two. If only she had been as cautious as she was pessimistic.

But all the paranoia in the world wasn't going to help her much in her current situation. She had a weapon that would allow her to defend herself to some degree, but if danger did show, she had limited mobility -- the term "sitting duck" came to mind. She had been swallowed far enough into the mud that if some nasty, blade-toothed monster chose to creep up on her from behind, it could probably chomp her head off before she would have a chance to react.

And not all of the potential threats would necessarily come from behind or above. Daniels had heard tales of mud-dwelling parasites boring their way through a victim's enviro suit and laying their eggs in the exposed flesh on the other side. While she waited, the captain developed a persistent twitch, one in response to perhaps imagined prods and stings, or perhaps real ones. She couldn't tell.

"Come on, Fields -- make it snappy."

The captain grumbled under her breath about the cold and damp as a means of distraction. The fact her enviro suit protected her from both of these unpleasantries didn't dissuade her. Complaining was the past time that brought her the most joy.

And at that moment, her life was otherwise joyless.

Hours passed with no sign of the ensign's return and Daniels began to wonder if the inexperienced woman had even managed to make her way back to the ship. She was now hip deep in the muck, continuing to sink very slowly even though she had been going to great effort not to move and make the situation worse. Gloomy scenarios and outcomes persistently gnawed at her stressed and tired brain, most of them concluding with her death. She was older, but not that old. She still had some good years ahead of her.

The potential end that bothered her the most was one where nobody ever came back to get her out, sinking bit by bit until the mud engulphed her completely. That would be a slow and miserable death; not the going out with a bang she had hoped for.

Because this was the scenario she dwelled upon, she almost welcomed the sound of something large forcing its way through the brush. She readied her gun and held her breath, aspiring to at least go down fighting.

"Bring it on," she urged.

She barely managed to refrain from firing when the foliage before her collapsed, exposing the disruption. Ensign Fields had returned, accompanied by the ship's doc-bot.

Daniels lowered her weapon. "Mother? You brought Mother?"

"Like you said, the rest of the crew were as weak as kittens, so they weren't going to be any help. I had to make other arrangements. After securing the soil samples as you instructed, I made an appeal to Mother to initiate a rescue mission. To get the doc-bot to leave sick bay, I had to convince her it was a medical emergency. I had to look up triage protocol. It's not easy to override primary programming to get her into the field," Fields said.

"Hopefully, drowning in muck qualifies."

"Well..."

"I understand you have been suffering chest pains, shortness of breath, and tenderness in your left arm," Mother said. "At your age and stress-level, it could be a cardiac event. Ensign Fields was correct in seeking assistance. I will extricate you and deliver you to sick bay for a thorough examination and treatment," droned the doc-bot.

Daniels glared at the ensign. "A heart attack? You told her I was having a heart attack? How old and out of shape do you think I am?"

Fields shrugged and smiled sheepishly. "Desperate times."

Although its efforts were slow and cumbersome, the doc-bot soon had the captain dislodged from the mud. It also insisted on carrying Daniels back to the ship.

Ensign Fields walked alongside them, matching the doc-bot's snail pace.

"I have to say, Fields. I may not be a fan of your methods, but you came through," the captain said. "And we should still have just enough time to make it to the rendezvous point by deadline. Inexperienced or not, catch me in a good mood and I may have to consider you for a promotion."

The ensign shot her a sideways glance. "So… not anytime soon then."

Daniels actually chuckled as they trundled their way back to the ship.

Afterword
Ellen Curtis

In 2016, we re-launched the *From the Rock* anthology series to resounding success. *Sci-Fi from the Rock* was, in many ways, our way of celebrating the Atlantic Canadian science fiction and fantasy community. Released to coincide with the 10th anniversary of our local convention, Sci-Fi on the Rock, the collection showcased incredible speculative fiction from all genres, much like the convention always has. In the years that followed, we chose to narrow our focus in order to showcase the best fantasy, the scariest chillers, the most sobering dystopias, and daring stories of flight. It was with great enthusiasm that we prepared to return to science fiction, zeroing in on the time and style that drew so many to the genre. *Pulp Science Fiction from the Rock* has been a joy to produce, from start to finish. Our hope is that, within these pages, you have found stories that awoke your curiosity, sparked your imagination, and reminded you that anything is possible. Time keeps spinning on, but you are living now, and that makes you just as miraculous as some of the scenarios you've just read.

We would like to thank all of the people who have made this collection possible. Our sincere gratitude goes out to our authors, whose modern takes on pulp have given us incredible joy. To our readers, we giveour thanks too, as without you we would simply be shouting into the void. Our sincere admiration also is owed to our amazing cover artist, Ariel Marsh, whose work elevates our own beyond our wildest dreams. To all of you, our love a thousand times over and God bless.

Ellen Curtis and Erin Vance
Editors

ON THE COVER

 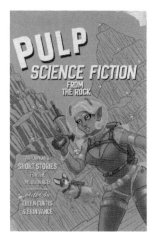

The cover to this year's anthology was was done by artists Ariel Marsh (www.sweetloots.com) and Karn Kirk Ratanasin (www.digiflohw.com).

It was based on an original illustration by Marsh, seen above and an the left, of the character Emma Awesome and her cat Butterscotch, and was as an exclusive print for the Sweet Loots table at the Ottawa Geek Market in 2017.

The image was recrated was an original character based on a sketch and input from From the Rock editor Ellen Curtis.

About the *Emma Awesome: Undead Rockstar* graphic novel: Created to be the perfect pop star, can someone undead breathe life into the music industry? *Emma Awesome* is a coming-of-age tale set against a rock & roll backdrop.

The Graphic Novel was written by Jay Paulin, illustrated by Ariel Marsh, and published by Ink'd Well Comics.

To learn more about Emma Awesome and her story, please visit www.sweetloots.com. Physical and digital copies of the book are available.

Reviews

"(Ink'd Well Comics') best book yet! Love the production values on it and the main character was especially fun."
                                                    - Border City Comics

"Emma Awesome stitches together a tale of following your dream even if you have to reanimate yourself... err... re-imagine yourself..."
                                                    - Josh Rodgers (Mushface Comics)

"Great book! (Ink'd Well Comics) put such a great polish to (their) stories. The art and the craft and the actual physical quality of the book is amazing!"
                                                    - Steven Charles Rosia (Muskoka).

ON SALE SOON FROM ENGEN BOOKS

Fans of the From the Rock series should be sure to check out *Slipstreamers*, a new monthly adventure series from Engen Books. The series follows the adventures of Cassidy Cane as she slips through dimensions to strange new worlds, all in hopes of finding cures for the problems that plague her home Earth.

Each episode will be written by a new talent from the Atlantic Canadian genre fiction scene, giving a fresh take to each new world that Cassidy visits.

Featuring the words of many different From the Rock contributors and the astonishing art of Ariel Marsh, this series is not to be missed!

PULP SCIENCE FICTION
FROM THE ROCK
A COLLECTION OF SHORT STORIES
EDITED BY ELLEN CURTIS & ERIN VANCE

A century ago, pulp magazines brought the fresh ideas of science-fiction and space exploration to the masses with its easily accessible format, and lit the imaginations of a generation on fire. Those inspired became the greatest storytellers of their time, producing stories that would shock, awe, and inspire the world.

That legacy of the new, the different, and the strange lives on today in the minds and pens of genre writers all over the world.

This collection honours that legacy with twenty-two short stories highlighting the best of the modern interpretations of Pulp Science-Fiction, from minds like Ali House (*The Segment Delta Archives*), Jon Dobbin (*The Starving*), and Sherry D. Ramsey (*Beyond the Sentinel Stars*)! With introduction from sci-fi legend Kenneth Tam!